KU-083-373

YOUR PLACE OR MINE?

When Bea's husband dies, she decides not to be a lonely widow. Instead, she chooses three tenants who, over the years, become a family, until the day they must find a new housemate. Will needs a place to stay and Bea's beautiful house seems too good to be true – then he meets the housemates. At least twenty years older than him, they range from outrageously camp to irritatingly raucous, but somehow Will finds he's taken the stunning spare room. His sister Harrie falls in love with more than just the house when she visits, and together they're caught up in Bea's final secret...

YOUR PLACE OR MINE?

YOUR PLACE
OR MINE?

by

Julie Highmore

Northamptonshire
Libraries

Magna Large Print Books
Long Preston, North Yorkshire,
BD23 4ND, England.

British Library Cataloguing in Publication Data.

Highmore, Julie
    Your place or mine?

A catalogue record of this book is
available from the British Library

ISBN   978-0-7505-2745-3

Northamptonshire
Libraries

First published in Great Britain in 2007 by Headline Review
An imprint of Headline Publishing Group

Copyright © 2007 Julie Highmore

Cover illustration © Head Design by arrangement with
Headline Book Publishing Ltd.

The right of Julie Highmore to be identified as the author of this
work has been asserted by her in accordance with the
Copyright, Designs and Patents Act, 1988

Published in Large Print 2007 by arrangement with
Headline Book Publishing Ltd.

All Rights reserved. No part of this publication may be
reproduced, stored in a retrieval system, or transmitted in any
form or by any means, electronic, mechanical, photocopying,
recording or otherwise without the prior permission of the
Copyright owner.

Magna Large Print is an imprint of Library Magna Books Ltd.

Printed and bound in Great Britain by
T.J. (International) Ltd., Cornwall, PL28 8RW

All characters in this publication are
fictitious and any resemblance to
real persons, living or dead,
is purely coincidental.

For Rose and Ava

ONE

Will took the scrap of paper out and double-checked. Fifty Bibury Road, he'd written down, but this couldn't be right. No festering bin bags. All windowpanes intact. Plus, it was huge. There were shrubs and flowers galore and, parked on the gravel, a beautiful old Saab with an out-of-date tax disc.

From the tiled steps, the house towered above him. A semi-detached Victorian mansion built in warm yellow brick. A very nice house, but the wrong house. He pressed the bell anyway, hoping someone could direct him to the right address. A body approached the stained glass and the door opened.

'Hi,' said a chubby old pony-tailed guy with an earring. His jeans were tight, his feet were bare and his T-shirt said *Out of my mind, back in five minutes*. 'Here about the room?'

'Oh. Yeah, I am. I spoke to someone earlier. A man?'

'That would be Hugh. I'm Terry.'

Will introduced himself and they shook hands. 'Are you the landlord, then?'

'Uh ... come in, but mind the floor. Joy's had the bloody polisher out again.' Terry's

11

feet squeaked down the hall until he stopped at a door, pushed it open and sort of waved. 'This is my pad,' he told Will, either inviting him in or wanting him to inspect.

Will poked his head round and saw a colossal room the length of the house, with posters on the walls – generally women on motorbikes – and, propped between the open French doors, an actual bike. An entire drum kit filled the front bay window and computers and bits of computers were scattered everywhere. On an unmade futon lay *PC Pro*, *MOJO* and *Loaded*. 'Nice,' he said, backing out.

'And this,' said Terry, squeaking on down the hall, 'is where we tend to hang out and try to bear each other, don't we, Joy? Joy, meet Will, who's here to size us up and see the room.'

They were in a kitchen-cum-dining-cum-living area, again huge. A blonde woman on a set of steps was swiping at cobwebs. 'There,' she sighed before swivelling his way. Joy was heavily made up and younger than Terry – somewhere in her forties. Late forties, he'd have guessed. She peered at Will over the top of reading glasses, gave him a friendly smile, then made her way down the steps in pink trainers that matched her shorts and lipstick.

'As soon as you turn your back, the blinkin' things are weaving again. I don't know.'

She gave Will a high-pitched giggle that would get on his nerves in no time. 'Fancy a glass of sangria? I made some earlier. Nice and refreshing on a day like this.'

'It'll be heavy on the brandy,' warned Terry. 'The woman drinks like Oliver Reed.'

'Watch it,' said Joy, batting him with her feather duster. This time the screechy giggle had an actual physical effect on Will. No way could he live in this house, but the sangria sounded good. It was a blisteringly hot day and he'd cycled at full whack to his two o'clock appointment.

'Yeah, OK,' he said. 'Thanks.'

'Did I hear Joy's sangria?' came a new voice, emerging from the basement. An almost bald man in brown loafers and no socks, dazzling white trousers and a polka-dot shirt appeared on the top step and stopped dead. 'Golly,' he said, giving Will the once-over, only he did it twice. 'What have we here? And is it my birthday?'

'This is Will,' Terry told him. 'You spoke earlier, remember? Will, this is Hugh.'

'Hi,' said Will dubiously. The person on the phone had sounded quite young. A limp hand floated his way and he shook it.

'Very Daniel Craig,' said Hugh. 'Don't you agree, chaps?'

'Oooh, yes,' said Joy, approaching him with a glass. 'Here's your drink, Will. Shaken not stirred!'

'Thanks.' He laughed awkwardly, feeling quite out of place. Their ad – 'Delightful accommodation in easy-going shared house for right person' – hadn't exactly been misleading. He was sure the room was going to be nice and, yes, the atmosphere seemed relaxed, despite Terry. But Will felt he was hardly their 'right person'. It would be ages till he had to check his cholesterol. He took a gulp of sangria and felt his throat burn.

'Anyway,' Terry was saying, 'this is the communal area.'

In the distance was a bit of a den: armchairs, a sofa, large TV and a computer. Halfway along was a lengthy dark wood table, polished to mirror standard, with six matching chairs and a vase of roses. Beyond that, the country-style kitchen was clean and, apart from a myriad of water stains on the ceiling, free of anything unsightly.

'Nice,' Will rasped, eyes watering. He sniffed and said, 'So, what do you all do? If you don't mind me asking.'

Joy drained her glass and filled it from the jug again. 'I'm at the local surgery Drs French, Briggs and Imani.' She did the giggle again. 'I always say I work for the FBI. French, Briggs and Imani. Get it?'

'Yes.' Will managed a laugh. 'Very good.'

Terry took a glass from the draining board and dried it on his T-shirt. 'Joy's one of the dragons on reception,' he said. 'The doctor will see you in a month,' he added in falsetto, 'unless you'd like to die in the meantime.'

'Oh, ignore the old grump,' she said. 'We always do!'

'Are you lot going to pig all the sangria?' Hugh asked from Will's side. Either he was one of those people who get personal space wrong or he liked Will's aftershave. Not that he was wearing any.

Will took a step away and swung round to face him. 'And how about you?' he asked. Hugh looked like someone who'd never worked, but maybe spent a lot of time on yachts sailed by others.

'I, er...'

Terry helped him out. 'Failed art history lecturer. Now giving one-to-one tuition, and God knows what else, in the basement.'

Hugh shrugged, then reached across and wrestled the jug from Joy. 'It keeps me in food and some of the students are adorable.'

Not keen to hear more, Will turned to Terry.

'Me?' Terry asked, an unattractive grin forming. 'Drum legend and part-time IT expert. How about you?'

Will gave his stock joke answer. 'I'm in environmental retail.'

'Ah, a proper academic,' said Terry, obviously hearing 'research'. But then many a drum legend was a bit deaf. 'Unlike old

15

Hugh, ha ha. So, you're working in some dingy Oxford establishment, then? Rooms full of cobwebs that would give our Joy paroxysms.'

'Are you being filthy again?' asked Joy. She was leaning hard against the fridge-freezer, perhaps guarding a second jug.

Will decided to keep quiet about Neil's Wheels, the cycle shop, his place of employment for the past four years. It was a pretty dingy establishment and it was in Oxford, so he said, 'Something like that.'

'I expect you'd like to see your room?' asked Hugh. It was clear from his face he already had Will's spices in the food cupboard, their toothbrushes side by side in a rack.

'Just a minute,' said Joy, eyes narrowing above her glasses. 'The decision is not yours alone to make, Hugh. And besides, this young man might not take to us.'

Will looked at his shoes.

'What's more, Hugh,' chipped in Terry, 'I think you'll find you're barking up the wrong back alley there. Yes, now I am being filthy, Joy. If I'm not mistaken, the boy's hetero to the core. Aren't you, Will?'

'Guilty,' he said, wondering when he might wake up and find himself looking over a proper shared house. One with a stack of dirty pans and someone's bass shaking the walls. A guy with bed-head showing him the

16

vacant half-sized room with cardboard walls that the landlord managed to squeeze in next to the toilet. 'Got a girlfriend and all,' he told Terry, Hugh and Joy, but mostly Hugh.

It wasn't a total lie. He'd had a girlfriend until last week and it didn't feel completely over. Or maybe it did. Anyway, they were still texting each other – 'Where's my Nick Drake?' (Will); 'Did you take the blue table-cloth cos my mum gave me that!' (Naomi). He did have the blue tablecloth, what he didn't have was a table to put it on. He'd been sofa surfing for six days, having left most of his belongings (and some of Naomi's, it seemed) in a friend's lockup. He was desperate for somewhere to live, but not this desperate.

'Let's show him the gardens first,' suggested Joy.

Will thought 'gardens' sounded a bit grand, even for north Oxford, but discovered 'gardens' there were. Four of them, because that was how the substantial area had been divided. They came first to the quarter directly ahead of Terry's French doors. On it were a large shed, lots of oil-covered gravel and a plant pot of fag ends. 'Guess whose,' said Terry with a smoker's chortle.

They moved across to section two and a plethora of roses, many woven round a wooden-trellisy-frame, beneath which were

17

white chairs and table in ornate curly metal. A water feature tinkled in the background, while Will's hosts raised six expectant eyebrows at him. They really were playing guess whose garden.

'Yours, Hugh?' he asked, and Hugh groaned and held his head.

'He bloody hates Joy's patch,' whispered Terry.

'Sorry,' Will said to Hugh, then realised he was insulting Joy. This really wasn't fair. In most places he'd lived, the garden was for burned saucepans. 'Smells lovely,' he said, breathing in solid rose.

Joy thanked him and Hugh mumbled something about a tart's boudoir, then they headed along the central path to section three. 'It's part Arthur Rackham fairyland,' Hugh explained, 'part Monet pond. The sculptures are after Antony Gormley, the figures on the shed Chagall.'

'Wow.'

'A touch OTT, I confess. But if one must have a hobby, it's preferable to buffing a motorbike that never *ever* sees tarmac.'

'I took her out in May,' protested Terry.

'Actually, it was March,' said Joy. 'You gave me a ride to the surgery when my ankle went. Frightened me to death.'

Terry shrugged. 'You into bikes, Will?'

'Yes, I am.' Five days a week, in fact.

Terry gave Hugh a nudge. 'See. Straight as

a Roman road.'

'And this,' said Joy, leading them to the last quarter, 'belonged to Beatrice – Bea, as we called her – but would now be the new tenant's. We'd like whoever took over to keep up what Bea established, in memory of her, sort of thing. In fact, it was one of her last requests.'

Will gawped at a messy overgrown vegetable patch. 'She died?'

Terry nodded. 'Sadly, yes. A few weeks ago.'

He had to ask. 'In the house?'

'Hospital,' they all said at once.

'She'd been ever so poorly,' Joy told him.

'Hence the state of her garden,' said Hugh, looking pained.

'None of us can be bothered with vegetables, not when Joy gets them dirt cheap at the Wednesday market. We were thinking of fencing it off. Such a ghastly eyesore. But perhaps you'll knock it into shape, Will?'

'Hugh!' snapped Joy, making Will wonder if she had a friend lined up for the room. Which would have been fine by him.

'Have you interviewed many people?' he asked, and all three suddenly found things to do. Joy whacked a cobweb off Bea's bean frame, Terry lifted a foot and picked gravel out of it. Hugh hummed, examined his cuticles, then finally said, 'One or two remarkably unsuitable types have paid us a

19

visit, yes.'

'To be honest,' said Joy, 'none of them wanted to move in. You're number nine and I can see Hugh's scaring you off before you've even seen the room.'

'Not at all,' said Will. They were all scaring him off. In fact, since being shown his vegetable patch, he was pretty keen to be out of there. He decided to speed things up. 'Talking of the room...'

Hugh said, 'Follow me,' and he did; the others tagging along like chaperones.

En route, they showed him Joy's first-floor 'suite': two big rooms, connected by a narrow arched opening and containing furniture of the 'Hurry, sale must end soon!' kind. There were several framed chocolate-boxy prints that must have pleased Hugh no end.

'Lovely,' Will pronounced, and they moved on to the bathroom, where a big cast-iron, claw-footed bath sat right in the middle of the room on the original sanded floor with visible gaps between the boards. 'Great,' he said, picturing Hugh and a student causing seismic waves. Could explain the kitchen ceiling.

For some reason Will was shown the linen cupboard, then another cupboard where they kept the vacuum and spare bulbs, before all four turned to the final flight. Will was third in line as they trudged up the dark stairwell, Terry panting in front of him, Hugh watching his rear at the rear. He couldn't help feeling trapped and claustrophobic, desperate to be back on his bike and heading for a drink and a laugh with flat-stomached people under thirty. Not much longer, he told himself. Then, one by one, they stepped into a spacious open-plan attic full of, presumably, the-late-Bea's stuff, where Terry, Hugh and Joy took time to get their breaths back.

While Will nonchalantly scanned the room, hands on hips, sceptical frown on brow, he was surprised to find his head going *Wow!* and his body wanting to punch the air and do celebratory cartwheels on the long oriental rug. The space was huge. And beautiful! Full of antiques and books and character and light. *And* a piano. Not that he could play. There was a balcony! What a room! He loved it. He wanted it. More, even, than he wanted his CD back.

'So...' he said, as casual as a pair of very casual Hush Puppies, 'would the furniture be staying?'

Hugh said, 'Anything you want, dear boy.'

'I'd give it all a jolly good going-over,' said Joy.

'No need,' Will told her.

'Um...' she said tentatively, blinking her blue-lidded eyes at him. 'So you think you might...?'

'Yes. I think I might.'

Hugh slapped a hand on his chest and said, 'Oh my,' while Joy gave a whoop and giggle, and Terry plonked himself on the lovely cast-iron bed.

At this point, second thoughts began creeping in. Joy's laugh. Hugh's needy eyes. Terry's crudeness. Vegetable gardening...

'Word of warning,' said Terry, jiggling the bed noisily. 'If you're thinking of shagging, they'll hear you in Cambridge.'

TWO

After Bea lost her husband in May 1994, following what the *Oxford Times* delicately referred to as 'a long illness', she'd felt that she too would most likely pass away within months of her spouse, as elderly devastated widows were prone to do. When, towards the end of the year, this hadn't occurred, and in fact Bea felt in excellent physical health, she sat herself down with a cocoa and contemplated the future she now appeared to have.

She was sixty-eight, a retired music teacher who still kept her hand in with private lessons, and a keen walker. It was, she felt, her music and her rambling group that had kept her going these past seven months. Even so, she still mourned for Donald and longed for the anniversary of his death to pass, so she could really move on. Meanwhile, the gloomy months of January and February loomed, and although she'd been stoical since May, she was now dreading first Christmas, and then the dead of winter.

As she sat beside her coal-effect fire, eking out the cocoa, Bea thought of Simon, and how, at such a time, she might have relied upon the love and support of her only son, particularly as she had no siblings to lean on. But this wasn't to be. Simon had turned up for his father's funeral, but had almost instantly whizzed back to some far-flung place to carry out whatever destructive and exploitative business he did for his ghastly conglomerate. 'Snowed under,' he'd explained, luggage in hand, his lips barely touching her cheek. She'd heard only once from him since – a short strained call with a bothersome echo on the line, telling her he'd moved. When she asked for his phone number, he said it would be better if he did the calling, since he was rarely at home.

Simon had never been easy, even as a child, and on top of that he bore a thirty-year grudge. When his father had decided, after a good deal of soul-searching, to leave the hugely successful family business in order to work with Oxford's down-and-outs, poor Simon had to be wrenched from his cosy private school and thrown to the lions of St Stephen's. They may have had a large north Oxford house, but they were now having to live on Bea's teaching salary and the pittance Donald brought in. Belts had to be tightened and, truth be told, she and Donald had never felt comfortable with their son's private education. Bea's nouveau riche father-in-law had more or less coerced them into sending Simon to prep school, and once their child was on that track ... well.

Bea had been fully behind her husband, agreeing that a life in paper products was never going to be fulfilling for someone with Donald's social conscience. However, she'd also felt for her thirteen-year-old son, who simply couldn't adjust to state-school life. He made no new friends, so far as she could tell, and after school still met up with his old ones, now all attending St Edward's.

Simon began to ridicule his parents – their clothes, their shabby house, their political beliefs – things he'd once found rather amusing and perhaps quirky, Now it was, *'Nobody's* parents belong to the Labour Party. How can you *like* Harold Wilson?' It was all so embarrassing, he told them more than once, especially his father's new tendency to offer a temporary roof to 'tramps'. Simon's best friends made only rare appearances at the house, and he began to confine himself to his basement room for unhealthily long spells. The thing that had made him most furious, he revealed several years later, was that his father had got himself written out of his grandfather's will.

Astonishing! Bea thought now, her mug of cocoa drained, her heart becoming less guilt-filled and more angry and disappointed with her son. Already, at thirteen, Simon had shown signs of the materialistic, uncaring adult he'd turned out to be. Thank heaven he'd never married and had children. Well ... surely, he'd have told her?

Bea pulled herself from her slumped position, straightened her cardigan and returned to the matter in hand. Her future. What was she to do with this enormous house? Rattle around in it for twenty years? And then there was the upkeep. The two pensions ensured she ate and paid her bills, but the roof was missing slates and there were signs of woodworm. Ought she to sell? No, not with Donald only so recently gone. There was his much-treasured vegetable patch to keep going. His greenhouse. And so many of his books to move. Donald had taken an Open University degree in his late forties and early fifties, and, as with many a mature student, had thrown himself into his subject with far too much enthusiasm; even teaching himself Latin.

She couldn't sell. Not just yet. And where would she end up? In some soulless retirement flat with incontinent, complaining old biddies for neighbours? No, no. What was needed was another source of income. Her friend Meg took in students from the language schools, but it wore the poor woman out. All that cooking and washing, and having to get up at two a.m. when they'd forgotten their keys. Although the company was probably nice. Rambling and piano lessons were all very well, but one still had to come home to an empty house. And in Bea's case, it was a very large empty house.

She took a look around her drawing room at the two empty armchairs and the long and empty couch, and imagined people seated in them. Not young foreign language students, but adults. Someone was reading out crossword clues, another told an amusing anecdote. A person was tinkling on the piano and singing along badly. What fun, Bea thought, before blinking the images and sounds away and staring again at her empty furniture.

She'd advertise for lodgers, she decided, picking up her reading glasses and making her way to the bureau. It wasn't the first time she'd had this idea but now she was going to take action. Sitting at the desk, she composed an advertisement for both the *Oxford Times* and the *University Gazette*. 'Rooms

available in north Oxford for mature professional persons with impeccable references.'
She knew she was being discriminatory and
that Donald wouldn't have approved, but it
was her house now, to fill as she pleased.
And, after all, one couldn't let penniless
people in when one very much needed the
rent.

'There,' she said, when she'd sealed both
envelopes, the appropriate payments en-
closed. 'Let's see what comes of this.'

THREE

The cast-iron bed may have been noisy, but
Will's plans were more along the lines of
reading in it for as long as he liked, laughing
out loud if need be. Maybe drinking a beer
as he did so. It was an exciting prospect, not
being beside an I-need-my-eight-hours
person, who snapped her beside light off at
eleven, then tossed and sighed and often
quietly growled till he did the same.

He and Naomi hadn't had a big theatrical
break-up. They'd been in the middle of a
mini row and he'd just decided to leave.
Actually, she told him to, and he really
couldn't see any reason for staying. After a
year of living together, they just bugged

each other. *Aargh, why does she go into baby voice on the phone to her dad?* – that kind of thing.

From her lofty position as Retail Banking Advisor – bank clerk – Naomi looked down on his trade. She also thought it dangerous, if not suicidal, to ride a bike in Oxford and insisted he wear a helmet. 'I am *not* nursing a vegetable for the rest of my life,' she'd said emphatically and quite understandably. But Naomi was behind him now, and Bea's room beckoned, with its books and its bureau, its antique bits and bobs, and pen-and-ink drawings of Oxford.

'Don't touch a thing!' Will told Joy, when he popped in on Monday evening to pay the deposit and rent. 'Well, the cobwebs, if you want.' He worried at first that his laptop would look out of place, but there was a tall screen on wheels, he noticed on his second visit. It was black-lacquered and oriental-looking, and would hide his computer nicely. And maybe a microwave, so he needn't venture downstairs often.

Hugh and Joy – Terry was out gigging – said his cheque would have to clear before he could be given the keys. He was told to make it out to Joy, as she dealt with that side of things.

'So who's the landlord?' Will enquired as he scribbled, wondering if a less impulsive person might have asked earlier. There was a brief silence, then Hugh shouted, 'Shoo! Shoo!' to a fly, and Joy suffered a series of hacking coughs.

'You know,' she gasped finally, clutching at her slim powdered neck. 'You pick up everything going in my job.'

'I can imagine.'

'Shall we give you a ring when the cheque's cleared?' she asked.

Hugh slipped from the room, then Joy strode past Will and down the hall.

'Er, OK,' he said, following her. 'You've got my mobile number, yeah?'

'Yes, yes.' She opened the front door and gestured him out of it with a high-pitched, 'Byyyeee!' The door slammed and Will chuckled to himself as he unlocked his bike. Old people!

Cycling along with the cool evening breeze in his hair felt great after a year of helmet wearing. No one would expect Naomi to nurse a vegetative ex, so over the past week he'd slowly weaned himself off his hard hat, nervously at first. Bus drivers still played *Get out my cycle lane!* and parked cars still waited for him to approach before springing a door open, but Will persevered unprotected. And now, as he belted towards the pub, it felt quite normal. On reaching the Scholar, he locked up, flattened his hair and found a pint waiting for him, as per his text message.

'How's things?' asked his little sister.

He sat down beside her on the pew, cupped his glass and took a swig of cold lager before answering, 'Good, yeah. You know, that's one *amazing* room I've found.'

Harrie tapped her mouth in a mock yawn.

'Sorry to go on,' Will said, 'but honestly, you should see the–' He stopped because her hands were round his throat. 'OK, OK,' he wheezed, and she let go.

'Will, you've convinced me it's a nice room. So now can we talk about me?'

'I'm not sure. Won't it be dull?'

'The good news is...' she said, swinging her long blonde shiny hair a hundred and eighty degrees, so that it all hung over her right shoulder and she could stroke it lovingly. A guy at the bar was transfixed, but Harrie never noticed such things. '...I've had *loads* of job offers.'

'Oh, yeah?'

'Well, loads more extras work.'

'Ah.' Harrie could be seen in more films than Judi Dench, Oxford being a popular film set. Often she was on a large wobbly bike, cycling to lectures with other improbably beautiful extras. Or in fist-shaking angry-crowd scenes, which, being a type-A personality, she did really well.

She said, 'Rumour has it, one's a big Hollywood film.'

'Again?' A few months back, Harrie had made an unexpected appearance at the

Oscars. Completely unexpected to her. With matted hair and blacked-out teeth, there she was when they showed a clip, shaking her fist at the Oxford Martyrs. 'Know who's starring?' Will asked.

'Not yet, but Fran and I are praying for Jude.'

'You always do.' He went back to his beer. Poor Harrie. So clever – Oxford graduate, annoyingly high IQ – but so directionless. 'No proper jobs, then?' he asked, wiping froth from his mouth.

'You can talk.'

Will sighed. Why was everyone so down on him about his job? He really quite liked the bike shop, and with the commission Neil gave his staff on sales, it didn't pay badly. Plus, bicycles were a good thing to be selling and repairing as the world heated up. 'Listen,' he said, 'do you know anything about growing vegetables?'

'Did a bit at school.' Her hair swung back towards him and dropped on her left shoulder. 'But do you mean in mud?'

'Soil,' he corrected her. 'Of course in soil.'

'Ah. I've only done blotting paper. You know, mustard and thingy.'

OK, sometimes she wasn't that clever. He'd just have to get a book on it, or talk to his stepfather.

Harrie said, 'Are we back on this *amazing* place of yours?'

'Yeah. Sorry.'

'So when can I come and see it?'

'After my cheque's cleared, I suppose. I'm not sure, but I think Joy's barred me till then.'

'They sound a weird lot.'

'No, no, they're not,' he said, almost convincing himself.

'And who owns the house?'

'No idea. Cheques are made out to Joy, but I'm not sure receptionists have huge houses in leafy north Oxford.'

'Oh, you never know. Maybe she inherited it. Want another drink?'

'OK.' Will nodded towards the bar. 'But watch out for maroon shirt.'

'*Eeew*,' said Harrie, 'and with cream trousers.' Her standards were so high, she never actually went out with anyone. 'You go, will you?'

Since they had nothing else to do and Will only had a sofa and rucksack to return to at Pete's place, he and Harrie cycled from east to north Oxford, so she could see the outside of his new home. After parking their bikes on the Woodstock Road they walked to the corner.

'Bibury Road!' cried Harrie. 'Will, you're way too scruffy for this.'

'You should see Terry.' He pointed down the lush green street. 'Number fifty's just round the bend on the left.'

'OK. Back in a tick.'

When Harrie hadn't returned in ten minutes, Will had visions of her knocking on the door and being shown around. Then falling in love with the attic room and telling Terry, Joy and Hugh that, actually, her brother couldn't take it after all, but that she would. He got his phone out and called her.

'I couldn't turn back,' she said, panting, 'so I'm having to do a huge square. I'm in Grandthorpe Avenue.'

'Right.' Will walked north along Woodstock, turned into Grandthorpe and met up with her. 'What happened?'

'God, are you sure you want to live there? They're only having a drink in the front garden. Who does that?'

'It is their only communal bit of garden, I suppose. I told you about the back–'

'Yes, yes, but it's still weird. Anyway, the old fat guy ogled me when I walked past. He said something under his breath and the woman hit him. Then I couldn't turn round and walk back.'

'No, I suppose not.'

'What I did, though,' she said, when they reached their bikes and were unlocking them, 'was to stop and listen for a while. Sort of hidden by the neighbours' hedge. They were talking quietly, almost whispering, so I didn't catch much. But they kept mentioning bees. Bees will do this, bees will do that. Weird, eh?'

'Maybe they've got some hives.' Will followed Harrie into the cycle lane. 'Didn't see any, though. God, I hate wasps and bees.'

'I know. Where are we going?'

'Home?' he suggested.

Home being where Harrie still lived with their mother and sensitive, right-on Patrick, but currently only Patrick. Their mother was away on what she was calling her 'half-a-gap year' – between twenty-six years as a mother and secretary, and the university place she'd been offered the coming autumn. She was currently staying with Kim, someone she'd befriended in Melbourne.

When his mum married six years ago, Will suddenly had a stepfather in his early thirties. To mask his embarrassment, and perhaps, deep down, because his own father had deserted them way back, he started calling him Daddy. Until, that was, Patrick said it made him feel undermined and could he call him plain Patrick. He was almost tearful, so Will agreed and called him Plain Patrick for a while. But then he grew up a bit and generally became a nicer person, and now he hardly ever laughed at Patrick's vegetarian shoes.

Patrick was out but had left Harrie a heap of interesting couscous, which she and Will shared and washed down with Patrick's homemade raspberry cordial. The east Oxford house Will had grown up in looked even smaller, after Bibury Road. He'd always loved it, though, with its unchanging pine furniture, batik wall hangings, painted floorboards and general clutter. There were things, such as the old dusty oil lamp, that hadn't moved his entire life. Same seventies Habitat rug in the living room, every now and then bashed on the washing line. Same dark cork notice board, same dried flowers. The magnetic letters were still all over the fridge, and paintings he and Harrie had done at nursery hung browning and curling above the larder door. The only part of the house that had changed was his old bedroom, now made into a study. If they hadn't done that, Will might have asked to move back home, if only for his stepfather's cooking.

Patrick had an allotment that he cycled to with a trailer full of tools, and returned from with the fruits and vegetables of his labour. It was an all-consuming passion and, being a freelance herbalist, he had plenty of time for it.

'Mmm, that was good,' said Harrie, leaning back in her chair. 'Did you hear Patrick won a prize for his sugar snaps?'

Will laughed. 'Good for him. I wonder if I could entice him down to my new garden.'

'I still don't understand why you can't just

grass it, or something.'

'Me neither.'

'I mean, are you going to let a bunch of oddball tenants dictate to you? God, you might end up being just like them.'

'Hardly,' Will scoffed. Bea had obviously been specific about her patch before she died, though. Put something in her will, even. 'Ah!' Will cried with a sudden realisation. 'Bea's *will*, not *bees* will. Bea's *will*.'

Harrie's eyes widened. 'Oh-oh.'

On the Tuesday, ten days after first seeing the room, Will moved just a few of his belongings into the house. As he'd sifted through things in the lockup, it was clear that, for a while at least, he'd have to do without the rowing machine and his half-life-size cardboard Angelina Jolie. He took mostly clothes. The plan was to check out how it felt to be amongst Bea's things, then take it from there. It was a bit of an experiment too. Could a different environment make him a different person? Would Bea's tasteful, cultured but old-fashioned bits and pieces soon have him hanging out in antiquarian bookshops with a terrible hairstyle. And would that be such a bad thing?

Harrie drove Will and his stuff to Bibury Road, then came up to the top floor and proceeded to poke around while he unpacked. 'God,' she said, 'Bea read Latin.

What did she do, do you know?'

'Terry just said she'd been a teacher before retiring.' Will put a sheet on what he realised was a brand-new mattress. Still had a ticket on. 'But I'm sure I'll find out more.'

'Definitely a socialist.'

'Yeah?'

'Marx, Hegel. Oh, look – *Tractatus Theologico-Politicus.*'

'You what?'

'Spinoza. I only know it in the translation, of course.'

'Of course. Give us a hand with this cover, would you?'

Harrie slipped the book back and came and helped him put his king-size duvet in his king-size duvet cover – something he'd never found easy. 'Spinoza was a pantheist,' she said, like he'd know or care what that was.

'Hey, do you think you've got it in the wrong corner there? Look, the duvet's all bumpy and wonky.'

'Oops. Anyway, they excommunicated him because he said God was just nature rather than a personified being, and that the natural world had made itself. Pretty outlandish in the seventeenth century.'

'Really.' Will gave the duvet a good shake. 'That's better. Ta.'

When Harrie wandered back to the bookshelves, Will started unpacking his clothes and filling the, thankfully empty, drawers. Each one he opened gave off an aroma that no modern drawer ever could. It was something like polish and damp and mothballs and lavender all mixed together, and he was suddenly back in his great-grandmother's house, aged seven or eight.

'I love that cute drawing of the room,' Harrie said, pointing to the wall opposite the bed.

'Oh, yeah.'

'I wonder if she did it. Odd that there aren't any photos.'

It was true, Will realised. 'Maybe the others put them away. I mean, you wouldn't want potential tenants being spooked by photos of the dead person.'

'Or maybe she never married. Didn't have family... Wow,' she said, pulling another book out. '*News from Nowhere*. I *love* this book.'

Will stayed quiet, knowing she'd fill him in.

'The William Morris novel?'

'I thought he did wallpaper.'

'Yeah, among a zillion other things. Social activist, poet–'

'Knock knock!' came Hugh's sweet voice. They listened to his delicate footsteps on the stairs before his bald pate appeared through the banisters, followed by the rest of him. 'I've brought you a little house-warming gift.' He stopped and glowered at

Harrie and gave a disappointed, 'Oh.'

'This is my sister,' Will told him. 'Harrie.'

'Ah! Delighted.' He did a little bow, then handed Will a package. 'Will and Harrie, how wonderfully royal.'

The present was mug-shaped beneath the wrapping paper, and was in fact a mug. It had 'WILL' written on one side in pretty gold lettering and a painted image of the house on the other.

'A little hobby of mine,' said Hugh. 'Pottery. I've made everyone their own personalised mug.'

Will could see Harrie had her 'oh-oh' face, and he wasn't too sure about the gift either. It somehow made him feel obligated. He wasn't sure why, or in what way. 'Great!' he said. 'Really good. Thanks. Is it microwavable?' Will pointed to his new oven and Hugh's face fell again.

'Yes,' he said, 'it is. But why the microwave, Will? Surely you'll be joining us for meals. Joy does a spotted dick to die for.' He grinned and rolled his eyes in a swoon, and Will wondered if the door at the bottom of his stairs had a lock.

'Not a big eater, really,' he told Hugh. 'Am I, Harrie?'

'More of a big drinker.'

'And anyway, I expect I'll be out a lot, or I'll just zap something up here.'

'Well, whatever,' said Hugh. 'But if you're

fond of a drink, do come and have a tipple in the basement with me some time.'

The only part of the house Will hadn't seen was Hugh's floor, which he imagined to be a sensory-overload indoor version of his garden. 'We'd love to,' he told Hugh. 'Wouldn't we, Harrie? Listen,' he added, 'I've been wondering who owns the house. Just curious, you und–'

'Ah! The door!' cried Hugh, trotting to the stairs. 'Could be my six o'clocker, Joe. See you!'

'Did you hear the doorbell?' Will asked Harrie.

'Uh-uh. Don't you love this walnut piano? And look at all this sheet music. I bet she was one clever and interesting woman, this Bea. I wonder how she ended up living in a room in a shared house?'

'Hmm,' said Will, trying to decide where to put his stereo and speakers. He could, of course, just make do with Bea's charming old art deco radio. Probably broken, he told himself, but when he switched it on, a classical station filled the room with the rich and warm sound of a piano being played beautifully. Will went over to the bed and lay on it, hands behind his head, just listening. After a while, he said, 'Nice music.'

'You think?' asked Harrie. 'I've never been keen on Ravel.'

'Know-all.'

FOUR

The first telephone call in response to Bea's advertisement came from a gentleman named Hugh Lamb. He enquired as to the exact location of the house and how much the rent was. When given this information, he continued to show interest, so Bea asked if he'd like to visit the following day at four. She thought, but didn't say, that she'd offer him afternoon tea – Dundee cake, perhaps. However, when the phone began ringing non-stop, Bea realised she'd be out of pocket before she started, if she were to provide all potential tenants with cake, so scrapped the idea.

The next day, three didn't show up, one was completely barking, and the other two were approaching retirement. She certainly wasn't setting up an old folk's home. Bea wanted young blood around the place, but not too young. Hugh Lamb, her last interviewee, turned out to be around the correct age. He was forty, he told her, although he looked younger with his mop of golden hair. His story was that he taught art history in London but preferred to reside in Oxford, in order to be close to his nine-year-old son, Bruno.

The news that Hugh had a child came as something of a surprise to Bea, for she'd pegged him as a queer from the moment he'd sat on her couch and crossed his legs at the knees, then crossed them again at the ankles. Donald would never have sat that way, nor any man she could think of. Hugh confided that he was going through an acrimonious divorce and looked most distressed at times. Bea felt sorry for him, realising that divorce must often be akin to bereavement. She didn't ask for details, for they may well have been sordid, but she did put Hugh on her mental list of 'maybes', and even made tea and got out the Dundee cake.

'Beatrice,' he said, whilst sipping from bone china – his wedding ring, she noticed, now on his pinkie.

'Do call me Bea.'

'Thank you. The thing is, um ... well, in my favour...'

'Yes?'

He put his cup and saucer down, unwound his legs and stood up. 'Please don't take this the wrong way, but I can see that your house ... as beautiful as it is...' He waved an arm around, and Bea wished he'd get on with it.

'Yes?'

'What I'm trying to say is that I'm a dab hand with a paintbrush. I can wallpaper to a professional standard and, if I say so myself, have immaculate taste when it comes to décor. Honestly, Bea, I could spruce this place up in no time. Oh. Do say if I'm over-stepping the line.'

'Not at all.' This was rather a dream come true for Bea. As though her son had re-turned home and offered to help, albeit with a new camp persona.

She knew, before Hugh had trotted off down her path with a dear little wave, that she'd offer him the basement room he'd taken such a liking to. For Bea, Hugh's strongest asset wasn't his decorative ability, but the fact that he had a son, whom he'd have coming to stay on a regular basis. A child in the house again. How wonderful!

FIVE

Joy and Hugh came to the attic and invited Will, and even Harrie, down to dinner that first evening. But, feeling as though he hadn't yet mentally or emotionally installed himself in the house, Will declined. 'We're expected at home,' he explained.

'Are we?' said Harrie.

'*Yes.*'

'No, I'm sure Patrick said he was going to

43

the Youth Theatre.'

Will gave up. 'Really?'

'Yeah, definitely.' Harrie turned to Joy. 'We'd love to. Thanks.'

'Jolly good. I've just popped the potatoes in. Hugh, why don't you show our guest around?'

Harrie was duly given a tour of the house and gardens, during which Will got to see Hugh's basement. This turned out not to resemble a decadent den of iniquity in any way. It was fantastic, in fact, and quite unlike the rest of the house, with its chic white brickwork and solid wood floor. Although an art historian, Hugh had only a couple of modern pieces on his walls, perfectly placed. The room had a window at the front and French doors leading to the garden at the back. Tucked into a corner was an ensuite bathroom. There wasn't a semi-naked student anywhere.

After the tour, they were joined by Terry, then all sat having an apéritif – Joy's sangria – around the dining table, waiting for the potatoes to brown. Terry was convinced he'd seen Harrie before. 'Probably on TV,' she said, and explained about being an extra. 'You wouldn't believe how many cold and congealed meals I've pretended to be eating.'

Joy promised there wouldn't be anything like that this evening and checked on the potatoes. 'It must be ever so exciting and glamorous, all that filming.'

'Oh, yes.'

Will snorted. He knew it was a lengthy, deadly dull and uncomfortable business because he'd once been a bewigged, tights-wearing servant for a day.

'This is a fabulous house,' Harrie told her hosts. The three of them were seated on the other side of the table, making Will feel he and Harrie were at an interview. Only Harrie was the one asking all the questions. 'How old is it?'

'Built around 1880.'

'How long have you all been here?'

'Since the mid-nineties.'

'And who does it belong to?'

This one seemed to stump them. 'Erm...' said Terry.

'Well...' said Hugh.

'Oh, let's just tell them!' cried Joy, perhaps emboldened by her power drink. Shifty looks took place, then Joy said, 'The truth is, we're not sure.'

Will nodded. That seemed fair enough. He'd rarely known the owners of his places, only the agents collecting the rent. He was about to ask what day the dustmen came, when his sister said, 'What do you mean?'

Hugh was wringing his hands. 'It's all a bit ... delicate.'

'Oh?' said Harrie. 'Why's that?' Will gave

her a gentle kick and she kicked him back less gently. 'It's not about to be sold and everyone thrown out, or something?' She laughed but the others continued to look grave.

Terry stood, scraping his chair back as he did so. He picked up his glass, took a deep breath and cleared his throat. If it hadn't been for his T-shirt – *It only seems perverse the first time* – he might have been about to toast the bride and groom. 'It belongs ... belonged to Bea. We're pretty sure it now belongs to us, the three of us. But we don't have proof because we don't know where the fuck she put her will.'

'Isn't it with a solicitor?' asked Harrie.

'Oh, no,' chipped in Joy. 'She told Hugh she didn't want that, in case Simon was informed of her passing away, then con- tested the will. And anyway, we don't know who her solicitor is. Looked everywhere for a name, haven't we, boys?'

'Who's Simon?' asked Will.

Terry turned to Joy. 'Surely those potatoes are as brown as old boots now?' She shot off and he continued with the story. 'Simon is Bea's estranged son. We moved in after Bea lost her old man, and sort of became her family. Simon was too busy climbing some tacky career ladder in the Far East to bother with his mum. Apparently there was a rift. Began when he was a kid. Anyway, Bea

46

became ill and started worrying about Joy, Hugh and me, and what would become of us if she kicked the bucket. She saw fat-cat Simon, now a marketing director, she'd heard, coming home and needlessly selling off the house. Between us, we've invested a lot of time and energy in this place.'

'So,' said Joy, rejoining them, 'Bea sent me off to the post office for one of those DIY wills.'

Hugh said, 'The couple next door came round and witnessed the signing ... and, well, we've searched high and low for the blasted thing.'

'Wow...' expired Harrie. 'And does Simon know his mother's, you know...?'

'Nah,' said Terry.

'Well, not that we know,' said Joy.

'I take it you've looked through all her books and things?' asked Will, realising instantly what a stupid question it was.

Hugh tutted. 'Of *course*, dear boy. But we can't bring ourselves to pack her stuff away or give it to charity, just in case it's there somewhere and we missed it.'

'Is there an older will?' asked Harrie. 'One leaving everything to Simon?'

Terry shrugged. 'Dunno.'

'So basically,' said Harrie, 'you don't want Simon finding out his mother's passed away, at *least* until you've found this will. If you don't find it, and if there isn't an earlier will, then she'll be seen to have died intestate.'

Will sniffed. 'Can I smell burning?'

'Oops,' said Joy, leaping up again. She put a mitt on and opened the oven. 'Done!' she announced, and soon piles of lamb, potatoes, carrots, peas and green beans covered all their plates. A steaming boat of gravy was being passed round and all glasses were filled with red wine.

'Welcome,' said Hugh, raising his glass to Will.

'Welcome,' said Joy.

'And here's to serendipity,' added Hugh.

Joy giggled. 'Yes.'

'What do you mean?' asked Will.

Hugh took a small sip, then dabbed at his lips with the back of his hand. 'Your name, my love. As soon as you said "Will" on the phone, I had this feeling you'd been sent to us. The others agreed.' He chuckled. 'Will *will* find the will!'

Harrie laughed and clapped.

'Yeah, right,' Will said, taking what might have been more than his fair share of gravy. 'No pressure, then?'

'So,' said Harrie, 'if you've inherited this house, or think you have, why did you want another tenant?'

Terry grinned. 'That's easy. Cash. First, the house is always needing something done to it and none of us is earning a fortune. Far from it. Second, if we find the will and it gets contested, we'll need a good lawyer. And he won't come cheap.'

'Do you know who Bea named as executor?' asked Harrie. 'Maybe she gave them the will for safekeeping?'

'We think a friend of hers, Meg,' said Hugh, while Will wondered how Harrie got to ask all the good questions. 'They did a lot of walking together and were close. And, no, she doesn't have it.'

'Does that mean that if you find the will and I live here long enough, you'll all leave the house to me?' asked Will. 'Ha ha,' he added.

'Unlike Bea, we all have close relatives,' said Joy. 'Sorry, Will.'

'I wasn't being serious.'

'I've got two sisters,' she went on, 'and Terry has a grown-up daughter and grandson. Then there's your son, isn't there, Hugh?'

Will's fork stopped on its way to his mouth. He turned to Harrie and hers was poised too. He waited for her to blurt something out but, instead, he did. 'Aren't you gay?'

Hugh shook his head and smiled at Will. 'Ah, the young.' His pale gaze then fell on Harrie. 'Bruno's around your age. You'll absolutely adore him.'

No she won't, thought Will.

49

As soon as the meal was over and Will and Harrie were told not to dream of helping clear up, they went to the attic, two steps at a time in Harrie's case, so eager was she to find the missing will.

Once in his room they got a bit of a system going, taking blocks of six books from the shelves. Harrie would check through one, then dangle it to see if anything fell out, then Will would do exactly the same. All six then went back and another six got checked. By nine-thirty they were certain the will wasn't in any of Bea's books. Harrie was keen to start on the sheet music, but Will sent her home, saying he had work the next day and still had unpacking to do. After she'd gone, he put the radio on and lay on the bed. The unpacking could wait.

When he came round after dropping off, Will reached for his phone and sent Naomi a quick text, telling her where he was now living and hoping she was bearing up without him. He also mentioned the CD again.

A reply arrived within seconds. 'It's fucking midnight!'

What? He checked the time on his mobile – 12.03 – then on Bea's old clock – just after twelve. He couldn't believe he'd been asleep two hours, but then it had been a knackering day, what with work and moving house. 'Sorry!' he replied before realising he'd probably be waking her a second time.

In the shop the next day, his mind was on wills rather than wheels. You're a doddery, ailing old lady ... a bit forgetful, perhaps. You've started doing things like sprinkling salt on your cornflakes and watering the plants with milk. You can never quite get your shoes to match and you think Macmillan is still prime minister. You make out a will ... you get the neighbours to sign it... You don't want your evil son getting his hands on it, so you put it somewhere safe, but possibly a bit stupid. Under the floorboards? Behind a framed picture? Will had a sudden and horrible thought. Had Bea sewn it into her mattress? The one that was no longer there. He went out the front of the shop and called the house from his mobile.

Hugh answered. 'Don't worry,' he said, 'we checked. Not a darn to be seen. Ditto her pillows and eiderdown.'

'Do you think she deliberately hid it, or just did something silly with it?'

'There's no telling. She became so forgetful, you see.'

'Could have ended up in the dustbin, then?'

'Believe me, we've thought of that.'

'Listen, there's a customer waiting, so–'

'Customer?' asked Hugh. 'But I thought–'

'Ah. Tell you later.'

51

SIX

It took Bea a while to warm to Terry. She thought forty-two-year-olds, even female ones, oughtn't to wear ponytails. And then there was the earring. He had a daughter of fifteen, which was another impediment. Children around the house, lovely. But a moody adolescent? She and Donald had suffered miserably at the fifteen-year-old Simon's hands, and Bea was reluctant to let another into her house.

'The kid would only be here one, sometimes two, nights a week,' Terry said pushily. 'I could kip on the sofa here.'

Bea was mentally making notes: *Arrogant ... Ponytail... Troublesome daughter... Drum kit...* It wasn't looking terribly good for this applicant, but then he mentioned that he used to be an electrician, before 'switching to computers'. He said, 'I don't want to alarm you, but your wiring's crappy. Bordering on deadly.'

'Really?' asked Bea, eyes lowered as she added *Language!* to her list.

'Ancient. You know, I could completely re-wire the house for you. Sink everything into the walls, so it's not unsightly any more.'

Bea wasn't sure he should be calling her house unsightly. But then hadn't Hugh been saying the same thing, only more politely?

'And have you thought about getting a computer?' Terry asked.

'What on earth for?'

'Writing letters, keeping accounts. Soon every household will have one, you know. Ever heard of Netscape? The world wide web?'

Bea could do nothing but shake her head.

'They reckon we'll soon be using computers to communicate instantly with one another all over the world. I could set you up with one. Just think, no more bloody letter-writing.'

'But I enjoy writing letters,' said Bea. She added *Deranged, but possibly useful*, then steered him away from computers towards his recent marriage breakdown, for which, it appeared, he took full responsibility.

'You're out gigging,' he told her, 'there's the booze and the e's and stuff, and the chicks coming and chatting you up at the end of your set. The wife's safely tucked away back at your gaff. Well ... things happen.'

'I see,' said Bea, getting the gist if not the actual words.

Terry sighed. 'Seen the light now. Too late, of course. I've lost my gorgeous wife, my kid...' He sniffed and wiped an eye. 'Sorry. Get a bit chocked sometimes.'

Bea gave him a few minutes to dwell on the error of his ways, whilst she took in the big boots, the leather trousers, the denim shirt buttoned tightly over his paunch. His two chins were stubble-covered, his left ear studded. Terry was a long way from her fantasy crossword-doing lodger. However, when he raised his red-rimmed, rather kind eyes and said, 'I'd do it for free, of course. The wiring,' Bea felt a small tug. And then, when he said he could turn his hand to most maintenance jobs, she felt a slightly stronger one, and soon found herself offering him the ground-floor back room, subject to references, and on the condition that any newfangled computer equipment would be confined to his quarters.

'Wicked!' he cried, before she could say, 'Your daughter too.' He came over and scratched her cheek with a horrible kiss. 'You won't regret it,' he said, but Bea felt she was already beginning to.

It occurred to her, when first Hugh then Terry moved their possessions in, that she'd chosen these two because they were of a similar age to her son, but so refreshingly unlike him. For a start, they each presented her with a gift. In Hugh's case a rather super vase he'd made himself, all geometric reds and oranges. She thanked him, and because it was December, filled it with the dried flowers she'd last year sprayed a festive white, silver and gold. 'I'm quite touched,' she told him, embarrassed by the catch in her voice.

Two days later Terry was handing her more pottery. This time a mug. A fairly basic white mug, only it had on it, for most of its circumference, a picture of a handsome young man in a suit and tie. He was lying on his side, his head propped on one hand. 'It's... er, thank you,' she said, and went to put it in her crockery cupboard.

'No!' cried Terry. 'You've got to make a hot drink in it.'

'But I've just had one,' she protested. Goodness, he was bossy.

'Later, then?'

'Yes, yes. Now, do hurry and bring your drums in, dear. It's awfully chilly with the front door open.' Bea hadn't given this per-cussion business much thought, until it started making its way along the hall, piece by large piece. And so many pieces. She'd be sleeping directly above it too. Had inviting Terry to share her home been one enor-mous blunder?

'Fancy that hot drink yet?' he asked a little later.

Did he wink at her? 'Not yet, no.' In fact, she was trying to restrict her caffeine intake, since last week's rise in her blood pressure. As a terrifying pair of cymbals shot past, Bea knew she'd be off the scale if Dr French were to test her now.

At the end of a stressful, not to say cold afternoon, Bea finally made herself, Hugh and Terry a welcome cup of tea. Feeling obliged to use her new mug, she filled it from the pot, and having done so saw the suit of the man lying on his side slowly fade, until the actually rather attractive chap was completely starkers. She howled with laughter and showed it to Hugh, who said, 'Oh, I want one.' Bea wasn't sure if he meant the mug or the man – both, no doubt – but what she knew for certain was that the dull Simon would never have come up with such a splendidly inappropriate gift.

It became evident, over the following week, that Bea's lodgers were wholly incapable of feeding themselves properly. Hugh knocked together only cold snacks of salami, hummus and a variety of breads, all from the local delicatessen. Sprigs of parsley, olives, slices of tomato were dotted around for artistic effect, making his dishes terribly appealing, but *really* Bea thought, non-stop cold food must be a danger. It wasn't fear of the cooker, she guessed, but a lazy streak. With regard to his revamping of her house, Hugh had so far only examined the drawing room, finger on chin, saying, 'I think a lovely mucky blue, don't you?'

Terry lived on delivered pizzas, which smelled delicious on arrival but quite foul later, as the stack of not-quite-empty boxes grew steadily in his room. Bea had been in twice and cleared them out, but it couldn't go on. Mind you, she mused, a diet of pure carbohydrate hadn't stopped him tackling the wiring within days of moving in, on top of his daytime job and evenings spent all over town, bashing away at a second set of drums.

It unsettled her, though, this disregard for a proper diet. But what was she to do, offer to feed the two of them? Bea had never been an enthusiastic cook. She'd been happy to produce good basic meals for her family but always left the more exotic curries and risottos and things to Donald, who'd had a creative flair in that department, if not always the time. Perhaps, she thought, with the rent she was now receiving, she could pay a woman to come and cook for the three of them.

Bea quickly did her sums and thought not, then got on with her Christmas shopping list. Terry and Hugh were going to be around on Christmas Day, something she was grateful for but also faintly fearful of. For all three it would be their first Christmas without their immediate families. Bea imagined them sitting around the table in a horribly maudlin state, dwelling on past turkey dinners in a palpable silence – but then quickly decided it was up to her to see that wouldn't happen.

'Good-quality crackers,' she added to her list. Ones with useable gifts and challenging riddles. 'Lashings of alcohol!' She'd be cooking the dinner, of course. But that was fine, and would be more than worth the effort, just to see Terry get a fresh vegetable inside him. She'd ask the boys to organise a tree, she decided. It was something Donald always saw to, arriving home with a six-footer in the back of the estate, even when it had been just the two of them; sorting out the lights that would never work at first. She honestly wouldn't know where to begin.

A board game? she wondered. They'd be sure to hammer her, but then Bea had never had a competitive bone in her body. Well, apart from that one time when she'd been forced to save her marriage after Donald had attended a particularly lively OU summer school. Nothing had happened, he swore, whilst the youngish-sounding woman bombarded him with calls. They'd simply shared a love of Marx, he'd added limply. Bea finally told the harlot to sling her hook, requested a change of telephone number, then asked her husband to please, in future, act his age at such events.

'Trivial Pursuit' she wrote down, perhaps with Donald's escapade in mind.

SEVEN

Harrie rolled up on Saturday after a day of filming, keen to carry on the search for Bea's will and just in time for Joy's goulash. Will suspected his sister of deliberate timing, especially when she handed Joy a bottle of wine.

'Smells yummy,' Harrie said with a big grin that made both Joy and Hugh reel back and gasp. 'What?' she asked. 'Oh God, is it the teeth again? I *always* forget. Will, can I use your toothbrush?'

'Certainly not.'

'Here,' said Joy, sliding open a drawer and handing Harrie one, still in its packet.

'Got any like Jif or Zif or whatever?'

'You poor child,' said Hugh, bending and reaching into the cupboard under the sink. 'Surely there's a safer way of earning a living?'

'Maybe. But not one where you get to stand within *this* distance of celebs.'

'Ooh, such as?' asked Joy.

'Such as... OK, well, today wasn't so good.

There was that woman who plays Inspector Knight's sidekick's wife. What's her name...?'

'Not Delia Moran?' cried Joy. 'Well, I never.'

Will sensed a cackle coming on so aimed for the door, saying, 'Come on, Harrie. I'll give you a hand.'

'So what exactly did Bea die of?' Will asked during the main course.

Terry said, 'In the end it was her heart.'

'It just sort of gave up the ghost,' said Joy, 'according to Larry ... er, Dr French.'

'He signed the death certificate, then?' asked Harrie.

'Mm,' Hugh sighed. 'On this very table.'

Will came over cold. 'I thought you said she died in hospital?'

'Ah.' Hugh grimaced. 'Bit of a porky. We ... well, we thought you might not take the room if you knew she'd passed away ... you know...'

'In her room?'

'Ye-es.'

'In that *bed?*' Will plonked his knife and fork down in disgust. 'Jesus, that's gross. How could you lie like that?'

'Yeah, well, pots and kettles,' said Terry, 'You told us you were an academic, not a pushbike mender.'

'Mechanic. Anyway, I'm not sure I did. But this is different. She *died* up there.'

'Oh, chill,' said Harrie. 'Look, you go to an

antiques shop and buy a Victorian, or what-ever, bed, and you think no one's ever died on it? Or given birth to a stillborn baby, or something?'

Now everyone's knives and forks were being dropped.

'Think about it,' she carried on. 'This house is, what, a hundred and thirty years old? I bet at least six people have died here. Maybe a servant or two up in the attic.'

Terry pulled a yeah-you're-probably-right face and picked up his cutlery again, then the other two followed suit. Will reluctantly did the same, wondering why his sister didn't have something better to do on a Saturday night. He'd arranged to meet Jon for a drink later and was hoping Harrie wouldn't tag along. Maybe he could slip out while she was prising up his floorboards, or whatever she had planned.

Oh God, he thought, while his appetite faded, Bea *died* in that room. Her spirit probably left her body and floated to the ceiling, then looked down on Joy, Terry and Hugh, and maybe this Dr French. Was she still up there? Sort of stuck? Didn't that sometimes happen? Could she now be look-ing down on him all the time? He hadn't heard any noises, but then some ghosts were maybe quite quiet.

'Will, you've gone ever so pale,' Joy was saying.

Terry shook his head. 'Hardly bloody surprising.'

'We shouldn't have told you,' said Hugh.

'Want a drop of brandy?' asked Joy.

'Yes, please.'

Later, while Harrie was digging into Joy's upside-down cake, Will sneakily made his phone ring under the table. He then pretended to talk to Jon, who was supposedly waiting for him in a pub. 'Gotta dash,' he said to the others. 'Sorry. Great meal. Bye, everyone.'

He left his sister with a mouthful of cake and that old familiar scowl, then hurried out the back door. Grabbing his bike, he pedalled it down the passageway, through the front garden and over to east Oxford in what could have been record time. Once at the Scholar, he had an hour on his hands until Jon arrived, so watched the football and got through the first three pints of the evening.

Will woke up on a familiar sofa (his mother's) in a familiar living room (his mother's again). He knew, almost before opening his eyes, where he was because he could smell something herbal being wafted under his nose.

'Artichoke tea,' whispered Patrick.

'Grrhhmm,' said Will.

'Vietnamese,' Patrick added, as though that made it better. 'With a dash of milk thistle. Great for hangovers. Gets the bile flowing.'

Just the words were getting Will's bile flowing, and he had to swallow hard before sitting himself up and taking the large and heavy cup. 'Cheers,' he said, knowing he'd drink the foul concoction because Patrick was never wrong about these things. 'Don't open the curtains!'

Patrick padded off to do kitchen things and Will tried to recollect the past twelve hours. He had a fuzzy memory of not being able to unlock his bike at closing time ... no keys ... then Patrick opening the door in a sarong ... handing him a blanket... Christ, his head hurt. He held his nose and managed to get some tea down, then felt in a trouser pocket for his phone. It was there. He checked the other pocket. No keys. In future, he'd lock his bike in the back garden, then he couldn't leave home without them. Idiot, he thought, when suddenly the curtains were swished back and light seared through his eyes.

'Here,' said Harrie, chucking a bunch of keys at him. 'Sneaky lazy bastard.'

'Why? What'd I do?'

'Leaving me with that lot. Leaving me to go through Bea's things alone.'

'Find anything?'

'I'm not telling you.'

'Oh, go on.'

'How's the tea?' asked Patrick from the doorway. He had a sort of Vietnamese look himself. Off-white collarless shirt and calf-length baggy shorts, shaved head and a pestle and mortar in his hands. 'Doing the trick?'

'Maybe.'

'Can you stay for lunch? It's yam curry.'

'I think not,' said Will, the bile definitely flowing now. He hauled himself from the sofa and made for the stairs on rubbery legs. 'Thanks, anyway.'

He did, in fact, stay for lunch – the tea having done its business and the curry smelling pretty good.

'So?' he asked Harrie, once they were settled at the table.

'So what?'

'Did you find anything?'

'Like what?'

Will sighed. This was Harrie's way of telling him to apologise, so he did. 'I just got freaked by the whole dead-in-the-bed business. Sorry.'

'Oh?' asked his stepfather, and Will told him the story, including the will business. 'Hey, cool,' Patrick said, when he'd finished. 'You don't think they did her in, do you?'

Will laughed, then turned to his sister. 'Surely the doctor would have been able to tell?'

Harrie bobbed her eyebrows. 'You mean the doctor that Joy's on first-name terms with?'

'No *way*,' said Patrick. 'He could have been in on it!'

'You're both being ridiculous,' snorted Will. 'Joy works at his surgery. And anyway, *did* you find anything?'

'Yep. But not the will, obviously. Otherwise I'd be over at Bibury Road trying to extort money for it. What I came across, hidden in a sort of secret compartment in her desk, was a five-year diary.'

'Of Bea's?'

'Yep.'

'How did you find the secret compartment?'

'I can't tell you.'

'Why not?'

'Because you'll laugh.'

'No I won't. And neither will Patrick, will you?'

'Cross my heart,' said Patrick.

Harrie took a deep here-goes breath. 'I went and lay on the bed for a while, in complete silence ... and... No, you'll laugh.'

'*And?*'

Harrie breathed out. 'I asked Bea to guide me.'

Will laughed. 'Yeah, right.'

'Far out,' said Patrick. 'You mean, like your own one-to-one séance?'

'I suppose. Anyway, something – maybe Bea, maybe not – sent me to the writing desk. Only in my head it suddenly became a "bureau", which is why I think it could have been Bea. While I was searching – of course, it was all your boring stuff, Will – I knocked the pot of pens over, and when I got down on the floor to retrieve them, there was this tiny knob on the side, and hey presto, the diary.'

'Wow,' said Patrick. 'Fate. Don't you love it?'

'I've had a quick look and it seems to be mainly appointments, but I'll go through it more thoroughly when I've got time. It was really late when I found it and I had to get home.'

'So the others don't know?' asked Will.

'Uh-uh. I think Terry was still up, so I crept down the hallway. I'm not sure we should tell them. What do you think?'

'Absolutely not,' said Patrick. He looked over at Will's barely touched plate. 'Did I overdo the tamarind?'

'Maybe a tad,' said Will, wondering what the hell tamarind was, and whether Patrick had won a prize for it. Which reminded him... 'You couldn't come and give me a few tips, could you, Patrick? You know, this vegetable patch I was telling you about?'

Patrick's face lit up. 'Sure. When?'

Will realised he needed someone to go

back to the house with, and maybe hold his hand up to the top floor. 'This afternoon?'

'OK.'

'Great. Thanks.' He started making headway with his curry, then stopped. 'By the way, you're wrong, you two.'

'About?' said Harrie.

'Bea.' He put down his fork and clasped hands under his chin. 'Why, tell me, would they have bumped her off if they hadn't first got the will in their hands?'

'Hmm,' they both said, while they had a think.

'Shall I bring my tools?' asked Patrick.

'Good idea.'

EIGHT

For Bea, the very best part of Christmas came on Boxing Day, when a woman with hair as black as night and beautiful slanting eyes arrived at the house with a dear little child with similar colouring and features, although the eyes were a little rounder. She introduced herself as Mimi and her son as Bruno, and asked if Hugh was in.

'Very much so,' Bea said, for Hugh had been pacing all morning, occasionally stopping to rearrange the gifts awaiting his son's arrival beneath the tree, or to peer again through the front bay window.

'Bruno!' Hugh cried, edging Bea aside. 'Happy Boxing Day! Come in, come in!' He hoisted his nine-year-old in the air and gave his cheek a kiss before just as quickly dropping him again. Boys could be heavier than they appeared, remembered Bea, and Hugh was hardly Charles Atlas.

Mimi was invited in, but made it only to the bottom of the stairs, saying she was expected for lunch. She helped Bruno out of his jacket and from a bag produced a pair of indoor shoes for him. She was slim and around thirty, and for an oriental woman was quite tall. She wore a long coat in burnt orange with a red and purple scarf, all above a pair of bright green boots. It was an outfit only an exotic person could carry off, and it brought a dash of exuberance to the taupe-coloured hallway.

Bea was intrigued and would have liked the woman to stay longer, if only to explain what she'd seen in her effete husband. However, the atmosphere felt thick with resentment, and who knew what else, and Bea was quite glad when, a matter of seconds later, the door closed on Mimi and it was just the three of them heading for the Christmas tree. Terry had gone for the day and night to his parents' house, taking young Melanie, whom Bea had yet to meet, with him.

After lunch, Bea ventured through the door on the landing and up to the attic rooms to hunt through the toys and games she'd never been able to part with. The gloomy front room housed a lot of Donald's things – clothes, binoculars, a fishing rod, yet more books – whilst the room at the back, with its much-larger south-facing window, contained Simon's entire childhood. His first paintings and crayoned drawings, school reports, football boots galore, his Boy Scout uniform. If Simon became excessively famous, Bea thought as she rummaged, she'd be able to open a museum. She decided on a train set and a compendium of games, but because the train set came in an enormous box, she had to enlist Hugh's help.

'Bea!' he exclaimed on reaching the top floor. 'I had no idea these rooms were here.'

'Originally servants' quarters,' she explained. 'Now full of my departed family's belongings.' She tried to sound blasé but felt a tear sting each eye.

Hugh gave her a look that oozed with pity, and as Bea couldn't abide being pitied, she drew herself to full height, which was slightly taller than Hugh, and pointed at the box. 'It's not so much heavy, as cumbersome.'

'Golly,' he said, hopping from one room to the other, 'this would make a terrific living space. Just picture it. Wall knocked down, a dormer window in the back here. Or a darling little balcony...'

Bea waved an arm. 'But where would all these things—'

'They *have* to go, Bea, if you want to move on. You know that, don't you?'

'Yes,' she said heavily. She breathed in hard, in order not to embarrass herself with further tears. 'But not just yet.'

Bruno was a poppet. The three of them played snakes and ladders and ludo and tiddlywinks, and Bea taught the child how to play draughts; surprised that he didn't know. She allowed him to win four or five games but then, because he was clearly as bright as a button, beat him in the final one. It was a very special afternoon for Bea, and perhaps the more so for Terry not being there. For her, two adults and a child would always feel a comfortable family unit.

After batteries were found, the train set took over the drawing-room floor. It was late afternoon and the electric fire glowed in the grate. The Christmas tree twinkled warmly and the Choir of St Martin-in-the-Fields sang festively on the wireless. All they needed was Ovaltine, thought Bea, taking in the scene when she returned from the kitchen. But instead she handed Hugh a dry sherry and Bruno some pop, then placed a tray of sandwiches in the middle of the circular track.

'Dig in, chaps,' she said.

Before tea was over, Bruno had lost interest in the trains, climbing into an armchair with the electronic present his father had given him. It was called a Game Boy, and had the dinkiest screen – impossible for Bea to see clearly, even with her specs. She wondered how good that could be for a child's eyes, but held her tongue.

Little Bruno was to sleep on the old Z-bed, once regularly used by Simon's friends, now rather rusty and creaky when opened up in Hugh's basement room. Around eight-thirty, with some prodding from his father, Bruno came into the drawing room and thanked Bea for a nice day. He looked so adorable, with his droopy eyes and his cartoon pyjamas, that she wanted to give him a hug and a kiss. But, as no self-respecting nine-year-old boy would let a strange old lady do that, she said, 'Would you like me to read you a story?' He said yes, of course, and up on the top floor, they plumped for a Famous Five.

It was hard to keep Bruno out of the attic the following morning and, indeed, on subsequent visits. Not that anyone wanted to. Simon's old toys – the soldiers, the farmyard, the cowboy outfit, everything – were endlessly fascinating and kept the child occupied and off his Game Boy for hours and hours. Often, he chose to play up there alone; other times, he'd cover the dining table in the things he'd brought down: post-office set, toy typewriter, walkie-talkie robot.

'*Promise* me you won't chuck any of it away?' Hugh begged Bea, three or four weeks into the new year.

NINE

Harrie was standing just behind the tenor miming to Mozart's *Requiem* – '*Liber scriptus proferetur, in quo totum continetur*' – in Dorchester Abbey, when her mobile rang. She quickly lifted her cassock and delved into her jeans, but it was too late, people were tittering.

'Cut!' yelled the director. 'Who the fuck was it this time?'

Harrie grimaced and raised the hand with the phone in it. 'Sorry. It's off now. Sorry.'

The director swore again and said, 'OK, let's take from ... *Liber scriptus*. Rewind would you? After three. One, two, three ... rolling.'

'*Liber scriptus proferetur,*' rang out the recording, while the choir of twenty or so looked solemn and the tenor mimed along. '...*in quo totum*—'

A guy behind Harrie sneezed, and this

time everyone cracked up.

'Cut! OK, one more chance, then you're all sacked. Rewind the tape again to *Liber scriptus*... Done? OK, one, two three...'

'*Liber scriptus proferetur, in quo totum continetur,*' Harrie's eyes darted about nervously, waiting for someone to go into labour or something, as did lots of others.

'Cut!' cried the director, before throwing his arms in the air and stomping off down the nave.

Harrie sat, put the sheets of music on her lap and checked to see who'd called. Number unknown, she was told.

'It's a tiresome business, isn't it?' said the white-haired woman beside her. She was nicely spoken and distinguished-looking, and Harrie felt this might be a come-down for her.

'Mm.'

'But at least it's beautifully cool in here.'

'True,' Harrie said, smiling and wafting her face with a hand. 'I could do without the cassock, though.'

'Yes,' the woman agreed. 'Do you think we'll ever get past this book business?'

'What do you mean?'

'*Liber scriptus proferetur, in quo totum continetur,*' she said without even looking at the sheet. 'A book will be brought forth, in which all will be written.'

'Hey, I'm impressed,' Harrie said. Are you

an academic or a doc...? I'm sorry, what did you say about a book?'

'A book will be brought forth, in which all will be written. It's the translation of–'

'Oh God.' Harrie flopped back in the pew. A diary was a kind of book. It had been brought forth. Was she being told to check it out? Something – someone? – had made the director move her from the second row of the sopranos to the front, right next to a person who *spoke Latin*. And whose was the unknown number, interrupting her at that very point in the *Requiem*? 'Bea?' she whispered, looking up at a stained-glass window, then turning to her neighbour. 'Thank you *so* much.'

'You're welcome,' said the woman, frowning.

When the minibus dropped her off in Oxford around nine, Harrie went straight home and got to work. She'd been busy since Saturday and had only skimmed through the diary. Now she went at it slowly.

She started by checking the later entries for 'I think they're trying to poison me' or 'Dr French has quadrupled my medication,' or better still, 'I've put my new will safely in the...' but no luck. Throughout most of the four and a half years it was mainly dentist, doctor, tuition and other appointments.

There were instructions to herself to send

74

presents and cards, and there were lots of walks mentioned. 'Five miles round Sapperton' or, 'Great Tew circular – meet at Falkland Arms'. She'd obviously been a robust old lady before the illness kicked in, and socially active too: 'Lionel's croquet party', 'Tea with Meg, St Aldate's Coffee House'. Also, there were lots and lots of references to a 'B', scattered throughout the years. 'B called round – lunched in garden', 'Seaside with B! B such a help in the garden today', 'B back from Taiwan – hurrah. Where would I be without my B?'

B was definitely a he, and sometimes the entries about him were quite lengthy. He was obviously important to the old lady. Good for her, thought Harrie. 'B' stood for Bertie, she finally decided, picturing a slim and adventurous, white-haired man.

Harrie noticed that for a period of several weeks, each day had assorted letters in tiny writing; always in the bottom left corner. 'WWTC', 'PLLJ', 'WTTC'. Sometimes the letters were repeated, other times not quite repeated; a letter or two different. A code maybe? She was about to call her brother, then thought better of it. What interest had he taken in the diary? None. Everything about Bea seemed to spook him these days. She was on her own, Harrie realised, scrambling around her messy bedroom for pen and paper. She wondered how you set about breaking a code without the mind of Stephen Hawking, so first, just wrote down the dates and the letters.

Half an hour later, with a brain as sharp as porridge, she had a page full of dates and letters in front of her and no idea what to do next. She thought about looking for patterns, then wondered if the letters simply stood for words: WTTC – went to the cinema. In the end, she knew she wasn't up to clear thought. How good could it be for you, miming to Latin all day?

She decided to turn in early. 'Night,' she said to Patrick as she floated through the living room with a glass of water.

'Good night,' he replied. He was lying on the floor with his head on two books. 'Oh, someone called Malc rang. I guessed you wouldn't want to speak to him.'

'No, I wouldn't. God, I wish Mum would go ex-directory.'

'He asked for your mobile number. Said I didn't know it.'

'Thanks, Patrick.' Malc was such a moron. 'I owe you one.'

TEN

On Sunday morning, Will set out to turn over the soil from where Patrick had left off a week ago. Joy offered him the communal fork. She also offered him a glass of sangria, but what with it being ten in the morning, he just took the fork.

'Thanks,' he said, while she relocked the shed.

Beside them, Terry straddled his Kawasaki in a helmet. *If you can read this, the bitch has fallen off* said the back of his T-shirt. Will wondered how many women had ridden pillion with Terry, and whether it just referred to Joy. When the bike was let down off its stand and started up with a loud crack and roar, Joy jumped out of her skin and Hugh slammed his French doors shut.

'Taking her out?' Will shouted.

Terry said, 'Maybe.'

But, ten minutes later, after Will had wandered down the path and turned over several forksful, Terry was still roaring away on the spot. It wasn't pleasant; the noise, the fumes. Will downed tool and approached Terry with a turn-the-thing-off gesture.

'Sorry, mate,' Terry said when it fell silent

again. 'Thought I heard a bit of a whine.'

Will nodded. 'Big bike. Very impressive.'

'Ta. It's a Ninja. Six hundred.'

'Nice blue.'

'Officially Candy Blue, but that's a bit friggin' gay, if you ask me. Cobalt, I call it.'

'So...' said Will. 'Going to take me out on it?'

Terry grinned. 'Sorry, no spare helmet.'

'I thought I saw one in the shed.'

Suddenly Terry wasn't grinning. 'Er, yeah ... but that one's useless.'

'Nah, it'll be all right. We'd only be going for a short spin. I'll just go and get the shed key.'

Terry's eyes went rigid with panic. 'OK.'

Will walked down the side of the house and into the kitchen, where he lingered for a while, hoping Terry would dismount, prop his bike up again and cover it. What he heard instead, was Terry wheeling the thing down the passage; over the crunchy gravel outside the back door and towards the front garden. He pictured him on tiptoe. Next came the crack and vroom of the engine starting up, then the gentle fading roar of Terry heading off somewhere. Not what Will had planned, but at least the machine would get some exercise.

'Did I hear Terry go out?' cried Joy, rushing at Will with alcohol-flushed cheeks. 'On his *motorbike?*'

'Yep.'

'Goodness gracious, he'll crash and die.'

'Terry hasn't taken his monster *out?*' asked Hugh, popping up from the basement.

Joy's head nodded frantically.

'Oh Lord,' said Hugh, back of a hand on his brow. 'Now does anyone know where *he* put his will?'

Joy seemed to be praying, and Will wondered if she might be a bit in love with Terry. He could think of odder couples, but not many. 'He'll be fine,' he said. And, sure enough, as he spoke, a motorcycle engine could be heard approaching the house, followed by the sound of something smashing. They all ran out and down the passage to find the silent bike propped awkwardly on the front door steps and Terry removing his helmet.

'My pot of salvia!' cried Joy. 'But who cares!' She went towards Terry but then seemed to check herself.

'Just as I thought,' Terry was saying with a shake of the head. 'Engine's buggered. Another time, eh, Will?'

All the weeds and old roots and things went in the wheelbarrow, just as Patrick had instructed, then Will turned the soil again and picked out yet more weeds before moving on ten inches.

Who on earth could find this fun? His

back ached already, and the slow progress and constant stooped position wasn't doing much for his mood. And what the hell was he going to do with the patch once it was turned over? Patrick said potatoes, carrots and the brassicas were easy, but growing nothing was surely a lot easier.

In the distance Joy called his name. 'Harrie on the phone!'

'Good,' he said, stabbing the fork in the ground.

'What do you think it means?' asked his sister. They were in his room, sitting on the oriental rug. Harrie peered at a page of the diary. 'For example, M R T P T C T.'

Will got her to repeat it and jotted down the letters, then chewed on the pen. 'Must remember,' he said slowly, '...to ... pay the...'

'Council tax?'

'Very good!'

Harrie frowned. 'But why not just write, "Pay council tax"?'

'Hmm,' said Will, growing bored with the game. He wondered if he could get Harrie to do some digging.

'I mean, that's hardly top secret, is it?'

'Yes,' he said. 'I mean, no. Listen, why don't I sit and look over the diary. Alone. I'll be able to concentrate better. You could go and do a bit in my garden, if you want?'

'Sure.'

Will came round when he felt something being tugged from his hand. The ghost of Bea was his immediate thought, but it was his terrifying sister.

'You've really been concentrating, then?' she said, waving the diary at him. 'God, Will, I've been digging over your garden in the baking sun. I even emptied Bea's compost bin and spread it all over for you, because Patrick's always going on about how brilliant composting is, in all senses.'

He was about to thank her but she charged on. 'Honestly, Will, I don't understand why you're not totally intrigued by Bea and the missing will and these strange letters. It's just bicycles and booze with you, isn't it? Bikes and booze, bikes and booze.'

Pulling himself up off the rug, Will wondered if life with Naomi had been heaven on earth compared to life with most women. 'Actually, I *am* interested,' he said, suddenly wanting a beer. 'I just think it's up to the beneficiaries of this so-called missing will to sort it out. Or the authorities, or probate, or God, or whatever.'

'What do you mean, "so-called"?'

'Well,' he said, lowering his voice, 'can we believe that lot? They told me Bea died in hospital and she didn't.'

Harrie pursed her lips and tapped the diary. 'Mmm,' she said. 'Are you saying they might have made up the will because they don't want you somehow informing Simon of Bea's death?'

Will shrugged. 'Maybe.'

'If that's the case, why tell you about Bea at all? They could have just let you a room and made up a landlord.'

'Obviously that occurred to me,' said Will, even though it hadn't. He sighed and rubbed at his back, wanting to escape. From the Bea business, the garden. 'Why don't we go to the pub? That one in North Parade, yeah? Did you come on your bike? We could cycle.'

Will started gathering wallet, mobile, keys, when Harrie said, 'See what I mean, Will? *See*.'

'What?'

After Harrie stormed downstairs, he sat on the bed and reflected on what she'd said. He went everywhere on a bike, worked on bikes and spent most of his spare time in pubs. It could be she was right.

And what had happened to the serious Will who was going to emerge from this new environment? The one who'd take in Coffee Concerts at the Holywell, and Ashmolean lectures on Renaissance pottery. Have discussions with pals in the Turf Tavern, using words like 'parameter', 'a priori', 'nascent'... He picked up his phone again and sent Jon a text– 'Sorry, loads to do, can't make pub later' – then went to look for Harrie, but she'd gone.

He wasn't sure if he was pleased or not but, rather than call her, he wandered down to his garden, where most of the area in front of the bean canes was now dug over. Beside the upturned compost bin, the fork stood in the ground. Surely his sister hadn't turned over all that soil? Or, in her case, mud. Good on her! He took his phone from his jeans and texted Jon, telling him he could make it after all.

ELEVEN

Bea grew to appreciate the company and the extra income, but not the extra work. Following her successful Christmas dinner, a food fund was set up, to which the boys, quite rightly, contributed far more than she did. Most days Bea would shop, then cook an evening meal, but she couldn't say she enjoyed it.

On top of that, Terry was untidy: shoes all over the place, used teabags, dirty cups, bits of tobacco, beer cans, scraps of paper with phone numbers on. When confronted, he was always apologetic, but Bea could see the chap was quite blinkered to the trails he created. In the end, she bought a large plastic tub, into which she threw each of his misplaced things. Once every week or so, he took it to his room and emptied it. Hugh, on the other hand, was tidy but wouldn't, for example, think of vacuuming the drawing room or scouring the toilet.

Increasingly, Bea felt like the housekeeper, and, at the beginning of February, she made the decision to bring in a fourth housemate. A woman, this time. A woman who wouldn't mind taking on the chores and the cooking, perhaps for a reduced rent. Discussions took place around the table, as to where to put her, and by late March, after consultations with an architect and the Council, and the cashing-in of a savings plan, work was underway to create an attractive and lettable attic room on the cheap. Terry was happy to sort out the wiring and help the builder knock down the middle wall, and Hugh offered to decorate – although Bea wasn't going to be holding her breath on the latter.

Not caring to witness the chaos, or indeed make endless cups of tea for workmen, Bea spent a fortnight with Meg in the Peaks. There, they read a great deal and watched rain lash at the windows of their holiday cottage. Every couple of days they ignored the weather and donned boots and anoraks for a bracing hilly walk. There wasn't a telephone in the cottage, but messages could be conveyed via the owner next door.

When, at the end of the two weeks, Bea hadn't heard a thing, she assumed nothing untoward had happened to her house and finally relaxed.

On her return, it was with a minor adrenalin rush that Bea lowered her suitcase in the hall and called out, 'Anyone home?' It was a Monday and early afternoon, so of course no one was. She was aware of an odd smell to the place, or rather, a combination of smells. Varnish, sawdust, wet plaster and – she poked her head round Terry's door – yes, pizza.

Someone had vacuumed the stairs, Bea noticed as she ascended, but hadn't got into the crevices, or tackled the banisters or skirting boards. Still, she thought, there must have been a great deal of dust to deal with. As she climbed the second flight, Bea found herself pitying the poor woman who'd have to trek all this way, simply to fetch a book or something. However, on reaching the final stair and stepping into the attic, Bea knew instantly that that woman would be she.

Furniture was moved, items were thrown out or given away – often painfully – and an advertisement was placed. Towards the end of April, Bea and the boys interviewed eight women of varying ages, backgrounds and ethnic origins, and emerged with a short-list of two, from which Bea alone was to choose.

It was an easy decision.

Joy was a bubbly blonde divorcee, who'd endured many a beating whilst married, one of which had resulted in a miscarriage. As she recounted her grisly tale, Bea sensed nothing of the victim in her potential lodger, and she liked that. Joy was from good, no-nonsense, pick-yourself-up-again working-class stock, sensed Bea. The other short-listed woman, again divorced, was amiable enough, but had given off a faint air of defeat. What really swung it for Joy, though, were the two freshly homemade and truly delicious chocolate éclairs she'd arrived with.

'I've brought along a pair of *chouxs*,' she'd punned with an infectious giggle. 'Get it?'

TWELVE

Harrie was trying to avoid Dan, a good-looking but geeky guy she'd somehow ended up in bed with after their graduation ball. Dan was still in Oxford, post-gradding, and just would not get the message. He had a present for her, apparently. Wanted to call round with it. After a long day as a wartime WAAF, it was the last thing Harrie needed. That was why she found herself pulling up outside Will's house just as he arrived home on his bike.

When his face dropped on seeing her, Harrie went into ultra-pleasant mode. 'Hi!' she sang, getting out of her old Renault and holding her palms in the air. 'Look, no diary!'

Will said, 'Good,' and she followed him in.

Joy was kneeling on the sink unit, cleaning windows with newspaper, Hugh was sketching at the dining table and Terry was distantly drumming. 'Ever tried this method, Harrie?' asked Joy over her shoulder.

Will broke into a belly laugh, which was preferable to the long face, even if it was at her expense. 'No,' said Harrie, who'd never exactly cleaned a window. Weren't there guys with buckets who did that?

'Try it next time, but only use black and white newspaper. The fancy coloured pages don't work.'

'Will do.' Harrie peered over Hugh's shoulder at a drawing of a woman cleaning windows.

'Do keep still,' he told his model. 'I'm almost there.'

Harrie was impressed, but didn't see Joy's arms as quite that muscular, her rear as quite that tight-bunnish. It reminded her of Michelangelo's women – men in frocks, basically. 'You're good,' she said. 'I'd love to see other stuff you've done.'

'Would you?' Hugh asked, looking up at her gratefully. He put down his pencil and turned the pages of his large pad. 'Let me see... Well, here's Terry at a gig.'

'Hey.'

'I think I captured the utter sweatiness of him.'

'Yes,' said Harrie. 'You certainly did.'

'This is my mother's Chihuahua.'

'Aaah, look at those ears.'

'Hideous. And here's the aftermath of our last Christmas dinner.'

'Wow, so many bottles.'

'Yes,' sighed Hugh, turning another page. 'Well, you know Joy...'

'Less of that,' giggled Joy. 'Can I get down now?'

'By all means. Oh yes, here's one I'm extremely fond of.'

Jesus, thought Harrie, no wonder. The drawing, in charcoal, was of a gorgeous guy arranged casually on a sofa. He wore jeans and a T-shirt that hinted at a firm chest and six-pack stomach. His feet were bare and just perfect, but not as perfect as his face: full lips, dark, vaguely slanting eyes and high cheekbones. His black hair was straight and made to look shiny. He was stunning.

'I can see you like my boy,' Hugh said.

What did he mean, 'my boy'? Boyfriend, perhaps. Only the guy looked too young. He didn't look gay either, but she'd often got that one wrong.

Joy came and joined them. 'He's a looker, your son, that's for sure.' She nudged Hugh, crumpled paper still in hand. 'Let's see the one of me, then.'

Harrie took herself off to the sofa to recover, only she couldn't. Her heart pounded, her stomach flipped, her mind raced. What was going on?

She was just as affected the second time she looked at the portrait, and the third, fourth... 'Bruno' was written in the bottom left corner; bottom right was Hugh's signature and a recent date. She slowly recognised the sofa. Only a few weeks ago, this lovely man was in that very room, sitting where she'd just been sitting. Something strange was happening in her chest, down her spine, in the pit of her stomach. It wasn't hunger. Joy was heating something in the oven, but even if invited to stay for dinner, Harrie knew she couldn't eat a bite.

She concentrated on Bruno's eyes – the windows to the soul – and sensed intelligence, creativity, integrity. She saw a guy with standards, who was fiercely loyal and maybe a champion of the world's underprivileged. He was a poet, she decided, even if he wasn't aware of it. He read only literary novels and informative journals and, unlike her brother, could go days without alcohol. He was fantastic with children.

'It's a good likeness,' Hugh said, sliding on to a chair beside her. 'I think it's the first time I've captured whatever all his women see.'

Harrie blinked at him. 'Women?'

Hugh raised his eyebrows. 'He does rather get through them, but then he will go for airheads.'

'Oh.' How disappointing. But maybe Hugh was wrong, or jealous or something. 'And what does he do?'

'Bugger all, as far as I can tell. Unless you count pulling pints in a seedy dive as doing something.'

'I see.' Harrie closed the sketch pad and threw Joy a big smile. 'Something smells good.'

'Steak and ale pie. Want to join us?'

'If that's OK?' She handed the drawings back to Hugh. 'I'm famished.'

After dinner, they talked about the will. About the urgency of finding it before someone – the Inland Revenue, for example – got on to Bea's son.

'Could be tracking Simon down to screw inheritance tax out of him,' said Terry. 'Trouble is, we're a bit ignorant about all this stuff. Joy got a book out of the library but we were none the wiser. We've really got to find this sodding will.'

'It sounded ever so fiddly,' Joy was saying,

'sorting out a person's pensions and things. Savings accounts, subscriptions... And it would be all for nothing if we didn't find the will.'

Terry leaned back in his chair, arms folded. 'Maybe we should have one last concerted effort to find it. Search the bloody house top to bottom again. What do you reckon?'

'Oh Lord,' Hugh groaned.

'Now?' asked Harrie enthusiastically.

Her brother wriggled. 'I'm not sure I can–'

'Yes, you can. Tell you what, why don't Will and I take the ground floor, and you lot the attic? Fresh eyes and all that.'

Will wriggled again. 'I, er, might just need to go and tidy up a bit.' He jumped from his chair and headed for the stairs. 'Give me five minutes.'

'We don't care about the Class A drugs!' Terry called out.

Joy cackled and said, 'Speak for yourself,' while she gathered up the condiments. 'How was my rough puff pastry?'

Hugh pursed his lips. A little more rough than puff, perhaps?'

'Oh dear. Terry?'

Terry was miles away, staring at the table-cloth. 'Come to think of it,' he said, 'maybe I should do some tidying too.'

After Hugh also disappeared, Harrie told Joy about the diary she'd found, tucked away in the desk.

'Did you really?' said Joy. 'Bea got ever so forgetful, couldn't find keys and her pension book, and what have you. So we decided, she and I – a place for everything, and everything in its place. A key hook by the back door. A compartment in the bureau for her pension book, another for her savings book, and so on. She obviously chose that drawer for her diary. I can't imagine it was top secret, though!'

'Actually, I'm not so sure. You see, for awhile she wrote these little letters down, like a code or something.'

'I expect that was her medication.'

'Sorry?'

'I suggested she wrote down what she'd taken, on account of the forgetfulness. Only she said she kept getting the names of the pills muddled or wrong, poor old love. Got herself into a right mess. Anyway, then we set her up a medication organiser. You know, one of those–'

'Yes,' said Harrie, gutted that the letters only stood for tablets, but pleased she wouldn't have to go on any more code-breaker websites. 'My granny had one.'

An hour and a half later, they gathered again in the kitchen/diner/den for hot chocolate. While the housemates used their personalised mugs, Harrie drank from one with a naked man on it. He was in good shape and nice-looking, despite the nineties hair. She assumed it was Hugh's but it turned out to have been Bea's. Having now seen photos of the late Bea, with her strong face and mischievous eyes, Harrie wasn't surprised.

'So,' said Joy, 'that just leaves the basement and first floor to recheck. But, to be honest, I've been through my rooms with a fine-tooth comb.'

Harrie said, 'You're absolutely certain she wrote this will, leaving you all the house?'

'Ask the bloody neighbours,' snapped Terry.

'But they only witnessed it. You don't actually, for sure, know what she put in it, do you? Maybe she left everything to … to…'

'Her rambling group?' chipped in Will.

'Quite.'

Hugh said, 'I doubt it. But I think we might have to accept that Bea simply changed her mind. Tore the thing up.'

In the gloomy silence that followed, Will drained his WILL mug and said, 'Anyone fancy a pint at the Rose?'

Joy perked up. 'Ooh, *ra-ther.*'

Terry said he was up for it, and Harrie thought she might be too. Hugh first declined but was easily talked round. Terry checked his jeans for cash, Joy took her compact out and Hugh ran a comb through his one or two hairs. When the phone rang,

Harrie jumped up for it, but Will got there first.

'Hello,' he said, then after a while, 'Will... Yes, I am... Oh, a couple of weeks now... Uh-huh... Right... Right...' Harrie wondered why her brother was staring that way; why he'd gone so very grey in the face. 'Just one moment,' he almost whispered, then held a shaky phone in the direction of his house-mates. 'Someone called Simon,' he told them, eyes wide. 'Wanting to speak to his mother.'

THIRTEEN

To Bea, a gig would always be a two-wheeled carriage pulled by a horse. For three years she managed to avoid Terry's 'gigs', but then came his forty-fifth birthday bash at the Rowing Club. Terry's band, the charmingly named Eaten Alive, were to perform to a couple of hundred people – friends and family – and Bea knew it would be churlish, rude even, not to go.

She consulted Terry's daughter, now eighteen, about what one wore. 'Black,' was Melanie's advice, but Bea felt nothing could be more funereal than an old lady in black. It took her a while to decide, but in the end she went for pink – as, coincidentally, did her escort. On arriving at the club, Hugh put a protective arm around her waist, despite the fact that Bea towered over him in her heels. She was astonished to find they had to pay to enter, but assumed that was the difference between a party and a gig. Once inside, Hugh found them seats, fetched two drinks and, for quite some time, ogled a particularly swarthy dancer in a singlet.

Bea, on the other hand, was fascinated by Terry and his wild intense stare as he thumped and thumped away at the rear of the small stage. Clearly, some deep primeval need was being tapped into, regardless of what it might be doing to his hearing. Slipping a finger in one ear, Bea wondered if it was an essentially male need, but then saw several young women in the audience, rhythmically flinging their heads back and forth, back and forth, in a similar way to people in asylums. Had her generation missed out somehow, never having bashed or banged in this way? In her teens, Bea had learned to tango, which, with its sudden jerky movements, probably came closest.

'Let me know if you fancy a bop,' shouted Hugh.

Bea laughed. 'I might fall and break a hip!'

'I'll catch you,' he promised, and before long Bea was trying to copy his movements on the dance floor. Her arms swirled, her head wobbled, her feet shuffled, but her bottom didn't wiggle – at least, not the way Hugh's did. One had to draw the line somewhere.

It had been fun, of sorts, but she didn't hurry to repeat the experience. The music wasn't to her taste – 'grunge', Hugh called it, which seemed appropriate – and she'd been at least twenty-five years older than the next oldest person there; possibly Terry. But at least she could now say she'd been to a 'gig', should anyone enquire.

Far more pleasurable, for Bea, was to spend time with Bruno, who'd now reached the awkward age of twelve. The boy had long since stopped playing with Simon's toys, and no longer wanted to potter in the garden with his father. He was still a sweet and engaging child but, when left to his own devices, would simply play video games in the drawing room; sometimes with a friend, often alone.

The secret, Bea discovered, was not to leave him to his own devices. She took him out, doing things that held no interest for his father. Men could be so selfish and rigid, Bea concluded, even the queer ones. Would it have killed Hugh to sit through 'Antz'?

She and Bruno started going to jumble sales and church bazaars, where he'd fill a carrier bag with items he'd pay attention to for a while, then abandon – strange futuristic models, a baseball bat. It was picking up things for a bargain that he liked. Bea would perhaps buy a sponge cake or a bag of sausage rolls, although once she found a bundle of ragtime sheet music, which led to hours of enjoyment; for her, if not for her lodgers and neighbours.

Yes, she thoroughly enjoyed Bruno's company. They did so much laughing together, that was the thing. Had Simon *ever* had a sense of humour? Aware of Hugh's relief that his son was being entertained with no effort on his part, Bea stopped feeling guilt at monopolising the child, and came up with ever-more-exciting trips. They'd go to all sorts of places in her Saab. Strapped into the passenger seat, Bruno would chat away, or they'd listen to a story on tape. It was fun, and Bea often felt Hugh was missing out on something special, for he chose not to own a car, claiming the train could shoot him into London in half the time it would take to drive.

Bea thought, if only for his son's sake, Hugh might have invested in a vehicle. But he hadn't, just as Terry and Joy hadn't either. Terry pleaded poverty but Bea suspected he liked his beer too much and didn't want to risk a conviction. Joy's excuse was that her ex-husband had drained her of any confidence she might have once had at the wheel. It was all very well, turning their back on car ownership, but none of her lodgers were averse to cadging lifts from her, often for no remuneration, just a quick peck on the cheek, or a 'Thanks ever so'. Did they think petrol was given away?

Not that Bea wanted to charge Hugh for driving Bruno around. In fact, she'd have paid Hugh, so enjoyable and varied were their outings. They had a day at the races, where Bruno placed bets via Bea and went home several pounds better off. She took him to the Railway Museum, and as they chugged along in a steam train, told him how things had been when she was a girl. About the war. He listened and even asked questions. Bea couldn't think of another person who might be interested in her childhood.

Back at the house he'd plug himself into a game again, giving his father only short monotone accounts of what they'd done– 'We went to the owl centre. There were loads of owls' – which often seemed enough for Hugh.

Always at the back of Bea's mind, though, was the thought that, at any moment, Bruno could go from endearing and interested, to unlikeable, critical and morose. She braced herself each time he visited, but he turned thirteen with no discernible signs of change, even helping plan and host her seventy-second birthday gathering.

'What an absolutely charming young man,' one old friend said, then went on, rather pointedly, to ask how and where Simon was.

'He's in Hong Kong,' Bea told her. At least he had been, the last time he'd contacted her. It was a call that, as usual, had left her reeling. He'd scolded her again for letting strangers invade their house. *Their* house? Primarily, he cursed his late father for forcing her to take in paying guests. Said he'd come and visit if it wasn't for them. Bea put down the phone, relieved that her son was on the other side of the world, and with a renewed gratitude for her housemates.

FOURTEEN

Will had sold two new mountain bikes, four expensive locks, a couple of helmets and a second-hand Raleigh Chopper, which were suddenly the rage. All this before lunch. Not bad. He checked the time again, not wanting to be late for the strategy meeting in the King's Arms. At twelve-twenty, he asked Neil if he could leave early, then zoomed and zigzagged his way to the pub, arriving just as the others were ordering drinks and food.

Hugh, Joy and Terry wore a shell-shocked, hadn't-slept appearance and looked grateful for the chairs they eventually lowered themselves on to. While three of them waited for coffees to arrive, Joy swigged her Malibu and said, 'I suppose one of my sisters might take me in.'

Terry groaned. 'You're hardly fucking destitute, woman. You've got a job.'

'Part time,' snapped Joy. 'And practically minimum wage.'

Will wasn't sure he liked the atmosphere. And none of them looked awake enough to talk strategy. He'd slept well himself, despite the bomb-that-was-Simon dropping. Will had no desire to move again, though. In fact, he was strangely happy in Bibury Road. Living with old people wasn't that bad. There was none of that pressure you got in a standard house-share – to be bitingly witty, listen to the right music, regularly drink till you fell over. If asked, he'd say he could be *more* himself with Terry, Joy and Hugh, which was a bit bizarre.

However, should it come to it, Will would easily find other accommodation. There were a zillion ads around town wanting a young professional to move in – professional meaning employed person, rather than chartered surveyor. Luckily. But what would you do if you were fifty-something and had a laugh like a car not starting?

'It might not come to that,' he told Joy, trying to buck her up.

'You think?' asked Hugh. He wore a pale lemon top with orange trim and flared three-quarter-length sleeves. It suited him well but wouldn't help him get a place in a shared house. Terry might struggle too, what with the grumpy face and the *No, I won't fix your computer* T-shirt.

'I mean,' said Will, 'all we know is that Simon was contacted by his mother's solicitor.'

'Bastard,' said Terry. 'Playing that "Can I speak to my mother?" trick on us.'

'And,' continued Will, who'd had Harrie on the phone to him first thing, 'even if there is a will, you might have a right to remain in the house as sitting tenants.'

'Oh, I do hope so,' said Joy. She stood up with her empty glass. 'Don't say another thing till I'm back from the bar.'

The coffees and food arrived and, in turn, Terry, Hugh and Joy talked about their contributions to the house. 'Nearly got myself killed knocking the attic wall down.' (Terry) 'All my cooking and cleaning.' (Joy) 'I've spent the equivalent of a small inheritance on the garden.' (Hugh) 'Gosh, these Malibus go quickly.' (Joy)

By the end of Will's precious lunch break,

101

the momentous decision they'd arrived at was to wait and see what happened next.

After work, he was locking his bike at the back of the house when he heard a loud public-school accent through the open window. Simon, he guessed, and reluctantly went in.

A tall, large-nosed man in his fifties, with auburn and grey hair, too long at the back, was leaning against the fridge-freezer, looking down on Hugh, Terry and Joy at the table. He was casually dressed in short-sleeved shirt and blue jeans, and didn't at all reek of wealth. He said, 'Will, I presume?'

'Yes.'

'Simon.'

'Hi.'

'Sangria, Will?' asked Joy.

'No, thanks.' What he wanted was a beer. 'Do you mind?' he said to Simon, pointing at the fridge.

Simon peeled himself off it, jangling the coins in his pocket as he walked over to lean against the broom cupboard instead. He obviously couldn't bring himself to sit down.

'So,' Will said as he pulled the ring off a can, 'shall I go to my room, or do you want me to stay?' He was addressing his house-mates but it was Simon who answered.

'This business affects you, so do take a seat.'

Will shut the fridge and leaned against it. 'Please. Carry on.'

Simon stopped jangling. 'I was saying how appalled I am that no one saw fit to inform me of Mother's passing away.'

'We're ever so sorry,' said Joy. 'Only we honestly didn't know where you were.'

'Surely a quick search through her address book would have found me?'

'But all the entries for you were crossed through.'

Jingle jangle went the loose change, then it stopped. 'Lucky I've stayed in touch with Bagshaw, then. He only heard about Mother last week.'

'Bagshaw?' asked Will.

'Ma's solicitor. Old school pal of mine. Recently replaced Rogers senior, only I don't suppose Ma knew that. Anyway, we're all to go and see him at four tomorrow for the reading of the will. I believe he's contacted you lot now?'

Joy managed a nod, while Terry, with his clenched white-knuckled fist, looked close to violence. Hugh sat back in his chair looking unbothered, or maybe just defeated.

'And which will would that be?' asked Will, chuckling to himself.

'What do you mean?' said Simon. The background noise had stopped again, and

Will suddenly got it – Simon jangled when others spoke, stopped when he spoke. 'My mother's will, of course. That old Rogers drew up for her.'

The others were glowering at Will; their faces saying *No, don't go there*. 'Er ... yeah, of course. Sorry, long day at work.'

Simon announced that he needed to use the little boys' room, and while he was gone, Will grabbed another beer and joined the huddled whispering at the table.

'Golly, he's scary.'

'Arrogant bloody wanker.'

'Black brogues and jeans, *really*.'

'Oh-oh, here he comes.'

'So,' boomed Simon, striding back in and whipping a sports jacket from the back of a chair, 'see you all tomorrow. Not you, of course, Will.'

'No.'

'I'm at the Wayside Guesthouse, should you need to get hold of me.'

'Right,' said Terry, who did look as though he wanted to get hold of him.

Simon held a palm up, said, 'Toodle pip,' and left.

'Arsehole,' growled Terry.

Joy hiccuped. 'He's gone to seed a bit. So dashing last time he was here. When was that? The millennium?'

Hugh pulled a face. 'Brogues, jeans, mullet *and* a sports jacket. How very ex-pat.'

Later, Will lay on his bed, ankles crossed, hands behind his head, Radio 3 on. He may have only had the room a couple of weeks, and he may have been sharing it with a ghost, but he was going to miss it. He'd even started reading some of Bea's books – *Silas Marner, Das Capital* – and wondered if he'd be able to slip some into his packing boxes. Simon didn't look the reading type. Just the business pages, maybe, or the odd annual report. Strange bloke. Not at all what Will had expected, apart from the arrogance. He pictured him now, irritating other guests in the hotel dining room with his coin jiggling. Hotel? No ... hadn't he said a guesthouse ... the Wayside? No, surely not the Wayside? That place he cycled past every day, that was one up from sleeping rough? Where there was always at least one guy with a can out the front?

Will shot up and galloped down the stairs to look in the Yellow Pages. 'Hotels and Guesthouses' he found. 'Wayside Bed and Breakfast.' There was only the one in Oxford.

'How strange,' he said.

'What's that?' asked Joy from behind the cooker. She and the others were having a last-ditch attempt to find the will.

'Simon.'

Her head appeared. 'What?'

'Well, wouldn't you think he'd be staying

at like the Randolph or somewhere? Not the cheapest, roughest B and B in town?'

'Oh, I *say*. Is he?'

Terry heaved the fridge-freezer back in place. 'Maybe that's how he got rich, by being a tight arse.'

'Maybe,' said Will.

Hugh reversed out of the large broom cupboard and brushed down his clothes. 'So,' he said, hands on slim hips, 'there can only be the U-bends to forage through now. And forgive me if I pass on those.'

FIFTEEN

Harrie sipped cold water from a flowery cup and chatted to fellow extra Jill. They were in an old city-centre teashop, closed for the day for filming, and they'd been there for hours. Harrie's hair was rolled and tucked up in 1930s style, and round her shoulders lay a dead fox. A fake one, and firmly stitched to her jacket, but good enough for the faraway cameras. Jill had told Harrie all about her father's knee operation, and Harrie was now filling Jill in on her mother's half-a-gap year.

'Action!' they were told, and off they went again, trying to look elegant and animated while they drank their pretend tea.

'Anyway,' said Harrie, 'she's gone to stay with some new friend of hers, Kim, who lives in Melbourne.'

'*Golly!*' said Jill, as though Harrie had just told her something fascinating. She tilted her head and smiled. 'And what does he do?'

'He?'

'Kim.'

'Oh, right. It didn't occur to me it could be a bloke's name.'

'It usually is in Australia.'

'*Really?*' said Harrie, also cocking her head and beaming for the camera that might just be on her. One day she'd get spotted, be given a few lines ... find herself screen-testing for Ang Lee. 'I'll have to read Mum's email again. Maybe I just assumed it was a female friend.'

Jill poured milk in her cup of cold tea. 'No way would my dad let my mum go travelling.'

'Oh, my stepfather's cool about it. He's a feminist.'

'Cut!' they heard. 'OK, that's a wrap.'

'Thank God,' said Jill, flopping back in her seat. 'How did they wear these tiny fitted jackets? This one's killing me.'

They probably weren't a fourteen squeezed into a ten, thought Harrie, just as a familiar face walked past the nearby window. Terry.

But an unusual Terry, for he was wearing a suit and tie. Then came Hugh and Joy, nattering to each other and also dressed up. It dawned on Harrie that they were off to the reading of Bea's will. How exciting! Or maybe depressing? If only she could be there too. When everyone in the café stood up and started milling around, stripping off or going out for a smoke, Harrie wondered if perhaps she could be.

'Excuse me,' she said. 'Scuse. Sorry. Oops, sorry. Excuse me.' And then she was out on the pavement, Terry, Joy and Hugh marching onwards in the distance. Her pencil-slim skirt wouldn't allow her to run, but she managed a trot, turning into George Street just in time to catch them going through a door. Harrie sped up on her thick but high heels, and once inside the building, examined the list of firms. 'Rogers, Hope and Bagshaw,' she saw. 'Solicitors'. They were on the third floor, which was where the lift now was.

Harrie pressed the button and waited. She pressed it again when the lift didn't shift from the number 3. And again. Were they stuck up there, she wondered, while she jabbed away. Trapped in a lift with Terry – nightmare. But then floor 2 lit up, then 1, then G. When Harrie finally reached the offices of Rogers, Hope and Bagshaw, there was no one in sight but the receptionist, who let out a small wail.

Harrie tapped her fox's nose. 'Don't worry, he's friendly. Um, I'm here for the reading of Mrs White's will?'

'Oh,' the girl said, dragging her eyes from the animal and towards her screen. 'I fought everyone had arrived. What's the name?' Harrie told her, and she did some scrolling. 'You're not on the list Mr Bagshaw gave me. Are you like a relative or whatever?'

'Er, no. I'm a friend of the people who've just arrived. Couldn't I sort of, you know, creep in?'

'Sorry, no. I'll get a bollocking, then they'll get another temp. But have a seat if you want to wait for your friends.'

Harrie sighed and made her way to the sofa. 'I've been filming,' she said.

The girl stayed glued to her screen, as though actors were always dropping in to exchange contracts, or whatever. 'Right.'

'Big BBC production.'

The receptionist slid her mouse around with her maroon-talon nails and her eyes stayed on the screen. Harrie wondered if she was on eBay. 'Not another one,' was all she said.

Jealous, decided Harrie. She picked up a country-lifestyle magazine and flicked through, choosing the two-million-pound house she'd buy, once the Ang Lee deal was signed. She then discovered how to make wine from root vegetables, and how to grow and weave a willow fence. She read half an article on an organic-farming earl, and the whole of her stars for seven months ago.

What *were* they doing in there? Harrie had never been good at waiting, unlike Patrick, who'd sometimes sit and watch a cake through the glass oven door. 'How long does it usually take?' she asked the receptionist.

'Depends. If it was, like, Richard Branson's will, then, like, all afternoon. My nan's took, like, three minutes.'

'I see.'

Harrie went back to the magazine, where 'Twenty Quince Recipes' held her attention for a while. Who knew you could stuff a quince? In fact, what was a quince? Some way off, a door opened and someone, possibly Joy, called out, 'Simon!'

A tall man with a murderous expression then strode through reception, pushed the glass entrance open and disappeared down the stairs. The receptionist's eyes darted briefly to the closing door, then back to her screen. Harrie drummed fingers on the mag and thought *interesting*, then stood and tried to get a glimpse of the others. What she saw was Terry, walking towards her, head hung low, hands in his trouser pockets.

'Hi, Terry,' she said.

He looked up and stared. 'Is that you?'

'Yes, it's me. I've been filming.'

'Ah,' he said, and glumly made his way to the lift.

The other two appeared. Hugh nodded at Harrie and moved on, while Joy stopped and managed a smile. She smelled faintly of booze, but then it was four-thirty. 'Well, I never,' she said, patting Harrie's arm before joining the two men.

'What?' said Harrie, to no one in particular.

Two elderly women and a white-haired man then passed and went through the door. Harrie was about to follow them to the lift, when a couple of guys came down the corridor from the offices. One looked like a young solicitor and the other looked like a young god. The hair was slightly shorter than in Hugh's sketch, but the eyes were the same.

The solicitor shook Bruno's hand. 'If we can be of any further help, Mr Lamb, do let me know. Our conveyancing fees are very competitive, should you decide to sell.'

'Thank you,' he said in a deep soft voice. 'Obviously, I'm in shock at the moment. I'll need time to absorb all this.'

Harrie was pretty traumatised herself. If gods could talk, they'd sound just like him. Her heart thumped, her knees had completely gone. She picked up the magazine again and fanned her face, unsure whether to introduce herself.

'Goodbye,' Bruno said. 'And thanks again.' He pointed at the door. 'Better catch up with my father.' On his way past Harrie, he stopped and blinked at her fox. He then looked up and his eyes lingered on hers for a while. 'What's his name?' he asked.

'Basil,' she told him, amazed she could speak, but then wishing he'd been more original.

SIXTEEN

After five years of accumulation, Terry outgrew his space and persuaded Bea to let him knock down the wall between his and the drawing room. Since they all had their own domains, and Bea's precious piano was now up in the attic, she could see no reason to object. Particularly as Melanie was at university and no longer camped in that room, next door to her father's. Bruno always slept behind a partition in Hugh's basement. For some time, the drawing room had barely been used, the couch having mysteriously made its way into the large breakfast room.

Terry said, 'Think what a brilliant through-room I'll have. And it'll increase the value of the house no end when you come to sell. Not now, of course. Later. When we're all out your hair.'

'But why would I want to sell?' she'd asked.

'For the dosh, Bea, the dosh. Get yourself a nice cheap-as-chips villa on some costa del and live on the difference. Sorted.'

Bea had laughed at the very idea – surely one had to be blonde, bronzed and like peach bathroom fittings? – but she did agree to the removal of the wall. Clive and Valerie next door had done the very same thing, creating a room they could hold a ball in.

So down the wall came, causing elation in Terry and a touch of resentment in Bea. Such a glorious space had been created, only to house her lodger and his general detritus. Not that she ought to complain, for Terry had acted as builder's mate, so saving her a 'wad', apparently.

The residents now had an entire floor each. Bea's attic, with its sloping ceilings was, naturally, less spacious than the others, but when one took into account her balcony – just big enough for two chairs and a tiny table – it all appeared to be fair. Yes, Bea was quite content with the arrangement, even after her disapproving son made an un-expected appearance on the eve of the millennium.

'Felt I had to be home for the momentous occasion,' he said, frightening the life out of her. 'If you can fit me in, that is.'

Simon hadn't seen any of her birthdays as momentous enough for even a phone call, but Bea swallowed her bitterness and said, 'Yes, of course. Come in, come in. Terry's staying with family, so you can use his room.' They gave each other an awkward kiss. Simon wore a long woollen coat and had with him a large suitcase bound with straps. His face was more gaunt than five years previously, and his hair thinner. He wasn't losing it as rapidly as poor Hugh, though.

Bea's thrill at seeing her son faded within seconds of his entering the house. Nothing was right for him, and for two days she endured criticism after judgement after lecture, until the trains were running again and he left to visit an old friend.

On several occasions during his stay, Bea found herself gently weeping in the attic. Did Simon have some neurological disorder that made him so callous, so bullying? Donald's father, also successful in business, had been of a similar disposition. It was one reason, perhaps the main one, that Donald had felt compelled to break loose. As much as Bea believed Simon couldn't help being the way he was, she found herself desperately wanting to smack him, send him to his room, dock his pocket money. Alas, a little late in the day ... but an only child had been so easy to spoil.

Simon found it appalling that his mother was confined to the attic, was disgusted by Terry's mess and hated Hugh on sight. He bossed young Bruno around and treated Joy like the hired help. 'Honestly, Ma, you've got a slob on the ground floor, a charlady on the first and a fag in your basement. Then that kid comes and freeloads. Is this really how someone of your age and class should live?' Bea tried to tell him she was very happy with the arrangement and that she enjoyed the mix of people, but Simon wasn't a listener.

For tax reasons, he tried to pressure her into putting the house in his name. 'As soon as poss, eh? I'll get Rogers senior on to it. Should be quite straightforward.'

'No!' cried Bea, seeing herself thrust into a home before she knew it 'Don't.'

'Let me explain the–'

'*No*, Simon. I'm keeping my house and I won't sign anything. You can't make me.'

'Listen, Mother,' he said, affecting a kind smile. How duplicitous her son was. An hour earlier, he'd complimented Joy on her pork and bean casserole, whilst pulling a sour face at the others. 'It makes so much sense. The house will come to me, anyway. Why make me liable for inheritance tax?' He went on for another fifteen minutes or so, at one point making a veiled threat regarding power of attorney. Could Simon have her diagnosed insane because she shared her house with others?

'Well,' Bea said finally, 'let me think about it.' It was a ploy to get him off her back, but the subject arose several more times before, at last, he wheeled his suitcase towards a waiting taxi. What a dreadful thing it was to want to see the back of your only son.

'Goodbye,' she called out cheerily.

'Bye,' said Bruno beside her.

Both of them waved with fixed smiles until the taxi pulled away, then Bea sighed and flopped against the doorframe.

'Dickhead,' Bruno said quietly. He looked at Bea sheepishly. 'Sorry, but he really is.'

She laughed and gave him a squeeze. 'How clever of you, Bruno. That's the very word I've been searching for.'

The following morning saw Joy staring into space on the couch, nursing a glass of alcohol. It was the one day of the year when she allowed herself to be sombre, for it was the date her long-since-miscarried baby had been due. Bea sat with her for a while, patting her hand and reassuring her that having a child didn't necessarily bring one joy.

Joy shook her head. 'I know Simon's a bit of a plonker now...'

Another good word, thought Bea.

'...but I expect he was a sweet little boy once?'

'I'm sure he must have been. I simply can't recall it.'

'What really gets my goat,' said Joy, and Bea knew what was coming, 'is that my ex, Pete, has turned over a new leaf. Got a wife and two lovely kiddies now.'

'Life can appear terribly unfair,' Bea said, as she did each January the third. 'But they say a leopard never changes its spots.' Just look at Simon, she wanted to add. She took Joy's empty glass to the sink and rinsed it. 'Now, how about a little expedition into town? There's nothing like a new outfit to boost the morale, and we might find a bargain for you in the sales. What do you say?'

'Oh, Bea,' cried Joy, suddenly cuddling her from behind. 'You're like a second mum to me, you are.'

'Well, that's nice to hear.' Bea broke free and thanked God this was only a once-a-year event. 'Now go and put your face back on.'

Joy was always made up, from first thing till last thing each day – generally for Terry's benefit, Bea realised. The only time Joy bared her broken capillaries was when he went away. Tragically, it was a crush that was bound to go nowhere. Judging from Terry's occasional overnight guests, with their ghostly faces, matted hair and leather clothes, Joy was far from his type. For one thing, she wouldn't dream of going to the

117

lavatory without closing the door, as one girlfriend had regularly done. Bea couldn't decide if that was healthily uninhibited or plain uncivilised.

If only Joy would meet a suitable man and fall in love. This was most unlikely in her present job, Bea felt. One could hardly be swept off one's feet by a chap coming in about his prostate or a strange rash. Joy's home life was another barrier to her meeting Mr Right, for the place wasn't exactly awash with handsome middle-aged callers. Terry's 'mates' all looked as though they'd slept in their clothes, whilst Hugh's male visitors were on the young side and often had a furtive air. Was she damaging Joy's chances of future happiness, wondered Bea, by providing her with a safe and comfortable home at a peppercorn rent?

When Joy reappeared, all made up and with a whole different demeanour, Bea rather regretted her shopping suggestion, for the day was dry, crisp and bright and perfect for a country walk.

'First stop Debenhams?' asked Joy.

'Why not?' said Bea, unbuttoning the coat she'd just done up and taking her cardigan off. It was bound to be as hot as July in there.

SEVENTEEN

Will was in the Scholar with Bruno and Harrie. At least, he thought it was Harrie. It could have been a twin their mother had kept quiet about. One that flirted a lot, and made goo-goo eyes, and gave a gurgling, girly giggle at Bruno's witticisms.

Will and Bruno had left the olds wandering round the house in an eerie post-will-reading daze. Although Will had met Bruno only two hours ago, he'd taken to him straight away and suggested a drink, mainly to get the poor guy away from the atmosphere. He'd also called Harrie, who'd given a strange strangled scream, then turned up dressed like a hooker.

'You should have seen Simon's face,' Bruno was saying.

Harrie flung her head back and did the gurgling thing again, even though Simon hadn't said anything funny. Did she think it was sexy? Will wondered if he should tell her.

'So...' he said, as they were on the subject, 'when are you chucking me out, Bruno?'

'Not for a while, don't worry. And, besides, Simon might still contest things.'

Harrie, keeping up the inane grin and adding a concerned frown, said, 'Did his mother leave the poor guy anything?'

Poor guy? Yesterday he was an 'arse'.

'Just some personal belongings. Simon told the solicitor to shove them, then stormed out.'

'So, let me get this straight,' said Will. 'She wrote this will recently.'

'Er, I can't remember, to be honest. I was only half listening ... well, to begin with.'

'Was it witnessed by the neighbours?'

'Uh, I'm not sure.'

'What are their names, Harrie?'

'Clive and Valerie?' she said, smiling at the two men. She dipped a finger in her spritzer – where was her usual pint? – did little circles, then took it out and sucked it. Will was finding her scary.

'So,' he said, 'this is most likely the will she got Joy to buy for her?'

'Oh no,' said Bruno. 'This one was drawn up by the solicitor. I think Bea must have decided against the DIY one in the end. Obviously, I feel bad, but she must have had her reasons.'

''Scuse, guys,' said Harrie. 'Must powder my nose.' She stood up and smoothed her very short skirt over her buttocks, then wiggled her way across the room, flicking her blonde hair hither and thither, pink handbag hooked over one shoulder. She obviously thought Bruno was watching, but he was fiddling with a beer mat, miles away.

'So you know the conditions?' he asked Will.

'You mean in Bea's will? No, I don't.'

'She stipulated that if I sell the house, or if I ask them to move out, I must see that Dad, Joy and Terry are financially recompensed for the disruption. Bea left it up to me to decide how much. I was thinking of around thirty each.'

'Really?' Maybe Bruno wasn't that decent after all. Thirty wouldn't cover a man with a van. 'Listen, if you want to take over the attic room, just-let me know. Only, give me some notice, yeah?'

'Sure, but I'm OK where I am, especially now I'm there on my own. My girlfriend moved out a couple of weeks ago.' He raised his eyebrows and grinned. 'Thank God she left before all this happened, otherwise I'd have been stuck with her for life.'

'You didn't like her?'

'Oh, yeah. Carly's sweet, beautiful. Great fun, very soft and caring. But ... well, let's just say if she had another brain it would be lonely. And I think she'd just love to find herself a wealthy husband. Not work, have loads of babies.'

Will tutted and said, 'Know the type,' as though beautiful gold-diggers were the bane of his life. He and Bruno then talked about

121

women for a while, before Harrie eventually tottered back.

'Hey, you two,' she said, lowering herself on to her chair, unhooking her bag and crossing her strangely orange legs towards Bruno. 'You can stop talking about me now.' She giggled and batted some heavy-duty mascara. 'So, who's going to buy me another spritzer?'

Bruno said, 'Actually, I think I should be off. Bit worried about Dad.' He stood up and tucked his phone in a back pocket. 'Really nice meeting you guys. Might see you back at the house, Will?' He gave Harrie a quick smile and left.

'Oh, wow,' she went, kicking off her shoes and lifting her feet up, so that her knees were under her chin. 'Yuck, this fake tan smells rank.' She took some tissue from her bag and wiped lipstick off. 'Oh, wow.'

'What?'

'Oh, nothing. Get us a pint, would you?' She took a fiver out and handed it to him.

When Will returned from the bar, Harrie grabbed the glass and gulped some. 'Ta,' she said, plonking it on the table. 'So, what do you know about Bruno?'

'Well, we walked here, so quite a bit. He's sort of a struggling musician. Bea taught him the piano, then encouraged him when he took up the guitar.'

'Oh, wow, the guitar. It's so ... so...'

'What?'

'Romantic. It's said to represent the female body, you know. Mmm, Bruno and a guitar. Wow.'

'You all right?'

'Yeah, yeah. What else do you know about him?'

'He started an art history degree.'

'Wow.'

'Coerced into it by Hugh, but he dropped out. Since then he's had to take crap jobs while he tries to make a success of his band.'

Harrie turned and with wide nervous eyes, said, 'Girlfriend?'

'Not exactly. He's just come out of one relationship, but...' Will could see Harrie was anxious, and he didn't quite know how to put it. 'He said he thought he may have fallen for someone.'

'No!'

'Today.'

'What! Who?'

'He doesn't know. Someone he saw in the solicitor's office. Had a dead fox, of all things, round her shoulders. She looked like a really interesting woman, he said, and gorgeous with it. Wished he'd got her – hey, where are you going?' Will grabbed his sister's arm before her head could hit the floor, then yanked her upright. 'Harrie?'

Back at Bibury Road, Will found everyone

round the table, still looking tense, despite the four bottles of wine in their midst.

'Well, I never,' Joy was saying. 'You can't possibly give us that much, Bruno.'

'Sounds bloody reasonable to me,' said Terry. 'So long as you've got that left after tax. Simon told us you'll be stung something rotten.'

'And how cheerfully he said it,' chipped in Hugh.

Will took a seat next to an embarrassed-looking Bruno, who said, 'Actually, the tax is sort of taken care of.'

'Oh yeah?' asked Terry. 'Did she leave you an heirloom to flog as well?'

'No, but she took out this insurance policy, years and years ago, which pays out to me on her death. She told me about it once, and I thought maybe hundreds. She left the policy with the solicitor, and apparently it's ... well, worth quite a bit now. More than enough to pay inheritance tax.'

Will turned to look at the suddenly rich Bruno. If Harrie didn't marry him, he would.

'But, Bruno, dear,' said Hugh, 'despite that, could you really afford to give us thirty thousand each? What if we *all* moved out? That would be ... um ... er...'

'A fucking drop in the ocean,' said Terry courageously. Bruno could just as easily give him thirty p.

'I'd probably take out a mortgage,' Bruno told his dad. 'On the basis of future rent.'

'Like that lie-to-bet thing?' asked Joy, swaying on her chair. 'Pauline I work with does that with her husband. Always going on about her blinkin' portfolio, like she's chancellor of the s'chequer.'

'Buy to let? Yes, something like that.'

'My, we have thought it all through,' said Terry. He knocked back his red wine and reached for a bottle. 'From failed student, to struggling musician to practically property tycoon. All those years buttering up the old dear really paid off, didn't they?'

'Are you implying...' said Hugh, puffing up his chest.

Will mentally rubbed his hands together. Was Hugh about to pop Terry one? Or Terry pop Bruno one and lose his thirty thousand? And was Terry aware of Joy's hand on his thigh?

'...that my son,' continued Hugh, when a new voice crossed the room.

'Hello everyone,' it said huskily. All heads spun round to the back door, where Harrie stood with a hilarious hairstyle, deep red lipstick and a fox round her neck. With one hand stretched high and holding the doorframe, and the other on her hip, it could have been Bette Davis dropping in to stake a claim in the house.

Whatever it was, it was having an effect on

Bruno. He got up and walked over to Bette, beaming as he went. 'I didn't think I'd ever see Basil again,' he said, before they both disappeared.

EIGHTEEN

The kitchen window behind the sink provided Bea with a vista she'd once believed she'd never tire of. The vast lawn, the fine-gravelled patio, the fruit trees, the rose garden and the distant vegetable patch had, year after year, come together beautifully in a pleasing combination of light and shade. South-facing too, but with next door's acacia keeping the direct sunlight from her kitchen – luckily. Who'd want that blasting in when battling with cooker heat?

Although Bea thought she'd always love the view, the garden had slowly acquired a shabbiness that began to bother her. Mr Harris, who'd come once a month for years, was now down to once every three months, on account of his knees. Recently, Bea had phoned a chap who'd put a leaflet through her door offering gardening services, but she hadn't been impressed by his standard of work, nor the way he appeared to 'case' the house when she wrote him out a cheque. She'd made a point of telling him she lived with two men and didn't ask him back.

Bea took good care of the vegetable patch. However, when it came to the rest of the garden, she didn't have Mr Harris's deft hand, nor his stamina. He'd always prune symmetrically and edge neatly, barely stopping between eight in the morning and four in the afternoon. But once every three months wasn't adequate for so large a garden.

The subject came up over dinner one evening, and it was suggested by Joy that they all muck in. 'I was so proud of my roses in Edna Road, till Pete took his blowtorch to them.'

Hugh laughed. 'I may well have done the same. Not my favourite flower. Honeysuckle, wisteria, yes. I created the darlingest courtyard when I was with Mimi.'

'I'm good with gravel,' chortled Terry.

'Well, there you go,' said Joy. 'Panic over, Bea. Hugh, Terry and I will do our bit.'

Bea's heart didn't know whether to soar or plummet. She'd once loved her understated traditional English garden and didn't want to see it sprouting pampas grass and garden-centre Buddhas. On the other hand, was she being too conservative and unadventurous? 'Very well,' she said to her lodgers. 'And thank you. I'll reimburse you for any expenditure, of course.'

127

For several weeks she had to keep the kitchen window blind down, for half-empty bags of this and upturned wheelbarrows of that, and buckets and bits of trellis and goodness-knew-what, made her garden look like a hurricane had rushed through. Had it been reckless to say she'd leave it in their hands? Joy and Hugh had endless things delivered and Bea began to wish she hadn't offered reimbursement. No one had asked for money yet, but she imagined a mound of receipts a foot high.

Unfortunately, squabbles broke out about what to put where – for Joy and Hugh, it seemed, had quite different ideas. Meanwhile, Bea quietly got on with her fruit bushes and her vegetables and salad ingredients – or Donald's, as she still thought of them – and let the others battle it out.

Then, gradually, over the spring and summer of 2002, there came about a certain orderliness, together with some quite distinct divisions. Terry and his pals had erected two lengths of fencing, which chopped the garden in four and gave everyone their own patch, each one open to the central path. Although Bea might have liked a little more cohesion, the four sections did, almost pleasingly, mirror the arrangement in the house.

They also provided each housemate with an incentive to work on their own small, but still considerable, piece of land. Hugh treated his area as a huge canvas, while Joy expanded the rose section. Terry's input was, when asked, to pick up cigarette ends from the gravelled and paved quarter that he'd happily taken over. Bea suggested he use a large pot as an ashtray, suspecting she or Joy would be the ones to empty it.

When the dreaded bill was finally presented to Bea, she felt giddy with relief at how small it was. 'But surely...' she said to the retreating Hugh and Joy, both waving dismissive hands at her.

Hugh said, 'Terry knew someone who got things ... well, cheap.'

Bea deduced that 'things' had fallen off lorries, but chose not to enquire further, since the gardens could hardly now be undone.

Also to be seen from her kitchen window were Hugh's students and visitors. They'd come around the side of the house, then go down the steps and tinkle the little bell by his French doors. One chap, a man somewhere in his forties, became not only a more and more frequent visitor, but also an overnight guest. Bea often caught sight of him exiting the basement before nine on weekday mornings, and, if Bruno wasn't staying, a little later at weekends.

Bea found this upsetting, not because she disapproved of the dalliance, but because

Hugh felt the need for secrecy. If this fine-looking man were his boyfriend, then let him be brought up from the basement and introduced. Let him enjoy Joy's steak-and-ale pie and Terry's blue jokes. Bea could only guess that Hugh wanted to protect his son, but it was evident from her conversations with Bruno that he was quite aware of his father's leanings, and not at all bothered by them.

'Jamie's dad's got a sort-of husband,' he'd once said. 'Jamie and his brother and his dad and his sort-of stepdad all go camping and fishing and canoeing together.' He'd looked towards his father's closed basement door and added, rather forlornly, 'He says it's really good fun.'

Hugh and his friend's continued covert behaviour had the other housemates whispering and tittering, and Bea felt it time for a little more frankness on Hugh's part. They were, after all – Joy, Terry, Hugh, Bruno and herself – one big happy family, of a sort.

But when, alone in the kitchen with Hugh, Bea broached the subject of his 'nice-looking guest', he was far from forthcoming.

'When he's had a drink, it's difficult for Anthony to get back to Chipping Norton in the evening. The least I can do is offer him my Put-u-up for the night.'

'Ah,' said Bea, who'd heard some euphemisms in her time. 'I see.'

NINETEEN

'But I don't want to be cured,' Harrie told Patrick. She peered into her mug at the browny-green drink with bits in. 'I like being in love.'

'You'll waste away, though, if you don't eat anything. Here, try one of these sweet-potato burritos.'

'No, thanks. I had a biscuit for breakfast. Well, half one.'

Patrick tutted. At least take a sip or two of the tea. Passiflora, valerian. Great for chilling.'

'I don't want to chill and I don't want to be cured. I like feeling slightly sick with euphoria. It happened when I passed my driving test, but nothing like this.'

'Well, OK,' said Patrick. 'Only I don't know what your mum will say when she gets back and finds you anorexic.'

Harrie looked over at his long face. 'Have you heard from her recently?'

'Actually, no. I expect she's having a ball. No time to email home.'

'And do we know if Kim's a man or woman yet?'

'I did ask in my last message,' said Patrick,

reaching for Harrie's herbal cure. 'In fact, I haven't heard from her *since* I asked.' He knocked back the tea at quite a rate, then put down the mug. 'No connection, I'm sure.'

'No.' Poor bloke, thought Harrie. She quietly cursed her mother, who deserved a break, but not if she was going to find herself another husband. She also cursed her for being absent when Harrie finally fell in love with someone. Her mother often despaired of Harrie's choosiness, saying, 'Show me a perfect man, Harrie, and I'll show you one that hasn't been born yet.' The trouble was, their mum had never recovered from being deserted by their dad, Ken. But then, why do the same to kind Patrick?

Harrie took a bite of burrito and Patrick perked up and started spooning sour cream, chopped onions and salsa on to her plate.

'Best to have these with it,' he said.

Harrie nodded while she chewed. Maybe it wasn't good to be so flustered and fluttery over someone she hadn't even snogged yet. There was also the clothes and image issue. A person could only wear a fake dead fox so many times, and Bruno could go off her the moment he saw her in High Street gear. After all, he'd paid her no attention in the pub. In fact, when she'd explained who she was he couldn't believe she was both women. This had led her to pretend she'd gone to the pub straight from a film set, which meant she was lying to the man she loved, which wasn't good so early in the relationship. If there was a relationship.

Although, it was looking hopeful. This evening, they'd be going to see a Mexican film together at the Phoenix. Should she let Bruno know she spoke Spanish, or wait to find out if he found clever women threatening? Hugh did say his son went for airheads, but Harrie wasn't so sure. What to wear, what to wear...? Her black dress? It was shortish but inoffensive, with its Audrey Hepburn neckline and little cap sleeves.

'I tried calling her,' said Patrick, 'but was told the number didn't exist.'

'Oh dear.'

'I expect she got a digit wrong.'

'Sure. How's your burrito?'

'Really nice, thanks. Especially with the sour cream and salsa and ... *aaaghhh...* Patrick, you've made me eat raw onion! I've got a date tonight! I'll have to cancel and he'll think I don't like him!'

Patrick smiled. 'No you won't.' He got up and headed for the garden, then returned with a bunch of parsley. 'Works every time,' he said, and Harrie wanted to kiss him. But not till she'd had the parsley.

While Patrick did his post-lunch meditation, Harrie lay on her bed looking through Bea's diary. *A book will be brought forth, in which all will be written...* It all made sense now. 'B' wasn't a Bertie, he was Bruno. In a way, Harrie felt disappointed that Bea hadn't had a secret man-friend. However, she'd obviously got a lot out of her relationship with Bruno. 'Good Friday. B and I to St Matthew Passion at Bartlemas. Agreed J.S. Bach a genius.'

Harrie got off the bed and found an A4 pad. She put *'Liber scriptus proferetur, in quo totum continetur'* at the top, and underneath it, the English translation. She then wrote 'Bach' and flopped on the bed again.

B called. Says he may love the Dutch masters, Cézanne and Kandinsky, but doesn't want to deconstruct them to death. May well drop course and come home!

Harrie thought the exclamation mark said so much. 'Dutch masters, Cézanne, Kandinsky,' she wrote down.

One entry covered two days.

Will never get B to enjoy the countryside – lucky I have the ramblers, then! B says it's dull and he doesn't 'get' the views – that it's just grass and trees. He finds farm animals disgusting and when camping with the school, was terrified by the pitch-black silent nights. Villages, he says, are full of bored potential axe-murderers, who've only seen non-white faces on TV. I told him people in the Cotswolds are mainly professionals who spend their days or weeks in London, wheeling and dealing and drinking new types of coffee – but fear that put him off even more.

'Thank you, Bea,' whispered Harrie. 'Thank you, thank you.' She wrote, 'Hates countryside,' and turned the pages.

Dear B has encouraged me to read books I might not have considered, nor even heard of. Currently enjoying Donna Tartt's The Secret History, *which he highly recommended.*

Harrie rolled off her bed and pulled out the drawer beneath it. She rummaged through with both hands until she found her battered Tartt. 'Yes,' she said, kissing it and closing the drawer. She read the blurb on the back and jotted down the characters' names.

'So what did you think of the film?' asked Bruno.
They were in a pub near the cinema. Harrie, in her black dress, sipped a double vodka to calm herself. What she really needed was Patrick's chilling concoction, for she had the feeling her entire future would be determined by the next hour or so.

Their first real chance to chat.

'I'm always amazed by Alfonso Cuarón's versatility as a director,' she said. '*A Little Princess*, gritty documentaries, sexy road movie, *Harry Potter*.'

Bruno looked at her pale blue eyes with his dark brown ones. 'You're a bit of a film buff, then?'

No, she'd just gone on the Internet. 'Oh, not really,' she told him with a shrug. 'But I'm interested in lots of things. Art, music... All sorts of music, in fact. I *love* Bach. What a genius that man was, don't you think?'

'Yes,' he said, eyes now twinkling. 'Can I get you another drink?'

'I can't believe how much we've got in common,' Bruno said, when they were leaving. 'Music. Art. Both of us loving the Dutch masters.'

Harrie turned and looked up at him. 'Weird, isn't it?' She tried to guess his height. About five-eleven. Maybe six. Not too tall, anyway. Nothing was worse, when kissing at length, than standing on tiptoe with your head doubled back. And God, how she wanted to kiss him, but she had to be patient. Too keen was never good.

When Bruno asked if she wanted to come back to his place for a coffee, she said, 'Better not. But thanks. It's been a long day. Think I'll go and snuggle up with a good book. I'm reading a brilliant novel called *The Secret History* at the moment.'

'No!'

'Oh,' Harrie said. 'Do you know it?'

TWENTY

'I think we just feel a bit foolish,' said Joy. 'All that running around looking for a will Bea must have changed her mind about. Popped it in her waste-paper bin, I expect, and I never noticed.' She wrung out her cloth and hung it over the mixer tap. 'Now, anyone for an apéritif?'

'No, thanks,' said Terry, Hugh and Will.

Will looked at the two long faces beside him and was tempted to slap them. No way would he turn up his nose at thirty thousand pounds. In fact, he might even be a bit happy and grateful about it.

Joy said, 'Well, I might have one myself,' and tiptoed over a wet patch of floor to the fridge. 'Maybe a small glass of white,' she added, reaching for a very large glass on her way.

At the table, Hugh nodded at his clasped hands. 'Yes, I'm sure Bea simply changed her mind. Rather amusing, really.'

'Oh, yeah, hilarious,' said Terry. 'One

137

minute we're going to be joint owners of a great big north Oxford house, the next we're being palmed off with a paltry bloody thirty K, and then only if we vacate. Mind you,' he added, scratching at stubble, 'it would buy me a bike or two... I could do them up, flip them over for a nice profit.'

'I'd *love* to set up a gallery,' said Hugh dreamily. 'Contemporary work, photography, ceramics.'

'Do you know what I've always fancied?' asked Joy, joining them at the table. 'Opening a little tea shop.'

Terry snorted. 'Don't you mean distillery?'

'Oh, stop it, you.' She tapped his hand. 'The real thing, with scones and toasted buns and doilies and what have you. I might look for a partner to go in on it with me.' Her eyes roamed to Terry, of all possible partners. *Today, the voices told me to clean the guns* said his T-shirt.

'It's rather depressing and unsettling,' sighed Hugh, 'but at the same time quite exciting.'

Terry got to his feet. 'Maybe I will have a drink. Helps me think straight.'

'Pour me a sherry?' asked Hugh. 'What about you, Will?'

It was five fifty, so Will said he'd stick to tea. He could sort of understand, though, why they might want to hit the booze. It had

138

been a roller coaster of a few days – weeks even. All the more so when you took into account their ages, and how set in their domestic ways they'd become. Keys on hooks, letters stacked in separate piles, shoes left directly under the owner's coat hook, Joy in the bathroom first each morning, dinner on the dot of seven. On the other hand, the three of them weren't really all that old. Will found himself swinging between pity and anger. For one thing, none of them seemed concerned about his future domestic arrangements.

'So, what do you boys think you'll do?' Joy asked, and for a moment Will thought she might be addressing him too. 'Stay put or take the money and run?'

Hugh said, 'It's so bizarre that my son is about to determine my future. I mean, if he decides to sell the house, we'll simply have to go.'

'Aren't you fucking furious?' asked Terry. 'I reckon you're much more entitled to this place than Bruno is. All that effort you put into the basement. Not to mention your poncy garden.'

'I know, I know...' said Hugh, almost impatiently. They'd all heard Terry ask that so many times now. 'But, you know, Bea was terribly ... well, helpful, when one had ... difficulties. Particularly of the, er, financial kind.'

'She certainly was generous,' sighed Joy. 'She must have paid me back my rent over the years, what with all the treats in town and driving me here, there and everywhere.'

'So you actually paid rent?' asked Terry. 'I was never sure.'

'Oh, hardly anything, because of the cooking and cleaning. And then, when they rationalised at the surgery and made me part time, she said just to give her what I could, when I could. Bless her.'

'Did you pay rent?' Hugh asked Terry, in a way that made Will wonder if he should leave the room. He didn't want to, though.

'Um...' stalled Terry. 'Did you?'

Hugh blushed and wriggled in his chair. 'I, er... Actually, Bea and I came to an agreement. After I lost the lecturing post. We sort of put the rent on hold for a while, then...'

'Never got it going again?' asked Terry. He rocked back on his chair and let out a long smoker's wheeze. 'Fuckin'ell. There I was, racked with guilt all this time.'

'You mean you stopped paying too?' asked Joy. 'Golly, what on earth did Bea live on?'

'She must have had a pension,' chipped in Will, still trying to imagine Terry racked with guilt.

'Yes,' said Joy. 'She was all right for pensions. And then I suppose we all paid our way with the food and bills and so on.'

At the sound of bike brakes by the open

back door, all heads turned. Will waited for Harrie to charge in, but instead Simon appeared, looking windswept, despite the calm day.

'Sodding bus drivers,' he said, pulling bicycle clips off his lower calves.

'Tell me about it,' said Will. Simon, he felt, was becoming quite an enigma. No posh hotel? No big hired car? On top of everything, he didn't look clean. Will imagined the washing facilities at the Wayside were minimal, but all the same...

'Just thought I'd drop in,' Simon puffed sweatily, 'to let you know I'll be contesting Mother's will.'

Terry went to leave his seat but Joy grabbed his arm. 'Oh, Simon, are you sure?' she asked.

'Absolutely. Thing is,' he said clearing his throat, 'I ... er ... to tell the truth, I'm skint.'

Everyone gasped, except Will. The Wayside and the bicycle now made sense.

'How come?' asked Terry, sinking back in his chair. 'Thought you were high up in some mega company?'

'Yes, well, I was.' Simon went to the fridge and opened it. 'Got a beer?'

'In the salad drawer,' Joy told him, and while Simon rummaged, the others swapped horrified what's-to-become-of-us-now expressions.

'There was a bit of a marketing cock-up,'

said Simon, pulling the tab from a can and closing the fridge with a shoulder. 'A year or so back. Cost the company a fortune. Wasn't my fault but I did the decent thing and took ultimate responsibility. Ended up resigning, or rather, being asked to.' He came and joined them at the table, sitting between Hugh and Terry. 'I went it alone after that. Set up a management consultancy with my not-so-golden handshake, officially based in London, but with a Far East clientele.'

'And how did that go?' asked Joy.

It was pretty obvious how it had gone. Will guessed Simon had even run out of loose change now, since he hadn't jangled once.

'Let's just say I was considering declaring myself bankrupt, when I heard about Ma.' He knocked back beer, then wiped his mouth with a hand. 'Anyway, she was clearly demented towards the end, to have left her entire house to that little–'

'Hugh's son,' Will said quickly.

'What? Oh, yeah.' Simon turned to Hugh. 'You probably thought you'd be all right for life, then? Eh? Sorry to spoil it all, old bean, but this house should be mine, and no sane court's going to deny me it.'

Terry lurched forward, put his elbow on the table and his head on his hand, then looked Simon in the eye and gave him his version of a friendly smile. 'Sorry to hear your story, mate. Got a few debts to clear, have you?'

'You could say that.'

'And in a bit of a hurry?'

'Things have become rather pressing, yes.'

'So you need to get your hands on some dosh, like pronto?'

Simon sighed. 'In a nutshell.'

Will could see where Terry was heading, and said, 'Just contesting the will could take months and months.'

'Then, if you win,' said Terry, 'there'd be a few more months while the property was being put in your name.'

'Huh,' said Simon, getting up and making his way back to the fridge. 'I'm sure things could happen more speedily that that.'

'And have you thought about inheritance tax?' asked Hugh.

'I have been in business my entire adult life,' scoffed Simon. 'Of course I haven't forgotten the tax. But I'm planning on selling the place, so no problemo.'

Joy put her hand up, obviously wanting to say something, and obviously thinking she was back at school.

'Yes?' asked Simon.

'It's just, you know, that your mum put in her will that me, Terry and Hugh should be reasonably compensated for having to move. We're sort of sitting tenants, you see. And as Bruno's offered us– *Ouch*. Terry, that hurt.'

Terry did the friendly grin thing again at Simon. 'Look. Think about it. By the time you've been through the whole challenging-the-will business, then you've put the house on the market... What's it worth? Not that much. Seven hundred thousand? Seven fifty?'

'And the rest,' snorted Simon.

'Think eighteen months down the line, mate. You've finally found a buyer, you've paid us off, you've paid the tax and the legal fees and the fucking estate agents ... but you're still broke because, while all this was going on, your debts got bigger and bigger and big–'

'All right, all right!' growled Simon. He put down his beer and patted at shirt and trouser pockets. 'Listen, I don't suppose anyone's got a ciggy?'

'Follow me,' said Terry, standing up and leading Simon through the back door to the shed.

Joy flopped back in her chair with an, 'Oh, my giddy aunt.'

'My sentiment exactly,' said Hugh. 'Will, dear boy, you're young and intelligent and an impartial bystander. What do you think?'

Will got up and went over to the window. Simon and Terry were puffing away in their terrible outfits. They looked like a couple of winos, rather than a company director and a drum legend. 'I think the poor bloke's desperate,' he said. 'Why not get Bruno to give him a one-off payment, on the basis that he doesn't make a claim? Ever.'

Joy came and stood beside him. 'I wouldn't mind having a bit less money, if that's any help.'

'Me too,' said Hugh.

Terry pulled the cover off his motorbike and Simon did a lot of nodding at it, then sat astride it for a while. That would be one solution, thought Will – Terry taking Simon out for a fatal spin. Simon then dismounted, the cover went back on and the two men chatted again while they puffed on a second cigarette.

'One can't help wondering,' said Hugh, 'if Terry's wheedling his way into Simon's affections. Before we know it, they'll be in cahoots over some house deal.'

'Don't be so daft,' said Joy, her brow creasing itself into a frown. 'Honestly, Hugh, the things you come out with.' She leaned further towards the window and cocked her head as though trying to hear them. 'He wouldn't, would he?'

When the two men stuck their cigarettes in their mouths and shook hands, Will heard two intakes of breath beside him. Then, while Simon stubbed out his cigarette, head bowed, Terry turned to the three at the window and gave them either a reassuring, or a worrying, thumbs-up.

TWENTY-ONE

One beautiful spring morning in 2003 was spoiled, very first thing, by not one, but two dishevelled women emerging from Terry's room and entering the kitchen. The first was a platinum blonde, the second had hair dyed the colour of peonies. Both wore studs between their nostrils that made Bea's eyes water and quite put her off her muesli.

The women, who were of indeterminate age but probably hadn't seen thirty, chatted amiably about the best pubs and music venues in Oxford. It wasn't a subject that held great interest for Bea, but she listened politely and asked questions, whilst waiting for Terry to show his face. When he finally did, it wasn't a pretty or indeed happy one. He was curt with his guests while he made coffee, then ushered them out of the house in an uncivil manner. 'Get your slaggy arses home,' Bea thought she heard from the hallway.

Was this really the way to treat ladies? Even ones who'll happily *ménage à trois* with a middle-aged drummer at the drop of a hat? Bea shook her head and when her lodger slouched back in for more coffee,

146

said, 'Could I have a word, Terry?'

'Er, yeah. What about? Is it the rent? Only, I've had to replace half my drum–'

'No, it's not the rent. Now, why don't you sit down?' He did so and Bea took a deep breath. 'Would you say you're happy?' she asked.

'I dunno. Yeah. No. Maybe.'

'Would you say that your lifestyle is appropriate for a man of... How old are you now, Terry?'

'I always tell women I'm thirty-eight.'

Bea did her sums. 'For a man approaching his fiftieth birthday?' She suddenly felt like a headmistress and didn't like it. 'Far be it from me to judge, and on the whole I feel people should lead the lives they choose. But tell me, Terry, if you could have absolutely anything right now, what would it be?'

'That's easy,' he said croakily. 'A fag.' He pointed at the back door. 'Do you mind if...?'

'No,' Bea sighed.

After he'd gone, she scraped her muesli into the bin and rinsed out her bowl at the sink, watching Terry inhale with relish. Was he aware of the pretty patch of crocuses, just yards away in Joy's garden? Or the charming and abundant birdsong? She knew some people's souls appeared devoid of beauty and poetry, but couldn't help thinking those souls simply needed a little nudge in the right direction. Away from smoke-filled clubs and strumpets, in Terry's case, and towards ... what? A kind-hearted, adoring but quite firm and sensible wife might be just the ticket. A woman who'd bring stability and an array of new interests to Terry's life, including one or two sports and an appreciation of nature and the higher arts. It was possible that such a woman frequented Eaten Alive gigs, but unlikely.

When Terry came in from his smoke, he said, 'I've been having a think, Bea. And I reckon you're right.'

'Oh?'

'Yeah. Too long in the tooth for all this chick business. Not to mention a bit short in the libido area. Those two last night. Would they let me read my Dan Brown?'

'Ah,' said Bea sympathetically. She'd often had a similar problem with Donald. 'Wouldn't it be wonderful if you met someone ... well, more suitable.'

'Yeah, it would. But who do you reckon *would* suit me? And where do I meet her? Not at work, that's for sure. Half the girls are straight from school, the other half are pregnant.'

'Perhaps you could develop more interests?'

Bea tried to think of activities that might attract a feminine, fun-loving but sensible type of woman. She recalled an advertisement – 'Aerobics for the Over 50s' – but thought Terry might fare better on the romance front fully clothed.

'Pottery?' she suggested.

'You having a laugh?'

'Well, let's have a think,' said Bea, and this they did, until a week or so later, when Terry announced that he'd decided to join a motorcycle club.

Bea was perplexed. 'One,' she said, 'you don't have a motorcycle. And, two, it's hardly a club that will attract women.'

'One,' said Terry, 'there's a bike on its way. And, two, you'd be surprised.'

Where Terry's previous overnight visitors had been a little scruffy and unsuitable, those that followed were enough to frighten the horses – tattoos galore, Gestapo boots, voices like coffee grinders. Then there was the motorcycle. Bea felt miffed that Terry found the monthly instalments for his new toy, but couldn't somehow scrape together the rent. On top of that, the monstrosity ruined her view of the garden.

After a while, a compromise, of sorts, was reached. Terry would squeeze his motorbike into the shed and Bea would find plenty of household and maintenance jobs for him to carry out, to make up for rent. In addition, his overnight guests were to spend a minimal amount of time in the kitchen and bathroom.

'You're a star,' he said, kissing Bea's cheek and making her feel she hadn't been quite tough enough.

Bea couldn't have afforded to be so generous, had not an endowment policy recently matured. It was a 'with profits' one in her own name, which Donald had insisted she take out forty years previously – 'in case you're left on your own, Bea' – and the sum assured, together with the profits, proved a timely and reassuring nest egg.

The substantial lump sum was put into an accessible high-interest account, which Bea dipped into once or twice a month. Sometimes she dipped in only lightly, perhaps to buy a good-quality coat or theatre tickets for herself and Meg. At other times, such as when the boiler was replaced, quite a chunk had to be withdrawn.

However, interest accrued and the balance stayed healthy, and Bea regularly thanked Donald for providing her, and her increasingly hard-up lodgers, with a lifeline. Not that she'd shared the news of her windfall with the others, for that would have created an atmosphere of patronage that might have rankled, especially with the men. Or perhaps it wouldn't have. Either way, Bea was happy not to have members of her household know every little thing about her.

TWENTY-TWO

'God, I really miss her,' said Bruno out of the blue.

They were in a restaurant having dinner and an invisible person had surely just passed their table and stuck a knife in Harrie's middle.

'Oh?' she said, confused as well as hurt. Hadn't Bruno told her he'd been overjoyed when Carly moved out? That he'd had a celebratory drink, all on his own, knowing he'd never have to listen to Enya again? Harrie carried on with her dainty feminine low-cal salad, while Bruno ate a best-burger-in-town and stack of perfect-looking chips – what she'd really wanted to order, but her dress was tight enough already.

Bruno dabbed his mouth with his napkin. 'She had such a brilliant sense of humour.'

'Did she?' Had he been lying then, when he said Carly loved *You've Been Framed* but didn't get *The Office?*

'Best of all, she managed to laugh at herself.' Bruno chuckled and shook his head, no doubt thinking of some cute Carly incident.

Harrie tried to frame a sentence that

would let him know this was totally out of order, but which wouldn't hint at chronic jealousy. *You know, I've always thought old girlfriends/boyfriends should be taboo at the start of a relationship.* Maybe not. It still wasn't clear they were in a relationship. What might be better, Harrie decided, was a bit of magnanimity.

'She sounds wonderful,' she said, giving Bruno a warm but slightly concerned 'poor you for losing her' smile.

'There was this one time,' he said still grinning, 'when her support tights sort of lost their way and ended up all wrinkled round her ankles.'

'I'm sorry?'

'We were doing a circuit of the lake at Blenheim and there wasn't much she could do to salvage the situation. Poor old thing.'

'So was she embarrassed?' Harrie asked, not missing a beat.

'Very. But the more crinkly they became, the more she laughed. She said it looked as though someone had been playing hoopla with her legs, and by the time we reached the palace and the Ladies we were both crying with laughter.'

Harrie chuckled along with him, but had the invisible man returned and twisted the knife? This was silly. How could she be jealous of an elderly – deceased, even – woman? 'You were very close, weren't you?'

'Yeah. She was my surrogate granny, I guess. The only real one I have lives in Taiwan, and I've only seen her twice. Still, I can't believe Bea left me her house.'

'Did you think she'd leave it to Simon?'

'Maybe.'

'Or your father and the others?'

'I don't know. I was always a bit sceptical about that. Bea confided in me, you see. Quite a lot.'

'Although she didn't tell you what was really in her will?'

'She might have thought I'd talk her out of it. Or tell the wrong person, or something. Plus, she was quite hazy about everything towards the end.'

'So how do you feel about inheriting the place?'

Bruno flashed his perfect teeth at her. 'Shocked, as I said. And honoured, I suppose. But guilty too. I dunno... How would you feel?'

'Thrilled, I think. And also ... well, really, *really* pleased that it was a house in the city, rather than one in some ghastly remote country area, surrounded by miles and miles of tedious fields and things.'

'Don't you like the countryside?'

'God, *no*.'

'I love it.'

'No you don't!'

Bruno's smile faded.

'I mean, you don't, do you?'

'Uh, well, I didn't used to, but Bea talked me round a couple of years back. Dragged me along on some of her walks, introduced me to the delights of cute village pubs.'

'Oh, *that* kind of countryside. I was talking about endless flat farmland that reeks of manure. I didn't mean the Cotswolds or anything. No, no, I love quaint little villages, tucked away in pretty valleys... and all that. Ha, ha, ha, no, I *adore* the countryside.' Stop, she willed herself. 'So, anyway, do you have a plan? For the house?'

Bruno finished his mouthful of delicious-looking burger. 'It depends on the others. I'm not going to sell and turf them out if they don't want to go. I mean, we are talking about my dad. On the other hand...'

'What?'

'I just think Bea might have wanted them to sort of move on. She once said she thought she might be killing them with kindness. That they were comfortably stuck and that wasn't such a good thing. She was very wise, Bea.'

'Mm.'

'But never in an in-your-face way.'

'Right.'

'She had this lightness of touch with people. Just seemed to *know*, do you know what I mean?'

'Emotional intelligence?' suggested Harrie.

154

'Exactly. Anyway, less of Bea and the house and me. Tell me more about you. What are you going to do, now you've got your Oxford degree?'

Harrie hesitated, trying to recall what her long-term plan had been before Bruno came along. Acting, that was it. But how frivolous that would sound. Bruno had been telling her about his voluntary work with depressives. And he obviously admired women with a bit of depth and moral fibre. Kind, caring, altruistic types. Women like his surrogate granny. 'Well,' she said, 'I think I'd like to do something, er, worthwhile. Work with ... um, oh, disadvantaged children. Or maybe, you know, do something in say ... the charity sector.'

Bruno raised an eyebrow at her, then put down his fork and leaned across the table. He tucked a finger under her chin and pulled her face towards him. 'I'd love it if you could be yourself,' he said, planting a soft kiss on her mouth.

He sat back in his chair and so did a stunned Harrie. Doing as Bruno asked was going to be tricky because, in post-kiss shock, she couldn't quite remember who she was. But then an idea came to her. She'd try to imagine that Will, not Bruno, was across the table. She was always herself with her brother. *Will, not Bruno... Will, not Bruno* ... repeated itself in her head, while her fork

155

made its way to Bruno's plate and stabbed his last three chips. 'You didn't want those, did you?'

Later, while Harrie polished off chocolate cake and cream, not giving a toss about her tight dress, they discussed Simon.

'Will tells me he's in dire financial need,' she said.

'Just a bit. Says he needs a chunk of money as soon as poss, but it feels like blackmail to me. He never lifted a finger for Bea. At least Joy, Terry and Dad helped around the house, kept her company.'

'Even if they were sponging off her. Oops, sorry, I know it's your dad...'

'That's OK. Anyway, let's not talk about that lot any more. We keep bouncing back to them and it's doing my head in.'

'What do you want to talk about?'

'I dunno. Music? Didn't you say you loved Bach?'

'Er...' *Will, not Bruno.* 'Sort of. Well, he's OK.'

Bruno laughed. 'Who do you listen to, then?'

'Um...' *Will, not Bruno. Will, not Bruno.* Harrie reached into her bag and took out her little player. 'Here,' she said, switching it on and handing it to him.

Bruno held a headphone to one ear, listened for a while and nodded. 'Yeah, she's good. And *Like a Virgin* was definitely a breakthrough in terms of female pop culture.'

'Seminal, I'd say.' They were both doing well at keeping a straight face. 'And you?' asked Harrie. 'Who do you like?' Bruno gestured to the waiter for the bill, then his beautiful dark eyes landed back on Harrie. How could she imagine him as her pale brother?

'Blues, jazz, classical.'

'Uh-huh?' *Will, not Bruno*. 'Hey, why don't we go and listen to some of it?'

'Now?'

Harrie stretched across the table and squeezed his hand.

'Definitely now.'

'Yeah, OK. Great. I thought the other day ... when you didn't want to come back–'

'Kiss me again?' said Harrie.

'Now?'

'Definitely now.'

TWENTY-THREE

'So who do I make the rent out to?' Will asked the group: Terry, Hugh, Joy, Bruno, Harrie and for some reason, Simon.

Will had walked into the kitchen/diner and

found them quietly pow-wowing round the table. There were no raised voices or cross faces and Will hoped they'd reached some sort of consensus about the house. One that would let him stay in his lovely attic for ever. He'd been casting an eye over 'Rooms to Let' ads and become more and more miserable. All the affordable ones meant an hour-long cycle to work. 'It's overdue now,' he added, wanting to sound conscientious.

Bruno shrugged. 'Although the deeds are being drawn up, it's not officially mine yet.'

'Shall I pay you, Joy?' Will asked.

'Oh, don't worry,' she told him with a flick of the hand. 'Why don't we just forget your rent this month?'

'No, I want to pay,' insisted Will, aware he'd never been given a tenancy agreement or anything in writing. If he stopped paying rent, Bruno might be more inclined to kick him out. 'Here,' he said, opening up his cheque book. He took a pen from his shirt pocket and filled in the date and amount but left the payee blank. He signed the cheque, tore it out and placed it in the middle of the table. 'Please. Someone take it.' A set of fingers began moving across the table. 'But not you, Simon,' said Will, and the fingers retreated.

'Well,' Joy said, reaching for the cheque and giggling. 'Since you're twisting my arm.'

Simon now drummed his fingers on the

table and turned to Bruno. 'So, how soon do we each get our ten thousand?'

'Ten?' asked Will, confused.

Terry shot him a look. 'Bruno's agreed to give us ten thousand each to move out. Very generous, don't you think?'

'Er, yeah, very.'

Deciding they'd do better at conning Simon without him, Will took himself back upstairs and read William Morris's *News from Nowhere*. It was all about a utopian society based on common ownership, and made Will think of his housemates' dashed hopes. Did he feel sorry for them? A bit. But they'd had it easy for years. Now they were, almost perversely, being offered a reward.

No, the only person Will really felt sorry for was himself. Increasingly, the talk amongst the housemates was of where they'd move to and when. Before he knew it, there'd be a 'For Sale' board and a stream of high achievers and their families trailing through the house and working out where a cloakroom could go.

Will went back to his book, in which the narrator had come across an inhabitant of Morris's utopia who'd never heard of schools, or even education.

I said, rather contemptuously, 'Well, education means a system of teaching young people.'

'Why not old people also?' said he with a

twinkle in his eye.

Will was thinking of some old people, not that far from him, who could do with educating, when Harrie shouted, 'Are you decent up there?'

He dropped the book and got off the bed. 'I am,' he called back, 'but the eighteen-year-old twins aren't.'

'Yeah, right.' She clomped up the stairs. 'Bikes and booze, that's all you're– God, you're not reading a book?' She went over and picked it up.

Will tried to think of a clever comment about *News from Nowhere* for his sister. He knew she was bound to have one. What had Jon said about it in the pub?

'Mmm, gorgeous cover,' Harrie sighed, then flung herself on the bed, cuddling the book. 'Don't you think?'

'Yes,' Will agreed, then, after gathering his thoughts, said, 'You know, it's hard not to see William Morris as the first anti-globalisation activist. This book, for example, was an obvious response to the industrial dystopia of the nineteenth century. A call to return to cottage-industry society and the use of natural and beautiful materials.'

Harrie sighed heavily and Will waited to be shot down, trying to remember what else Jon had said. But then his sister sat up and smiled at him dreamily. 'Don't you think

Bruno's got the most perfect wrists?'

Will said he hadn't noticed, then inspected his own. Were wrists important to women? He hoped not, since his were pale, bony and flecked with the odd girlie blond hair. 'So what's going on downstairs?' he asked.

'Oh, Simon's going to get ten thousand. He asked Bruno if he'd take out a bridging loan, so he could pay him a.s.a.p. Bruno's thinking about it. Seems Terry, Hugh and Joy all want to move out and have the money. Not ten, but thirty thousand, of course. Only Simon mustn't ever know that.'

'And what's Bruno going to do with the house?'

'Give it a makeover, he says. I've offered to help.'

'So, are you and Bruno an item?'

Harrie did the heavy sigh again, but this time she rolled her eyes too. 'Yeah, since three nights ago. And let me tell you, physically it's *fantastic*.'

'Ugh, enough already,' said Will, putting his hands over his ears. Who'd want to hear about his sister's sex life?

'That guy's got the best bod.'

'Have I?' asked Bruno. He was taking the stairs two at a time in bare feet. On spotting Harrie, he made for the bed and threw himself beside her noisily. 'Yours isn't bad either.'

Harrie planted her lips on her new boyfriend's and Will, feeling uncomfortable, made his way to the stairs.

'Hey, don't go,' said Bruno. 'I came to tell you, you can keep this room for ... well, quite a while, I guess. What with all the legalities, then doing the place up. I'm going to live here while the work's going on, and it'll be nice having you around. If you want to stay, that is.'

'Definitely.' Will felt almost as excited as the first time he'd seen the place. 'Cool.'

'God, this bed's noisy,' Harrie was saying, wiggling back and forth on it. 'Let's not have this one when we move in.'

'We?' said Bruno stiffening.

Harrie nudged him playfully. 'Oh, you know what I mean.' From the look on Bruno's face, Will thought perhaps he didn't.

'I can stay, I can stay, I can stay,' Will sang as he cycled to work the next morning. Weaving his way through cars and other cyclists, he tried to picture the house emptied of Joy, Hugh and Terry. With Bruno there – and if she got her way, Harrie too – it would become a much younger place. The parties they could have! He imagined reggae booming out and skimpily dressed girls dotted around. There'd be heated all-night discussions around the table, about whether

162

Blur really were better than Oasis in the end, or if the table was really there. In other words, it would be a proper shared house, only a big attractive one in a posh street. And, of course, they'd be very selective about who they let in.

Harrie had told him the current tenants were to all move at the same time, rather than drag the business out. Better for Bruno, they'd agreed, and so much less painful for themselves. Joy and Terry had no immediate plan, but Hugh thought he might stay with his friend Anthony in Chipping Norton.

Anthony was the blur of a person Will had once seen hurrying up Hugh's basement steps and round the corner of the house. It was a Sunday morning and Will had been filling the kettle and admiring the way Joy's roses cleverly formed a red heart behind her table and chairs. Hugh's guest had been wearing quite a lot of black, that was all he could remember. When Terry stumbled into the kitchen, Will mentioned the guy.

'You mean Bin Laden?' Terry had wheezed. The wheeze turned into a horrible rasping laugh and then a long phlegmy cough. Terry was at his most unwholesome first thing. He'd scratched himself through his shorts and said, 'Fucking impossible to catch sight of.'

When he reached the shop, Will took his bike through to the back.

'What are you looking so pleased about?' asked Neil. 'Won the lottery?'

'I'd hardly be coming to work if I had.'

'Oh, yeah, what would you being doing then?'

Will grinned at his boss. 'Opening my own bike shop, of course. Can't be your assistant for ever.'

Neil frowned and rubbed at his unshaven chin – perhaps wondering how he'd cope with only the late-and-hungover help of Jake and Shaz.

'Only kidding,' Will said, even though he wasn't. There'd always be room for another bike shop in Oxford. Maybe he'd buy a lottery ticket in his lunch break. 'Coffee?'

'Let me,' said Neil, which was a first.

TWENTY-FOUR

When Bruno was whisked off to his university in the far north, Bea felt the bottom had fallen out of her world. This was the empty-nest syndrome people spoke of, but which she and Donald hadn't experienced when Simon left home. Possibly because he'd only moved two streets away, to a room in Robert's parents' house.

Rob was still at St Edward's taking his A levels, but Simon was already in employment. Already on a career ladder, in fact, having rather predictably and pointedly dropped out of his 'useless' school and joined the local branch of a building society. Rob's mother didn't care to do Simon's laundry, so Bea and Donald saw their son when he dropped off, and then collected, his clothes and bedding. It was embarrassing that Simon should choose to live with another family, but at the same time, Bea and Donald enjoyed a tension-free existence they hadn't known in years.

With Bruno, it was quite a different matter. Bea pined and she fretted, and often found herself waiting for the phone to ring. So foolish of her, she knew. In all the excitement of university life – getting to know people, dashing to lectures – he was hardly likely to stop and tap an old lady's number into his mobile. Although in two weeks, he had phoned her three times. Tell Dad this. Tell Dad that. Why Bruno hadn't called his father directly, Bea couldn't fathom.

Or perhaps she could, for the poor boy had undergone a change of heart about his chosen subject – art history – several months earlier and it grew to be something of a sore, barely mentioned point between father and son. When Bea enquired about lectures and so on, Bruno wasn't forth-coming. 'Fine,' he always told her flatly.

Over the years, the one activity Hugh and Bruno had persistently enjoyed – even through Bruno's adolescence – had been visiting art galleries. Mainly in London, but also in the provinces, as well as once in Scotland and twice in Paris. Hugh had been incapable of kicking a ball around a field with his son, but he'd planned and carried out trips to exhibitions, whatever the weather or the state of his health. It bonded father and son to an extent, which Bea was always pleased about. Then, when Bruno, aged seventeen, found he wasn't driven in any particular academic direction, an art history degree was applied for, almost by default.

It was clear that Hugh and Mimi would struggle to help their son through univer-sity, and so Bea set up a standing order for Bruno that might, at the very least, prevent three years of Pot Noodles. She'd also thrust four fifty-pound notes into his hand when he'd come to say goodbye.

'You'll need things,' she told him, unable to hold back the tears. How silly she'd felt, but then she saw Bruno's eyes redden too, and knew she had to jolly them both out of it. 'I'll be up next weekend to see you haven't blown it on an ePod!'

'I think you mean iPod.'

'*Why* not buy yourself a good anorak?'

'Yes, Bea,' he'd said, laughing and giving her a final hug.

Bea had always considered herself resourceful in times of crisis, and to fill the void she threw herself into assorted activities. For as long as she could bear it, she played the piano for the old folk in Sycamore House. Each Wednesday afternoon, she churned out 'golden oldies' and everyone sang along, or at least tried to. It was all rather merry, but when the residents lagged behind with the lyrics, or twitched or dribbled or, in one or two cases had a 'little accident', it brought visions to Bea of what lay in store.

After two months, she told a white lie about arthritis. The staff said they'd miss her lively playing, but not to worry, since they still had the CD compilation made especially for retirement homes. Bea doubted the inmates would notice the difference and asked God to take her sooner, rather than later.

She saw friends more often, helped at jumble sales and signed up for extra rambles. For a while, she joined a ladies' fitness class but found the constant 'legs, bums and tums' mantra tedious and off-putting. At least twice a week, she shooed Joy out of the kitchen and prepared dinner for everyone. She read all the Ruth Rendell's she could lay her hands on and knitted each member of the household a lambswool scarf.

When Bruno returned to Oxford in mid-December, Bea couldn't believe how the time had flown. At least, that was what she told him.

Christmas was jolly and, for Bea and Bruno, included an evening at *Puss in Boots*, for old times' sake. As for presents, she'd made him a sweater, which he genuinely seemed to like, and he gave her a mobile phone.

'I'll teach you how to text,' said Bruno. 'Easier than trying to call each other and cheaper too. And, anyway, you should have a mobile in case of emergencies.'

'You are a dear,' she told him, already dreading his January departure.

During the holidays, Bruno told Bea all about the friends he'd made and the girl he was interested in, but he avoided the subject of work. All wasn't well, Bea sensed, but it was really his father's place to enquire and resolve.

When they weren't chatting, they were texting. Even when Bruno was in an Oxford pub or club with his old friends, he'd respond to her little messages about Terry's latest horror of a girlfriend, or Joy's obsessive cleaning. Bruno had been the one person Bea could laugh about her lodgers with – even, on occasion, his father.

To great hilarity, Terry had coined the elusive Anthony 'Bin Laden', and the couple's clandestine ways were frequently remarked upon by the others – never in front of Hugh but often in front of Bruno. Bruno, however, didn't seem to mind. He'd met Bin Laden on several occasions and had actually visited his Chipping Norton home. A grand, five-bedroomed, seventeenth-century affair. Apparently, Anthony had inherited well a few years back. He shared it with two male cats named Babycakes and Flossie, and had several nude drawings of himself, in the distinct style of Hugh, on the walls. Bruno said he 'sort of' liked Anthony but found him a bit defensive. Based on the four occasions Bea had bumped into the man, she'd have said rude.

When the much-feared tenth of January came round, Bea braced herself for Bruno's departure and vowed not to devote the next twelve weeks to superfluous exercise and knitting. She couldn't believe she'd ever say it – so irritated had she always been by people and their mobile phones – but thank heaven for text messaging.

TWENTY-FIVE

'You've got psychic powers,' said Harrie, 'haven't you, Patrick?'

He nodded proudly. 'My hot flashes, as I call them.'

'So, tell me ... how does it work? Say, if I wanted you to see my future?'

'Hmm, it's not that simple, Harrie. Usually, I have no control. I just see something in my head. Maybe a journey, maybe a marriage–'

'Marriage?'

'Once or twice.'

Harrie slumped on to Patrick's beanbag. 'Wow. Listen, what if I give you something personal of mine, and maybe something personal of Bruno's. Would they bring about a hot flash?'

'I doubt it. Sorry. The first step might be a compatibility chart.'

'Astrological?'

'Mm. You know what time you were born, right?'

'Three in the morning.'

'Good. If you could find out Bruno's birth details, I'll take it from there. Also...'

'What?'

'I'm pretty good at tuning into people. Sussing them out. For example, I could tell you how Bruno felt about you from his body language.'

'Don't talk about Bruno's body,' said Harrie, fanning her face. 'Hey, shall I invite him to dinner this evening? Oh, but first, what are you cooking?'

'I thought I'd do asparagus, grilled aubergine slices with garlic, and a home-grown salad with a walnut and shallot dressing. Followed by organic fruit compote with a sugar-free custard.'

'And you'd do that even if I wasn't here?'

'Sure.'

Harrie got out of the beanbag and looked up Bruno's number in her mobile. 'Sounds good,' she said, grabbing the landline, 'apart from the sugar-free custard.'

'Sweetened with apple juice.'

'That's all right, then.'

Throughout dinner Harrie watched Bruno's body language. How he'd put down his fork and cross his arms when answering a question. How he'd more often than not, turn and address Patrick, rather than her. When they finished eating and retired to the sofa, he crossed his legs away from her, and those arms folded themselves again, despite holding a glass of wine. Harrie guessed this wasn't good, but thought she'd wait for

Patrick's verdict. Patrick was asking Bruno lots of questions about his interests and his childhood, and, having established his age, had now moved on to his birthday.

'What do you want to know that for?' asked Bruno. His legs crossed themselves away from Patrick and towards Harrie. Things were looking up.

'Patrick likes to make things for people's birthdays,' Harrie said. It was true. 'Chutney, painted gourds. All stuff from his allotment.'

Bruno gave a slow nod, probably thinking about whether he wanted a painted gourd. 'Well, it's not for a while. May the second.'

Patrick said, 'Hey, I've got a friend with that birthday. Same year as you too. Amazing. She was born on the last stroke of midnight. How about you?'

'Ten to ten in the morning. Apparently, Dad did that old thing of passing out. He insists it was because he hadn't eaten through the twenty-hour labour.'

Patrick nonchalantly reached for a pen and scribbled on a magazine.

'Would you'd like to listen to some music in my room?' Harrie asked Bruno, thinking Patrick might want to get on with his chart.

'Actually, I ought to be off,' he said. 'Sorry. Got a band practice at ten.'

'Ten?' cried Patrick, who often turned in before then.

Bruno laughed. 'Blues players, you know.' He knocked back the glass of wine he'd spent the evening eking out, thanked Patrick, and kissed Harrie goodbye.

'Well?' Harrie said when he'd gone, still kicking herself for the let's-shag-in-my-room suggestion. 'What do you think?'

'Um ... why don't I do a compatibility chart first?'

'No, I want to know *now* what you think.'

Patrick sank into his beanbag and looked up at her. 'I had a hot flash,' he said.

Harrie gasped. 'Really?'

'I saw you in–'

'The register office? A maternity ward with Bruno by my bed?'

'–a theatre,' said Patrick. 'On a stage. Centre stage, in fact. It was one of those gorgeous old places with lots of red velvety upholstery.'

'Oh.' Two weeks ago she'd have jumped from the beanbag and hugged him. 'I don't suppose you saw Bruno ... like, in the audience, or backstage, or...'

'Sorry.'

'Oh, well. Listen, what did you make of his body language tonight?'

Patrick rubbed his chin. 'He likes you but he's definitely cautious. Which can be a good thing. Commitment-phobes tend to charge into relationships at full speed, before going into reverse.'

'Like Dad?'

'Yes, like your dad.'

'Anything else?'

'He makes prolonged eye contact, which means he's trustworthy.'

'Uh-huh.'

'But the barrier thing he does with his arms means he's protecting himself from something.'

'Like me?'

'Maybe.'

Harrie collapsed on the sofa, put a hand over her eyes and went through what she'd just been told. Eventually, she sat up and looked down at her stepfather, now staring at the ceiling. 'Patrick?' she said, her heart racing.

'Mm?'

'This theatre...'

'Mm?'

'Do you think it was in the West End?'

'Um...' he said with a sniff.

'Patrick, are you crying?'

'A bit.'

'Is it Mum?'

'Yeah.'

'Kim's a guy, right?'

'So I'm told.'

'And they're like...'

He sniffed again. 'Yes. But I understand, totally. She needs a Virgo.'

'Oh, for fuck's sake, Patrick. She doesn't

need a Virgo, she needs you to go and sort her out and bring her home.'

'But you can't interfere with fate, Harrie.'

'Bollocks.'

Harrie was suddenly furious with her mother. But then, hang on, she told herself, when you fall for someone it's not so easy to control. And she should know. Mind you, she wasn't married to a nice caring man like Patrick. She was free, her mother wasn't. But then why shouldn't her mother enjoy herself after all the years of domestic and secretarial drudgery?

'You really think I could win her back?' asked Patrick.

He sat up in his beanbag looking much perkier but, down at that level, around four years old. If Patrick went to Melbourne, she'd chuck the unmanly seating out. Harrie pictured Kim – all muscles and tan and lager for breakfast.

'Go for it!' she said, waving an arm in the general direction of Australia, while her other hand perched on her hip. *'Carpe diem!'* she added with a flourish. God, she could be an actress.

TWENTY-SIX

At last, things appeared to be happening on the house front for Bruno. Will hadn't seen Simon recently and guessed Bruno had somehow managed to pay him off. Meanwhile, the housemates were in the process of packing.

'Anthony's got plenty of room, then?' Will asked Hugh. They were down in the basement, Will sitting with a coffee and Hugh dropping things in a big cardboard box with undisguised glee in his face.

'Absolutely. It's a veritable mansion.'

'And you think it'll be all right, do you? You and him living together?'

'You and *he*.'

'Sorry.'

'Oh, I'm terribly optimistic. I've been pressing for it for years, but Anthony's always resisted.' Hugh looked over his shoulder at the stairs to the kitchen. 'He and I have been ... well, partners. I don't know if it's common knowledge.'

'I think it might be.'

Hugh opened up a colourful beach towel, inspected it, grimaced and threw it aside. 'Now, of course, he has no option but to take me in. In the past Anthony always said there was no good reason to uproot myself from this house, it being so...'

'Cheap and convenient?'

'Quite. Anyway, I've told him that Bruno intends to sell, which I'm sure he will eventually. So, my imminent homelessness and destitution – I er, haven't mentioned the compensation – has forced Anthony to finally embrace the idea of us living together.'

'Isn't that *our* living together?' said Will. He gave Hugh a curt grin and both men laughed.

'I'm going to miss you, dear boy. No more Daniel Craig to light up my days.'

'Will drained his mug and got off the pristine cream sofa. 'No, you'll have Anthony for that.'

'At last,' said Hugh, clutching a giraffe pyjama case to his chest. After a little reverie, he held the case at arm's length and cocked his head. 'Do you think Bruno will still want this?'

'Hard to say.'

'I'd hang on to it, only Anthony and I have our own pyjama cases. I don't suppose you'd–'

'No.'

Working his way up the house, Will knocked next on Terry's open door.

'Come in if you can,' came the reply.

Where Hugh's packing was orderly and methodical, Terry had clearly lost the plot – among other things, no doubt. Bits of computers stuck out of dozens of far-too-small boxes. Everywhere, things had been half shoved into black bin liners. Piles of books, magazines, DVDs and CDs had mostly fallen over.

'Can I give you a hand?' he asked, not really meaning it and hoping Terry would have the sense to know that.

'Cheers, mate. Do you want to pack the DVDs and CDs?' He stood in his *I've got an inferiority complex but it's not a very good one* T-shirt and looked around 'Now, where the fuck's that roll of bags?'

Will searched too and found them inside another binbag. 'Not your forte, then?' he asked. 'Packing.'

'The blokes from the storage company said to get the stuff together and they'll sort it all out. Put it in containers, or whatever. I'm just going to hang on to some clothes, plus my bike, which Harrie said would be OK in their front garden, only I reckon it'll be safer left here for a while.'

'Harrie?'

'Ah. You haven't spoken to her since last night, then?'

'No, why?'

'Well, you know me and Joy's had a bit of

trouble finding anyone to take us – er, finding somewhere to live.'

'Have you?'

'Just a bit. I mean, where do you start at our age? Anyway, Harrie came up with the perfect solution. Temporary that is. Now your stepdad's gone off to Oz for a while and Harrie's moving in here–'

'Is she?'

'Bloody hell, Will. Keep up, won't you?'

'I've been really busy at the shop.' And the pub, and Jon's sofa...

'Anyway,' continued Terry, 'rather than have your mum's place sitting empty we're going to live in it.'

'You and Joy?'

'It's just temporary,' he repeated. 'Bruno's itching to get going here, we can tell. Anyway, it'll give us a bit of space to have a think. About what to do, where to go.'

'Have you seen the house?' asked Will. 'Because if it's space you're after...'

'You know what I mean – breathing space. A chance to see what's on offer. What our options might be. We've been a bit bloody cocooned here.'

'True. I'll probably have the same problem when I move out.' Only I won't have thirty grand, thought Will, as he gathered up CDs. Def Leppard, Motorhead, Black Sabbath. 'And you think it'll be all right, do you? You and Joy sharing a place?'

'Course,' said Terry. He wound a long cable round his arm. 'We've been together all this time, in a manner of speaking. So long as she turns a blind eye when I've got a, ahem, visitor. And so long as she keeps turning out the pukka meals.'

'Well, as you say, it'll only be temporary. Mum'll be back to start her course at some point. And who knows when Patrick might give up and come home. Mind you, he likes sleeping on floors.'

'Don't worry. Me and Joy will soon get our acts together. Even if we pool our resources and buy a canal boat or something.'

Will looked through another handful of CDs – Guns N' Roses, Kiss, Aerosmith, The Monkees... The Monkees? 'But where will the rock chicks go in a canal boat?' he asked.

'Good point,' said Terry, looking nervously at the last CD. 'Careful with that one, eh?'

'Of course.'

'Yoo-hoo,' he called out at the first-floor door. It too was open, and from the depths of the room came the sound of Joy singing 'There's a Place for Us'. She hadn't heard, so Will poked his head round the door. Joy was wrapping ornaments in newspaper and swaying to the song. It was coming from a music centre, circa 1979. 'Joy?' he shouted.

'Oh, crikey,' she cried, hand on chest. 'Excuse my caterwauling!' She reached

180

across and turned down the volume.

'Not at all. You've got a nice voice.'

Joy giggled. 'People used to compare me to Lynsey de Paul.'

'Ah.' Will nodded. Who?

'Heard the latest plan?' Joy asked, eyes dancing, sunset-pink lips smiling. 'Terry and I are only going to live together!'

Will toyed with the idea of telling her Terry hadn't quite put it that way. 'At Mum and Patrick's house, I hear?'

'Yes! What a stroke of luck it was, Patrick dashing off like that to save his marriage. Oh dear, listen to me ... but you know what I mean.'

'When's it all happening, then?'

'Friday. Harrie's moving in here that day, then there's the party on Saturday, of course.'

'Party?'

'Bruno's having a sort of open house. Seven onwards.'

'Nice of him to tell me.'

Joy picked up a mock-Fabergé egg and started wrapping. 'You haven't been around much, have you, Will? Busy mending punctures?'

'Something like that.'

'He wants a bit of a bash before he starts work on the house. While it's nice and empty. Told him I'd bring my *Seventies Party Hits* along, in case people want a bop.

Nothing like a bit of Adam Ant, I always say.'

'No.'

'And I'll be doing a few vol-au-vents and some things on sticks.'

'Great.'

'Sausage rolls are always a good filler.'

'Mm.'

'Cheese straws.'

'Good idea.'

'Do you know,' she said, leaning towards him and lowering her voice, 'I've always dreamed of Terry and myself setting up home together. And for the suggestion to come from him!'

Joy was in for a let-down, but Will didn't feel like bursting her bubble. And, besides, Jon was waiting for him at the Scholar. 'Probably good to take it slowly,' was all he could offer.

She stepped back. 'But I've been taking it slowly for years!' she said, no longer whispering. 'If you ask me, it's time to slam the accelerator and thrust us into top gear!'

This was fighting talk, and as Will reversed to the door, he thought about warning Terry.

The fire slowly faded from Joy's eyes and she went on with her wrapping. 'What do you think about devils on horseback?' she asked.

Will racked his brain. 'Was that Adam Ant?'

Joy giggled the giggle that Will had somehow got used to. 'You and your sense of humour,' she said. 'We'll miss that.'

They would?

TWENTY-SEVEN

How delightful it was to have Bruno back, but how worrying too. What on earth was he going to do with his life? He'd got himself a job in a pub and appeared content, despite his lack of direction. Many of his pals were in the same boat, even those who'd completed their degrees.

'Honestly, Bea,' Bruno had said in response to her concern. 'A degree's now the equivalent of like the Eleven Plus or something.'

He was exaggerating, of course, but it was evident from articles she'd read, that employers were seeking ever-higher-qualified youngsters. She could see that it might be tempting to throw up one's hands and pull pints and form a blues band. 'Sort of Howlin' Wolf meets Ry Cooder,' he'd tried, unsuccessfully, to explain to her.

It was a good fortnight before Hugh spoke to Bruno, then an almighty rumpus could be heard coming from the basement. As unpleasant as it was, it cleared the air and father and son resumed normal relations, but without the trips to galleries.

Within several months of his return, a good deal of Bruno's leisure time was being taken up with a new amour, Gina. In Bea's opinion, based on half a dozen conversations, the girl had the IQ of a doorknob. Bea tried suggesting to Bruno that he and Gina might not be mentally equal, but he'd just grinned and said, 'It's not her brain I'm interested in, Bea.'

Concluding that Bruno was just having fun, and praying that the fun didn't turn into an eight-pound bundle of responsibility, Bea resisted expressing any more opinions on his love life, even when he dropped Gina and started seeing the brash-as-Blackpool Nicole. Occasionally, Bea couldn't help wishing Bruno had stuck with his course and met a fellow art enthusiast called Francesca or Fiona. Someone with a thought or two in her head that didn't involve clothes or getting 'right bladdered' – one of Nicole's endearing phrases – on a night out.

The terrifying thought that Bruno might end up like Terry, once or twice passed through Bea's mind, but, on the whole, she had faith in him. One day he'd meet his perfect partner, God willing, but perhaps he'd need to move into a whole other sphere, in order to find her. That little bedsit of his ... the low-life pubs he worked in, the dingy places she imagined his band performing in ... the ghastly girlfriends... None of it felt right to Bea, not for the bright and socially accomplished Bruno, who, so far as she could tell, hadn't gone down Terry's drugs and alcohol route. Not yet.

Bea believed herself to be far from a snob – although never as far from a snob as Donald – but how she longed for Bruno to broaden his horizons. When Nicole disappeared in favour of the micro-skirted, long-legged, even dumber Becky, Bea began to wonder if she ought to do something to alter Bruno's direction. Pay for him to become a dentist. Set him up with a small-holding. If only she'd had the funds. Cashing in on the house was an option. She'd heard of schemes for elderly people in her situation. And Bruno was, after all, the person she'd consider most like an heir – Simon having bowed out of her life completely now, it seemed.

But no, it would be living too dangerously to hand over a chunk of one's house in exchange for a cash sum. What if the bottom fell out of the property market, as alarmist commentators were always predicting? What if she needed full-time nursing care and all her equity had disappeared into the coffers of some heartless company?

For the time being, she decided, she'd put her Bruno plans on hold and simply keep a quiet and watchful eye on him. When Becky was gone within a month and Bruno kept turning up unaccompanied, Bea allowed herself to relax a little. What heartened her further was that he'd become a volunteer at a drop-in centre for the mentally ill.

'It's something that could so easily happen to any of us, at any time,' he said. It was what Donald used to say about homelessness, and it touched something deep in Bea. To her mind, Bruno was increasingly becoming the son she and Donald should have had.

TWENTY-EIGHT

Harrie was knackered. Yesterday, she'd moved most of her stuff into Bibury Road and today she'd got up at dawn to go to Wallingford, in order to be a distant pedestrian in a small-town TV murder mystery. She arrived home around seven to find Bruno missing and Joy back in the kitchen she was supposed to have left, putting dinky things on baking trays.

Harrie groaned. She really didn't feel like a party. She wanted to lie in bed with Bruno all evening and night, watching DVDs and making occasional unenergetic love.

'Oh, good,' Joy cried, 'another pair of hands. Want to scoop some mushroom filling into those cases?'

'Sorry,' said Harrie, heavy-eyed and yawning. 'I *must* have a bath. I'll come and help afterwards.'

Upstairs she grabbed robe and washbag from her 'suite' and made for the bathroom. She and Bruno had decided to have separate rooms. Actually, Bruno had decided. 'May as well spread ourselves out,' he'd told her. 'All this space.' If asked, Harrie would have said Joy's old unfurnished rooms were a bit too much space, but Bruno would come round eventually. Maybe.

Harrie began filling the bath, pouring in her favourite salts and a few drops of lavender oil. While she waited, she plucked her eyebrows – almost too tired to feel the pain – and did her legs with her electric shaver. Then, once in the lovely creamy, salty, sweet-smelling water – head lathered with shampoo – she relaxed for the first time in days and tried to empty her mind.

This proved tricky. For a start, she realised she hadn't asked Joy how the house-sitting was going. Whether they'd worked out that you needed to lift the back door a bit before it opened, or that the washing machine got stuck mid-cycle and you had to move it on.

She'd ask later.

Harrie turned the hot tap on just a tad, then sank further into the water and tried again to think of nothing – only Bruno popped up. Where was he? Wasn't he supposed to be throwing a party? Perhaps he'd gone to that wine warehouse place he'd talked about.

And was Will upstairs? She hadn't thought to check. No doubt in a pub somewhere ... avoiding vol-au-vent filling... Harrie closed her eyes and listened to the hypnotic trickle of water... She could hear her breathing deepen ... in ... out ... trickle, trickle ... in ... out ... lovely. But when the trickle turned to a splash, then another splash, Harrie's eyes popped open to find the water at lip level.

'Omigod!' she gurgled, as it cascaded over the sides of the bath. She reached for the tap and turned it off, pulled the plug out and stood up, almost too terrified to look at the damage. In fact, it wasn't too bad. She stepped out, ignored her wet body and quickly mopped the floorboards with someone's bath towel.

The good thing was, she was suddenly wide awake. Ready for a party almost. Having rinsed her hair, she conditioned it, combed it out and moisturised her face and neck. After a day in heavy make-up, she thought she'd go *au naturelle*.

'Right!' she said and, wrapped in towelling

robe and with the washbag under her arm, opened the bathroom door to find a queue of three strangers on the landing. From downstairs came a hubbub of chattering voices. Either the party had got going rapidly or she'd been asleep some time.

'Sorry,' she said, as a girl with a grimace rushed past.

'Hey, there you are,' said Bruno. He hooked an arm around her waist and kissed her cheek. 'You look great. How was the filming? Phil, come here and meet my gorgeous girlfriend.'

There was no doubting Bruno could blow hot and cold. Yesterday, after helping her move in, he'd gone for an early night. Alone.

Harrie said, 'Hi,' to Phil, and while Bruno went off to see to other guests, she talked about her extras work, or rather, talked it up again. Rubbing shoulders with the stars, seeing yourself on the big screen. 'And what do you do?' she asked.

While Phil explained, at some length, just what being a hydrogeologist involved, Harrie's eyes scanned the kitchen/diner. There was Joy, going round with a platter of nibbles, and Hugh looking at his watch, as though counting a respectable hour before heading back to Chipping Norton.

Then there were the unknown faces of Bruno's friends, plus Will and his familiar mates. She gave his small group a little wave, while Phil rattled on about water cycles and rock formations and contaminants in ground water. He said, 'I expect you're wondering what the difference is between a hydrogeologist and a hydrologist?'

'Well, now you mention it,' said Harrie, catching sight of Bruno talking to a tall and pretty dark-haired woman of around thirty. Maybe a bit less. Terry was there too, paying her lots of attention. God, *men*, thought Harrie. They either bored you to death or drove you mad with lust and jealousy.

'Is that so?' she said to Phil, when he paused for breath. 'Listen, sorry, desperate for the loo.' She backed off, adding, 'Help yourself to food, won't you?'

'Ah, Harrie,' bellowed Terry when she reached them. 'Meet Melanie, my daughter.'

'No way!' Harrie was amazed that Terry could have produced such a stunner. Although aware there was a daughter somewhere, she'd heard nothing about her.

'Nice party,' said Melanie.

Bruno thanked her, then made his excuses. More guests were arriving. When Joy tugged at Terry's arm to come and help her, he too disappeared, saying, 'It's not like it's our friggin party.'

Left alone, Harrie and Melanie talked a bit about the house – Melanie saying how she'd spent some nice times there in her teens – then they moved on to jobs. She was doing her pre-registration training, in order to become a pharmacist. She had a little boy, she said, and often found it exhausting, working and being a single mum. This made Harrie feel lazy, self-indulgent and unfocused. After telling Melanie about work as an extra, she added that she'd really like to be an actor.

'Have you applied to drama school?' Melanie asked.

'Er, no.' Of course, it had occurred to her to do so, she just hadn't decided which one, or when, or who was going to fund her. 'But I'm planning to.'

'*God*,' said Melanie, leaning towards Harrie. 'There's this guy just staring and staring at me. I'm beginning to feel spooked. There by the table. Fair hair, black T-shirt.'

Harrie looked over. 'A bit like Daniel Craig?'

'That's the one.'

'Hang on, I'll go and have a word.'

'No, don't–' began Melanie, but Harrie was on her way.

'Put your tongue away, *please*,' she told her brother.

'Who is she?'

'Only Terry's daughter.'

'Christ.'

'Come and meet her.'

'Do I have to?' He knocked back some beer then put the can down. 'What will I talk about? She looks clever and confident.'

'Come,' said Harrie, dragging him by the T-shirt. 'Melanie, this is Will, my brother.'

'Ah!' laughed Melanie. 'Hi, Will.'

'This is Terry's daughter, Melanie.'

'Hi,' said Will. He rubbed the top of his head nervously.

Harrie smiled at her suddenly shy brother. 'Melanie's a pharmacist.'

'Right.' Will nodded and grinned, looking as though he'd like to be beamed up to his room.

'Will's in environmental retail,' said Harrie.

When Melanie said, 'Hey, that sounds interesting,' Harrie left them to it.

Things really took off after ten when more and more people arrived, some of whom were friends Harrie had called during the evening. 'Come to a party. Bring booze.'

People she hadn't seen in ages rolled up, said, 'Wow, great place,' then threw themselves into dancing in Bruno's huge ground-floor room. Someone must have brought along a seventies compilation for a laugh, but it was going down a treat.

For a while Harrie joined in, but gave 'Kung Fu Fighting' a miss and headed back to the packed kitchen. Will and Melanie were still in the same spot, heads glued together in an attempt to hear each other. In the mêlée, Joy was desperately trying to retrieve something from the oven. Harrie thought people were beyond wanting sausage rolls, so made her way across the room to tell her.

'Simon!' she gasped when he bumped into her. 'What are you...? What a nice surprise.'

'Didn't get an invite, old girl,' he said in a very loud drawl. 'Just happened to be parshing.'

Very, very pissed, thought Harrie, looking around for Bruno. 'Well...'

'Decided to come and join in the feshtivities. Watch sodding Bruno gloat.' Simon was swaying badly and puffing on an unlit roll-up, empty glass in the other hand.

'Shall I top you up?' asked Harrie, easing the glass from him.

'Cheers. It's the bottle of bloody fantastic Sancerre. Hid it in the shalad drawer, haw, haw.'

'OK. Back in a tick.' She gave Simon a pleasant smile and went in search of Bruno.

'Hey, beautiful,' he said, when she found him. 'This is a very old friend of mine, Frank.'

'Hello, Frank,' she said dutifully, then to Bruno, 'Did you know Simon's here?'

'Shit.'

'Mind your backs!' called out Joy, as she

passed with a mound of things wrapped in bacon.

'He's drunk,' said Harrie, pointing Simon's way. 'And a bit belligerent.'

Bruno pulled a face at his friend. 'Sorry, Frank. Something to sort out.'

Harrie followed Bruno, and they found Simon grabbing a handful of Joy's bacon things. 'Bloody starving now the dosh has all gone. An! There you are, Bruno. Thought you'd seen the back of me, eh? Ha! Thought you could get away with giving me ten grand, eh? Eh?'

'Why don't we go outside?' said Bruno. 'I'm sure people don't want to hear this. Come on. You can smoke out there too.' He got hold of Simon's arm but was thrust away.

'Hey, everybody!' Simon shouted, holding a hand in the air for attention and getting it. 'This was *my mother's* house, you know. Should be mine now, by rights. But this little pipsqueak–'

Terry appeared and quickly got Simon in an armlock. Harrie was impressed, but others looked terrified and began moving away.

'Why don't you all go and dance?' called out Harrie, and, fairly quickly, people made their way towards the hall. One or two stragglers stayed to see the fight, but when Simon took a limp swing at Bruno with his spare arm, he missed and looked pretty defeated.

'Lying bastards,' he said. 'I overheard her ... whassername, the charlady ... bloody Joy Stick... At the doctor's you see, for the old depression, I was. Heard her out the back, banging on to her colleague about the thirty thou compenshation. Ha! If you think ten grand's going to keep me off your back... Aarggh, that hurts!'

'Why don't you go home,' said Terry, looking every bit the nasty bouncer, 'like a good boy?'

'Thieves!' Bruno shouted to the small audience. 'They're all bloody thieves, this lot! *Aargh*, this is plain assault. I'll do you for this, you fat slob of a thieving– *Aargh.*'

As Terry manoeuvred Simon towards the emptied kitchen, Bruno hurried to hold the back door open. 'Let's just get him outside,' Bruno said. 'Then I'll call for a taxi.'

'I'll do that,' offered Harrie.

She wondered what Bea would have made of the scene. Whether she'd have felt a pang of remorse for disinheriting her only son. But then, what would Simon have done with the house? Just zapped it on the market and let anyoldbody buy it? Then squandered the profit on some dodgy business scheme? At least Bruno had compensated the others *and* he was going to make the place lovely. Now Joy, Terry and Hugh's things had gone, it was looking pretty shabby.

Harrie stood on the footstool and reached for her mobile on the top of the cupboard, where she'd hidden it from light-fingered gate-crashers. 'What do you think, Bea?' she asked, hoping to tune in to the old lady again. 'Any regrets about your decision?'

While Simon wriggled and fought against his eviction from the party, Harrie felt around for her phone but couldn't find it. She swore and clambered on to the worktop to get a better look.

'What are you doing?' asked Bruno, just as her head bashed the ceiling.

'Ow!' Harrie cried, making everyone look up.

'Fuck!' said Terry, letting go of Simon and stepping right back. 'Bruno! Out the door, quick!'

But Bruno didn't need to be told. He, like Harrie, could see, in the middle of the ceiling, the sagging plaster cracking in two, then three, then more. From their safe positions, they then watched a huge chunk fall on Simon's bewildered head and knock him to the floor.

When a second, then a third piece of plaster came down and practically buried the poor guy, Harrie looked into the gaping hole it had left and told Bea she could stop now. 'Message received,' she whispered.

TWENTY-NINE

Someone must have written a song about a Melanie, thought Will, lying in bed and listening to cleaning-up noises going on downstairs. Strangely, none came to mind. It was such a melodic name too. Melanie, melody...

If no one else had done it, perhaps he should. Song-writing wasn't something Will had attempted before, but then being a bit in love often brought out the poet in a person. He threw off his duvet, found a pen and a bank-statement envelope and returned to bed.

'Melanie' he wrote, then tapped at teeth with a pen. The sound of hoovering was a bit annoying but he concentrated hard. 'You and me ... were meant to be... Cos I love your...' He tapped at his teeth '...knee? glee?' He crossed everything out and started again. 'Melanie...You're like the sea ... a my-ster-y–'

'Oi! Will!' came Harrie's dulcet tones. 'Are you going to shift your lazy arse and help?' He pretended to sleep, but didn't seem to be fooling her. 'Alternatively, you could go to the hospital and check on Simon.'

It wasn't a great choice for a Sunday morning. A Sunday morning when you were a bit hungover too. He opted for Simon, and after a couple of strong coffees, found himself pedalling uphill to the hospital on very weak legs.

'He's all ready to go home,' said the nurse, once Will had found the right desk in the right ward on the right level.

'Pardon?'

'Only he mustn't be alone. Keep a close eye on him for the next forty-eight hours, won't you?'

'I'm sorry but–'

'Mr White,' she called into a nearby room. 'Your lift's here.'

Simon appeared with his arm in a sling and his head bandaged. His eyes were glazed and it took him a while to recognise Will.

'They tell me I had a nasty bump on the head.'

'Yes.'

'Can't remember a thing.'

'No? Listen, I haven't exactly got transport. Neither can I keep an eye on you for forty-eight hours. But, how about I get you a taxi and you can go directly to your guesthouse?'

'Guesthouse?' cried the nurse. 'I think not!'

'Well, can't you keep him in?' asked Will.

'Until a proper friend turns up.' He turned to Simon. 'Quick, who can we phone?'

Simon stared at a distant spot on the floor, then stared some more. 'I actually can't think of any friends.'

'Amnesia,' Will told the nurse. 'There. You'll have to keep him in.'

'Out of the question,' she said. 'The bed's already taken.'

'How come?' asked Will, just as a guy on a gurney was pushed into Simon's room. *'Look...'* he added forcefully, aware he was running out of ideas.

'Shall we go?' said Simon.

'It's just for forty-eight hours,' Will told an appalled-looking Harrie and Bruno. He'd put Simon on the old camp bed in the basement – carefully leading him through the garden entrance, so he wouldn't see the ceiling – and was keeping his voice down. 'If we're nice to him, Bruno, he might not sue you.'

'True,' said Harrie.

'Says he's a bit hungry.'

'We're out of everything,' said Harrie. 'Unless we give him leftover party food?'

Will looked at the mound of broken cheese straws and deflated vol-au-vents. He thought he could spot bits of plaster. 'I said nice to him.'

'Takeaway?'

'Good idea.'

After Harrie went off for an Indian, Bruno's mate Steve and a young sidekick brought several large bits of board into the kitchen.

'Shouldn't take long now the old plaster's off,' Steve said, and when he and the kid began work, Will and Bruno ventured downstairs to where Simon lay worryingly still on the narrow bed.

Mind you, thought Will – not for the first time – if he died it would make a few lives easier.

'Water,' murmured Simon, not dead.

'Sure,' said Bruno, leaping back up the stairs.

'So where was I?' Simon said in a whisper, barely audible above the drilling and hammering above, 'when it happened. And what did happen?'

'You were at our party. Do you remember that?'

'No.'

'You really don't remember?'

Bruno appeared with the water and Simon sat up. 'No. No memory of a party at all.'

Will and Bruno shot each other a look. 'You went into the garden,' said Bruno, 'to have a smoke, I expect. And, well, you must have tripped on something. We think you bashed your head on the shed, fell and landed awkwardly. Sprained your arm.'

'You were extremely drunk,' added Will, who'd not actually seen Simon till he lay under the rubble, he and Melanie having taken to the dance floor. *Melanie, melody...* Will sighed at the memory, then went back to the task at hand. He wasn't happy with the lies, but really, Simon had brought this on himself by being a dickhead.

'Did I drink masses, then?'

'You'd only just arrived,' said Bruno, 'so you must had got tanked up elsewhere.'

'Oh dear. I'm so sorry. Did I ruin your party? How thoughtless. Listen, awfully pushy of me I know, but I don't suppose you've got any grub I could have?'

'We'll go and see,' said Bruno, beckoning Will with his eyes.

Back in the kitchen, they discussed Simon's new personality and whether they believed it.

Will scratched at his head. 'Could be playing a clever game.'

'Or it's genuine, but he'll suddenly re-member everything and turn nasty.'

'Frightening either way.'

'Yep.'

'I wish Harrie would hurry up,' said Will as the drilling and hammering began to irri-tate. There was just something very com-forting about Indian food, plus he needed sustenance if he was to walk back up to the hospital for his bike. 'Cup of tea?'

'Love one,' said an unsteady bandaged-head Simon from the door to the basement. 'Ah, doing a bit of refurbishment, are you?'

Bruno nodded, Will held his breath.

'Super,' said Simon, smiling genially at the entire room. 'Ma would have liked that.'

THIRTY

Harrie realised just in time that she didn't have her debit card with her. After swinging the car out of the lay-by in front of the Indian restaurant, she steered it towards east Oxford, where she hoped to find the card on her mum's mantelpiece.

When she rang the doorbell there was no response, so she let herself in and found Joy and Terry huddled over the cooker, songs from *Evita* blaring out of the stereo.

'A touch more flour,' Joy was saying. *'That's enough!'*

'Hi!' Harrie called out.

Joy jumped and spun round. 'Oh, I say, our first visitor!'

'I did ring the bell.' Harrie stopped in her tracks and took in Joy's black leather sleeveless, sort of laced-up top.

'What do you think?' asked Joy with a twirl. 'Terry gave it to me. Said I'd look hot in it. I think it belonged to one of his bimbos, but what the heck. Want to join us for lunch?'

Terry turned down the music and went back to making gravy. He wore a T-shirt with ironed creases in the sleeves and no slogan on it. His jeans had been ironed too and he'd had a proper shave. 'There's plenty,' he told Harrie. 'I'm just steaming the carrots and broccoli.'

It was all a bit disorientating, and Harrie's first instinct was to find her card and get out – leave Terry and Joy to their strange new arrangement. But the smell of roast beef was making her swoon, so she said, 'Yeah, if you're sure.'

Over lunch she filled them in on Simon. Although Terry had gone in the taxi to the hospital last night, he hadn't actually seen Simon into A and E. 'He was conscious,' Terry said. 'What was there for me to do?'

'Well, I think you're a poor excuse for a human being,' said Joy severely. 'Now offer Harrie some more gravy, she's got hardly any.'

'Would you like some more gravy?' asked Terry.

'Er, yeah. Please.' This was too weird, Terry being obedient, not swearing.

As he poured, some of it went on the tablecloth and he said, 'Fuck.'

'Language!' cried Joy. 'Remember the

rule. Now, quickly, fetch a cloth.'

Terry rushed off to the kitchen, and while Harrie wondered if she'd shifted into a parallel universe, her mobile rang. 'Oh, hi,' she said into it, mouthing, 'Excuse me' to Joy. 'I'm at home. Had to get my debit card... Yes, I know there's nothing but stale leftover party... *No*. No way have I been that long. OK, I'll be there soon... Yeah, yeah, I'm just leaving the house now... Look, Will, there's no need for that... Will?'

Harrie hung up, rolled her eyes conspiratorially at the new Joy and said, 'Men!'

'Oh, they just need a firm hand,' said Joy. 'Listen, Terry's done a rhubarb pie for afters. Think you might like some?'

'I'll say.'

'What?' she asked Will and Bruno's thunderous faces. 'What?' She handed over the takeaway and while they ripped off cardboard lids and scooped up spoonsful, she looked up at the new ceiling. 'Hey, it looks great.'

Bruno said, 'Steve's coming back to put lino in the bathroom. From the dampness of the plaster, he thinks some idiot must have left a tap running.'

'Really?

Will said, 'Aren't you having any of this, Harrie?'

'I've eaten, thanks. Look, I'm sorry I was

so long, but you know what Joy's like. She forced me to stay for lunch.'

'Ha!' said Will. 'I said that, didn't I, Bruno?'

Bruno nodded while he ate. Harrie decided he looked gorgeous even when shovelling vast amounts of food in his mouth.

'It was all a bit odd, though,' she said, joining them at the table. 'For a start, Terry was cooking.'

'No!' Will shook his head. 'I've never seen him cook.'

'Me neither,' said Bruno. 'Not once in all these years.'

'And Joy was wearing a tight black leather top. There was cleavage everywhere.'

Bruno and Will pulled faces and carried on eating.

'And boy, was she bossing Terry around. Do this, fetch that. And he was jumping to attention. I tell you, it was surreal. Oh, yeah, and Joy was saying how she loved the lived-in feel of the house, and how Mum must lead a busy and interesting life. She said, "Boring women have clean homes!" and laughed, but not her usual annoying laugh. She ate the entire lunch with a cobweb just inches away. Can you believe that?'

'Maybe you went to the wrong house,' said Bruno. He wiped his plate clean with the last piece of nan bread and leaned back in his chair. 'That was great. And all the better for being two hours late.'

Will gathered up tiny bits of poppadom with a wet finger. 'Fantastic. Hey, listen, Harrie, we should tell you. Simon thinks he hit his head on the shed.'

'Oh, Christ,' said Bruno, looking round at the empty silver trays. 'We forgot Simon.'

They checked on him at regular intervals. Sometimes he was asleep and it was thought best to give him a nudge, just in case. When his eyes popped open then closed again, they left him to snooze. For a while, they had him out in the garden on a lounger, drinking tea and eating the things Harrie had finally been forced to go and buy. How charming Simon was being, she often thought. It was as though someone had slipped certain people at the party – Terry, Joy, Simon – a strange potion that altogether changed their behaviour.

Sadly, Bruno hadn't been a target. He wasn't exactly being horrible to her, but he was guarded and quiet, and there wasn't any touching going on. Harrie decided a confrontation might be called for, and when he said he was going for a nap, she joined him.

'I don't know what you mean,' he said, finally putting an arm around her as they lay on the bed. 'And anyway, it's all been a bit frantic, what with all the moves, then the party. Come on, let's just have a nice sleep.'

Harrie snuggled up and stroked his back, then he stroked hers, then one thing led to another. 'Wow,' she said when they fell back all sated and sweaty. 'So you do like me after all.'

'Of course,' Bruno panted. 'Only...'

'Yes?'

'It's just that I've never had a clever girlfriend before. It's a bit intimidating, even though you're not, you know, overtly clever.'

'I'm not?'

'A bit scatty even. Like over the lunch business today.'

Harrie felt she was being complimented and reprimanded at the same time, and as she lay with her back to Bruno, chewing on a finger, she tried to work out what he was saying. Did he want a genius or a dimwit?

'It's not just the house, is it?' he asked.

'You think I'm a gold digger?' She tried to sound indignant but just found the idea hilarious. 'God, Bruno, if you knew how little I care about money. I'll sign a pre-nuptial if you want, only without the nuptials, of course.'

'Hmm.'

'You don't sound convinced.'

'No, I believe you. It's my rugged looks and perfect body you like.'

'Yep.'

'I just sometimes wonder if inheriting property is a mixed blessing. I feel guilt at more or less turfing the others out. There's all the financing to arrange. Then I start questioning my girlfriend's motives. And no doubt Simon's going to be a pain in the arse for ever.'

'Oh, stop it,' Harrie said, rolling over to face him. 'You're sounding like a spoiled brat.'

'That's the other thing. I used to be so contented when I had nothing. I'd pull pints and help at the drop-in centre and play with the band. It was all so...'

'Carefree?'

'Mm. Now I'm worrying about ceilings falling down.'

Harrie took a deep breath. 'It was me.'

'What was?'

'I fell asleep in the bath with the tap on. I'll pay for the damage.'

Bruno laughed and kissed her nose. 'See what I mean? Scatty.'

'Look, not that scatty. Want me to say something clever?'

'Go on then.'

'OK, how about *Liber scriptus proferetur, in quo totum continetur?*'

'Hmm,' said Bruno. 'A book will be brought forth, in which all will be written?'

Harrie bolted upright. 'You know Latin?'

Bruno grinned. 'No, I was just nosing around your room earlier. Came across Bea's diary with all your notes stuck in it.

Bach, *A Secret History*, the countryside, the Dutch masters.'

'Oh, no, how embarrassing. I meant to chuck all that.'

'You did a thorough research job. Clever of you. But then you, a bit stupidly, hung on to the evidence.'

Was he calling her stupid? 'Tell me, Bruno,' she said, lying beside him again, head on elbow, 'what you think of Popper's criticism of Plato, on the grounds that his ideas were utopian? Mm?'

'I think ... we should check on Simon.'

THIRTY-ONE

For her seventy-eighth birthday, Bea treated herself to a trip to Rome with Meg. How she'd have loved Bruno to join them, but he was tied up with his bar work and the rest, and besides, why would he want to holiday with two old dears glued to their guide-books? Meg had her usual abundance of energy and the two of them took in as much as they were able in the five days and thoroughly enjoyed themselves.

Bea had previously visited the city in her twenties with Donald, shortly after they'd married. Unfortunately, her abiding memory was of a tiff they'd had over Donald's constant flirting – there was no other word for it – with waitresses and shopgirls. He spoke a little Italian, having taken two terms worth of evening classes. To say Bea felt excluded when Donald turned on the charm and the smarm and spoke in a different tongue to raven-haired olive-skinned beauties would have been a gross understatement.

Of course, he'd been devilishly handsome back then, before the hair loss and weight gain. It was perverse of her, she knew, but Bea was almost thankful when Donald, relatively rapidly, went to seed. For years afterwards, though, he'd continued, in coffee shops and other places, with the smiles and the winks and the utterances that smacked of innuendo, seemingly unaware of the impression he was creating – that of an unattractive ageing man humiliating his wife. Bea had tried to tell him, but Donald always insisted he simply couldn't help being nice to people. This was true, for he certainly had a heart of gold and spent his entire life feeling others' pain – although, in these instances, not Bea's.

'But, Donald,' she'd once said, 'there's being nice and there's being downright lecherous. When you find yourself in trouble, don't expect me to be a character witness.'

He'd laughed, told her she was being a

silly cuckoo and promised to be horrible to attractive ladies in future. Something he failed spectacularly at until, one day, in the feminist mid-seventies, a feisty young waitress threatened to report Donald to her boss if he called her 'my lovely' again. Bea wanted to rush after her and hug her, and couldn't help wishing she'd paid a waitress to say that years ago.

Still, on every other count Donald was a superb husband. Running up and down stairs with nourishment when she was unwell, massaging her temples when she suffered one of her 'heads'. In fact, he'd always drop everything to do a favour she asked of him. The flirtation business aside, they'd rarely quarrelled throughout their marriage. They had similar standards, agreed on most subjects, mucked in together around the house and garden, and — perhaps most importantly — always had plenty to talk about. Bea's friends would often complain about their husbands' lack of communication, their laziness and slovenliness, or their dictatorial ways, and Bea would thank her lucky stars that she'd found a man with just the one flaw.

On returning from Italy, she was disappointed to find Bruno had taken up with yet another pretty but empty-headed girl. Mona lived up to her name and complained endlessly – about her job, her parents, the weather, everything – until Bea had to ask Bruno to refrain from bringing her round. He took umbrage and she didn't see him for a while, but then he bounced through the back door one day with a bunch of flowers, telling her she'd been right.

He took her for a meal at Brown's, then they strolled around University Parks, Bea's arm hooked through his, chatting about everything under the sun. When they sat for a while by the pond, Bea spoke of her thwarted ambition. How, throughout her teens, as she'd impressed her piano teacher and others, she'd fantasised about being a concert pianist.

'It's always good to have goals,' she said, hoping Bruno might come up with one or two of his own, but he remained silent. 'Even if,' she continued, 'one ends up teaching clumsy-fingered adolescents for the rest of one's working life. And look at me now, I barely touch the instrument!'

'But you've been happy?' Bruno asked.

'Oh, absolutely.'

'Another person might have felt, well, a bit bitter. If you ask me, ambition isn't such a great thing. It can lead to egotism, disappointment. Best to be content with your lot.'

Bea sighed, feeling she wasn't getting anywhere. 'What would you do,' she asked, 'should you find yourself with a sudden windfall?'

'Depends,' he said, 'on the amount.'

'Say ... five hundred thousand.'

'Half a million? Oh, that's easy. I'd travel. Go to Taiwan first, see my grandparents. Then Japan, Australia, maybe India.'

'And if it were a million?'

He didn't think for long. 'I'd see those, then I'd go to South America. Peru and Chile, definitely. Then maybe Greenland, before the ice disappears, the Galapagos Islands...'

'I see.' Bea wasn't sure if she felt pleased or not that Bruno wouldn't consider buying property or starting a small business. Having suppressed a travel bug her entire life, she was sort of with him. On the other hand, perhaps now wouldn't be the right time to release any of her capital for this still very young man. She would, however, make substantial provision for him in her will.

This was something she needed to arrange soon, if she didn't want the whole shebang going to her son. Having had no response to her last three emails, Bea had tried telephoning Simon on the last number he'd given her. She'd got a woman with almost no English, who'd simply said, 'He gone.' Simon could have driven into a tree for all Bea knew. But wouldn't she have been informed?

Disposal of one's assets was hardly an uplifting subject, but Bea forced herself to give the matter some thought before making an appointment with Charles Rogers. Whom would she like living in her house following her departure? The existing tenants, she decided, for they were already established and attached and knew the house's little idiosyncrasies. In addition, they had, over the past decade or so, provided her with pleasant, if occasionally aggravating, company. They'd also put substantial effort into their rooms and gardens, if not into their rent payments. All three were somewhat down on their financial luck, and a move, Bea feared, could soon have them on social security and bowls of tinned spaghetti. She was far too fond of them to allow that to happen.

A will was drawn up. The house would go to Joy, Terry, Hugh and Bruno equally. Bruno might even like to take over her attic, she thought. Should one party want to sell their quarter, the others were to either buy that person out between them, or sell the entire house and divide the profits. Bea left Simon, should he still be alive, a few personal possessions.

Charles Rogers pointed out that there would be inheritance tax to pay, but Bea felt she could mollycoddle her lodgers only so much. And besides, Bruno was to benefit from a life policy she'd taken out, which would more than cover the tax, should he feel generous enough. Were she to pop off next week, however, Bea could see Bruno holding on to his lump sum and heading for distant lands. She'd have to keep going for a bit longer, for in a few years' time, Bruno might have an altogether different life plan. And, hopefully, an altogether different taste in girlfriends.

Her husband had always insisted that people don't change, but Bea had greater faith in a person's ability to learn from his or her mistakes. Donald, for instance, had spent the last two decades of his life limiting his exchanges in shops and restaurants to, 'Please,' 'Thank you,' and 'Yes, it was delicious.'

THIRTY-TWO

On a warm and sunny September Sunday, two weeks after the moves, Will, Harrie and Bruno were discussing the trip out to Chipping Norton. Bruno had been invited to lunch with his father and, since his son didn't drive, Hugh had extended the invitation to Harrie.

'And bring Will,' he'd apparently added. 'Anthony's dying to meet him.'

Will didn't feel the same way, but a trip to

the country sounded good.

What they didn't want was Simon tagging along, so when he emerged from the basement to make himself a late breakfast, they quickly changed the subject.

'I'll get Steve to take down the dividing fences then, shall I?'

'Definitely,' Will told Bruno. 'No point in having separate gardens now. Oh, morning, Simon. How are you?'

'Quite dizzy,' he replied, 'and a touch nauseous. The arm's still painful but otherwise I'm fine.'

This had become a fairly standard response from Simon to a 'How are you?' Will said, 'Right. Not up to helping in the garden today, then?'

'I only wish I could, since you're all being so jolly decent. But, you know...' He rubbed the so-called injured arm, made himself tea and toast and returned to the basement.

'Quick,' Harrie said. 'Let's go.'

Alone in the back of the car, Will's thoughts were on Melanie and her little boy. Sam was two and a half and a bundle of day-long energy. Sweet, though. And he seemed to have taken to Will. But not in a surrogate-father way, fortunately, for Sam spent half the week with his dad.

Anyway, it was all going pretty well and Melanie was everything Naomi hadn't been

– bright, easy-going, sensitive and percept-
ive, and never a babbler. In other words,
mature. Four years maturer than him, in
fact. Not that that mattered a jot to either of
them, mostly because the sex was great.
He'd never share that with his sister, of
course.

Will looked at her now, chatting away to
Bruno as she drove. She seemed happier
than he'd ever known her. Bruno looked
chirpy too, but then he had just inherited a
north Oxford villa. It often occurred to Will
that it was all a bit neat – Harrie with
Hugh's son, him with Terry's daughter –
and that at least one relationship was bound
to fail. If placing a bet, he'd have said –
based solely on boredom thresholds – that it
would be Harrie's.

'What do you think, Will?' she called back
to him.

All the windows were open and he hadn't
heard anything in the rush of traffic and
country air. He could see in her mirror,
however, that his hair was at ninety degrees
to his head. If he kept it that way, maybe
Anthony wouldn't molest him. 'About
what?' he shouted back.

Harrie closed her window. 'Asking Simon
to go.'

'Ah.' That again.

The guy who looked like Simon, but
wasn't really him, was still sleeping on the

camp bed. His bedside table was a cardboard box and beside it on the floor sat Bruno's old TV, which tended to be on all day. The not-really-Simon person claimed he'd cleared his debts with Bruno's 'extremely kind gift' but now had nothing to live on. Once recovered from the blow to the head, however, he'd look for work, then find a place to live. 'If I could just throw myself upon your generosity for a while' he'd said to all three of them, 'you won't even know I'm here. I promise.'

Of course, it was hard not to be aware that the bloke who should probably have inherited the house was lurking in the basement all day. But as Harrie had pointed out, at least they knew where he was and what he was up to. Watching *Cash in the Attic*, mainly.

'It's tricky,' Will told Harrie and Bruno. 'I mean, we don't want to shock him into getting his memory back and remembering the thirty thousand quid.'

'Good point,' said Bruno. 'Hey, we're almost there. Next left, Harrie, then second right.'

They pulled up outside a long stone house with lots of tasteful greyish-blue-framed windows and a matching front door. Either side of the door stood potted bay trees that, incredibly, no one had nicked. Will pictured Anthony taking them in every night, but then realised the skinny wan-faced guy who'd come out to greet them wouldn't have the strength.

'Will, I presume?' Anthony said, offering him a hand when he got out the car.

Will shook it. 'Yes. Pleased to meet you.'

'This is Harrie,' said Bruno. 'Harrie, Anthony.'

Anthony nodded. 'Hugh's just crimping the piecrust. Come.' In a kind of porch, he exchanged one set of flip-flops for another and said, 'Shoes off, if you don't mind.'

They did as they were told, then Anthony walked them through room after glorious flagstone-floored room. Fireplaces were filled with logs, walls with pictures, rooms with antiques. Will wondered if they'd ever reach the crimping Hugh, but there he finally was, in an apron with *I'm a Village Person* on it. Harrie went over and kissed him, Will and Bruno didn't. They were then offered sherry and, in shoeless feet, sat down on a patio that overlooked a fabulously kept garden, with trees and hedges that seemed as old and thick as the house.

'God, I *love* this place,' Harrie said. 'It's beautiful, and huge. And such a gorgeous big garden. You're so lucky, Anthony.'

'Oh, one somehow gets used to things. To be honest, it feels almost cramped with Hugh here.'

Everyone laughed, except Anthony, who looked to Will like a pretty humourless bloke. He'd had the one facial expression since they'd arrived, and it wasn't a friendly smile. Still, you shouldn't judged a man by his pinched mouth, Will decided, and instead, asked Anthony what he did.

'I lecture.'

'Me, mostly,' said Hugh with a nervous laugh.

'You will be such a slob around the place,' snarled Anthony.

Will thought back to Hugh's pristine basement, the way he'd wipe around, then under, everything on a kitchen surface, how his towels were perfectly folded in the bathroom...

'And what's your subject?' he asked.

Anthony sighed, as though this was way too much of an intrusion. Will's fear of being wooed and pawed by this man had been way off the mark He seemed to be boring him to death.

'Biology. Not that seat, Hugh. You know it was Aunt Celia's and precious to me.'

Hugh apologised, went into the house and came out with a stool. He perched himself on it and, towering above the others, lifted his glass. 'It's great to see you all.'

'You too,' said Harrie, Bruno and Will, while Anthony checked his watch, then put his head back and closed his eyes.

'How's the house sale going?' Hugh asked Bruno with a wink.

Bruno, momentarily stunned said, 'Er ... slow, actually. One or two viewings but no offers yet. Time of year, I expect.'

All eyes were on Anthony's eyes, still closed. He'd lifted his chin as though sunning himself. 'Shouldn't you be tending the *dauphinoise?*' he asked. 'It'll never brown on that bottom shelf.'

'Ah,' said Hugh, dismounting and trotting off.

Bruno got up and followed his father into the house. Will wanted to go too, but that would have left Harrie alone with horrible Anthony. Oh, sod it, he thought, and excused himself.

'Why's he being such a bastard?' he heard Bruno say. 'If he's like this when there are guests, what's he like when you're alone?'

Hugh's cheeks reddened with oven heat. He moved a large gurgling dish to the top shelf then took his mitts off. 'It's just since I moved in,' he whispered. 'He can be a frightful slave driver – I mean look at me, *cooking –* and terribly vicious, but I'm toeing the line for now. He'll get used to me being here.'

Bruno put a protective hand on his father's shoulder. 'There's always your old basement.'

'No there isn't,' said Harrie, padding over the quarry tiles. 'Simon remember?'

'Lord, is he still there?' asked Hugh.

'Anyway, Bruno, I'd have to give you back the...' he lowered his voice again, 'money.'

'I meant temporarily, Dad. Anyway, promise me you won't put up with this for much longer?'

'OK.'

Anthony appeared and everyone jumped. 'You're an unsociable lot, aren't you?' he said. 'Chop chop, Hugh. This is supposed to be lunch, not dinner.'

Harrie cried for a while as she drove. 'Poor Hugh,' she said several times. Will wished she'd stop because it couldn't be safe watching the winding road through tears. 'It just goes to show,' she continued. 'You think you know someone and *bam*, they change into an arsehole.'

'There's a sharp bend coming up,' said Bruno. He'd braced himself with a hand on the dashboard.

'Where?' sniffed Harrie.

'Here!'

'Whooahh...' cried Will, eyes closed.

Now on a relatively straight run, Harrie wiped her tears away with the back of her hand and with a few more sniffs, eventually composed herself. 'You won't ever turn evil, will you, Bruno?'

'Of course not. T-junction coming up!'

'I know. Now stop that. Hey, Will?'

'Yeah?'

'Why don't we check out what's happening at home? See how Terry and Joy are getting on.'

Will groaned. He just wanted to lie on his bed and dream of Melanie. Maybe grab a pint with Jon later. 'I'm sure they're fine. And anyway, you might start crying over hen-pecked Terry.'

'Yeah,' she said, driving properly at last. 'Crying with laughter.'

Once on his bed, Will thought more about Anthony than Melanie. Anthony's place, at any rate, and how come such a curmudgeon got to own and live in such a big beautiful house. This got Will thinking about where he'd be when he was late forties, early fifties. He'd want to have his own house, obviously. And if he wanted that, he'd have to start doing something about it soon. But no way could he get a mortgage on his wages. Then there was a deposit to save for.

Will felt a headache coming on, but continued with his train of thought. Mortgage, he told himself. That meant salary. That meant proper job. Could he get a proper job with just a General Studies A level? He got off the bed and switched on the laptop he'd left out on the balcony. Lucky it hadn't rained, he told himself, waiting for it to boot. He then typed 'Vacancies' and 'Oxford' into a search engine.

Twenty minutes later, with an even worse headache and a determination never to take a job with 'customer', 'support' or 'ledger' in the title, and a vague idea that he might become an accountant, Will gave up and checked his emails, pleased to find one from his mum at last.

Hi Will, glad to hear from Harrie that you're settled in your new place. Hope the bike shop's going well and that you're over that awful Naomi. I just thought I should email you and Harrie about Patrick, who's now on his way home and might need some TLC. I feel dreadful and I'm so sorry, but here's what's happened. Kim isn't Kim at all. He's Ken. Yes, Will – Ken, your father.

Will stood up and backed away from the screen, as if that would somehow make the message go away. He took some deep breaths and sat down again, heart pounding.

Sorry, if I've shocked you, sweetie. Hope you're sitting down when you read this! The thing is, we've had a bit of a reconciliation. Rekindled the flames, as it were. Oh dear, this must make me sound such a fickle floozie, but your father was always the great love of my lift, and when I looked him up, we instantly clicked again. After all this time – incredible. Anyway, I expect poor

Patrick will fill you in on the details. Take care of him till I'm back?

Must go now as it's stopped raining at last – Melbourne in September! See you in a couple of weeks. I'll be alone, don't worry. Your dad feels a lot of remorse for abandoning us, you know. Don't think too badly of him. Lots of love, Mum xxxx

Will read it again, incredulous. Don't think too badly of him? After all those years of her besmirching his name?

'Jesus,' he said as he ran down the stairs to see if Harrie had picked up her emails. When he heard a scream coming from her room, he guessed she had. Unless Bruno was in there and they were...

'Harrie?' he said with a gentle knock on her door.

THIRTY-THREE

Harrie phoned in sick. She wanted to meet Patrick at Heathrow, not spend the day as a wartime nurse. She got to Terminal 4 with half an hour to spare, so sat with a coffee and a copy of the *Stage* she'd found on a set. Just reading about the acting business thrilled her. Going through the jobs section, it all sounded so exciting. 'Wig Assistant at the National Theatre', imagine! One day soon she'd look into it properly – whether you really needed to go to drama school – but not just yet. There was Patrick to nurture, her mother to give a good talking to, Bruno to hook properly...

Ten minutes after the plane landed, Harrie made her way to Arrivals, prepared for a defeated, sobbing stepfather. When he pushed his trolley towards her, though, Patrick just looked knackered.

'Such a long flight,' he said, kissing her cheek and smelling of rosemary. 'But how fab that you're here.' He handed over the trolley, and, taking a bottle from his shoulder bag, splashed his face and neck with what smelled like more rosemary. 'Keeps you awake,' he explained. 'It's a natural anti-depressant too. Also a diuretic, so I've been peeing non-stop. No fun, I can tell you, in those rank little loos. But then walking back and forth does help prevent deep vein thrombosis. As I said to the woman beside me–'

'Patrick, are you all right?' Harrie had never heard him say so much in one go. Also, he was reeling this way and that as they walked. 'Why don't we go and have a cup of tea?'

'OK.'

Harrie sat Patrick at a table, then got them

both tea and a stack of carbohydrates. 'Here,' she said, thinking he'd be appalled, but he dug straight into a croissant.

'Barely ate on the plane,' he said. 'I ordered vegan, just to be on the safe side, but ended up with meat dishes. Not even vegetarian, but *meat*.'

'Didn't you create a fuss?'

'What would have been the point? They said there'd been a mix-up, and it was hardly the flight attendant's fault.'

'Oh, Patrick,' sighed Harrie, 'you're so...'

'Pathologically tolerant?'

'Nice, I was going to say.'

He laughed briefly, but then went gloomy and spacey again as he moved on to a hummus baguette. Halfway through, he stopped eating, unzipped the canvas bag on his lap and took out an envelope. 'Here,' he said, handing to Harrie. 'I'd expect you'd like to see what he looks like.'

'My dad?' she asked, not sure she did. She'd seen lots of ancient photos of her father, taken when he was young, slim and handsome. Was she in for a nasty shock? She took a deep breath and pulled out the picture. He was still handsome, but in a more stocky and lined way. His hair appeared a mix of fair and grey, and his eyes had a playfulness to them that made Harrie wonder if her mother was being taken in again. She could see a lot of Will in him.

'God,' she said, putting a hand on her churning tummy. 'Suddenly he's real.' She didn't like the smug smile. What did he have to be smug about, apart from avoiding maintenance all those years? 'I hate him,' she told Patrick, handing the photo back. 'And you must to?'

'No. Hating's such a waste of energy. And people do what they have to do. Your mum seems so happy, I can't bring myself to hate either of them.'

'Argh, you're so pathologically tolerant!'

'It's not such a bad way to be, Harrie. Most men become pathologically *in*tolerant as they grow older. And we know how unpleasant they can be.'

'Hmm,' said Harrie. He had a point. 'But, Patrick, honestly, didn't you, even for a second or two, just want to slap them both?'

'Yeah, of course.'

'Thank God, for that,' she said, just as her phone went. It was Will. 'Yeah, I've got him... Fine. A bit hungry... Really? *No!* I don't believe it. OK, thanks. I'll take Patrick there, then.' She hung up and put her phone away. 'That was Will,' she told Patrick. 'You know Terry and Joy are house-sitting, and there wasn't going to be room for you, so we thought you might have to come and stay in Bibury Road for a while?'

'No.'

'No, I don't suppose you did. Anyway,

Will's just popped in on Terry and Joy in his lunch break and ... you won't believe this.'

'They're sharing a bed and I can have your old room?'

'How do you know?'

Patrick shrugged. 'When they came to look round, I could see the signs.'

'You could?'

'The way Terry deferred to Joy.'

'He did?'

'How Joy put a possessive hand on Terry's back and his whole demeanour changed.'

'For the better?'

'Oh, yeah.' Patrick finished his cup of tea, wiped his mouth with the paper napkin and looked as though he'd come back to life. 'I think it's great, the way everyone's finding their soulmates. Even Will, I hear?'

But not you, thought Harrie. Still, Patrick would get snapped up, as newly single men always were in Oxford. There'd be a dozen women on the allotments with their eye on him. 'Yeah, even Will,' she said.

'Talking of soulmates,' she went on, 'you still haven't told me what was in my and Bruno's compatibility chart.'

'Ohh, er, let me think. No ... jet lag. You'll have to ask me later.'

This wasn't the first time Patrick had been evasive on the subject. Perhaps it was better not to hear.

During the drive, Harrie told Patrick about Anthony, and he said, 'Sounds like a commitment-phobe.' She told him about Simon, and he said, 'Could be a sneaky Scorpio. Wait for the sting.' About Bruno, he repeated what he'd said before. 'Cautious is good, Harrie. Believe me. And having separate bedrooms is a growing trend. We all need our space these days.'

Harrie didn't want her space. She wanted Bruno's body next to her each and every night, and couldn't understand why he shunned that kind of intimacy. After all, he'd lived with a couple of his girlfriends. He couldn't still feel intimidated by the Oxford degree. They'd definitely got past that. When they made love, he seemed to enjoy it. Whispered nice things, cuddled her and stroked her and talked to her for ages afterwards. From her limited experience, Harrie thought that might be rare.

'And how's Will?' asked Patrick. 'Apart from being in love.'

'I'm not sure. He told me last night he was thinking of doing this accountancy course.'

At last, Patrick laughed.

When she helped Patrick take his things in the house, Harrie couldn't help thinking about Terry and Joy having sex. Terry had lost some weight in recent weeks and Joy was dressing more sexily, so it didn't take too big a leap of imagination. Still, Terry and Joy ... at it. In her mum and Patrick's bed. Unreal, as Patrick would say.

While Terry put the kettle on and Joy arranged digestives on a plate, Harrie felt a wave of self-pity wash over her. Even Joy got to sleep with her man every night.

THIRTY-FOUR

On a walk along the Oxford towpath one late summer afternoon, Bea managed to sprain an ankle, quite badly. It was the fault of a large young man on a mountain bike, who came towards Bruno and herself at such a speed as to force them to jump on to the grass either side of the path – and in Bea's case, perilously close to the river. Although perfectly entitled to reprimand the young man, it was, in fact, he who hurled abuse at them over his shoulder for not moving out the 'effing' way quickly enough.

'Ouch!' cried Bea, when attempting to walk again. 'Oh dear. Do you think I might borrow your arm, Bruno?'

The ankle swelled and grew blue, and in the following weeks responded only mildly to ice packs, anti-inflammatory pills and being kept raised for hours on end. It put paid to any walking, both her jaunts into town and her country rambles. Once a day, Bea would limp to the end of the garden on her crutches, where she'd curse the weeds and feel sad about the fallen and rotting produce.

Twice, over dinner, she mentioned that a little assistance with her patch would be appreciated, and, although offers were made, no help ever materialised. She understood that her lodgers were busy with their own lives, and indeed their own little gardens, but it wouldn't have taken more than an hour of someone's time.

The subject then came up with Bruno one day, and before she could say, 'Oh, but I wasn't hinting,' he had her on a sun lounger issuing instructions, whilst he toiled with fork, hoe and trowel and improved things tremendously.

Although determined to be mentally, if not physically active, Bea failed to keep either boredom or despondency at bay. She tried daytime TV but found it left her spirits low. Protracted afternoon chats with Joy, over cups of tea and a fresh sponge, had the same effect. Sometimes, she'd simply lie on the bed it had taken her a good twenty minutes to reach – heaving herself up the stairs on her bottom – and think back to the past. It was an activity Bea had strenuously avoided for years, believing it did a soul no good to harp back to either the good or bad old days.

Often, she'd force herself to stop the reminiscing, sit up and sift through the dull sagas Meg had brought from the library, or Joy's inappropriate magazines – 'Ten days to get back into your jeans!' Invariably, she'd get up and put her old wireless on, then return to the dreaming and yet another doze. The painkillers Dr French had pre-scribed contained codeine and regularly sent her off.

The consequence of the sprain that Bea resented the most was her thickening waist-line. During her convalescence she'd become something of a sitting target for Joy, who always got a conveyor belt of pastries, pasties and biscuits going during the afternoon. 'Thought I'd try a lamb and mint filling, Bea. Here, tell me what do you think?' It got so that a cup of tea or coffee could not be enjoyed without a sausage roll or straight-from-the-oven choc-chip cookie. As much as she tried to decline, Bea was just too tempted by the sight and smell of Joy's evil little creations.

The sedentary lifestyle and accompanying frustration caused Bea's blood pressure to rise to the point of requiring medication. 'Cut out the salt,' Dr French told her, and she passed this on to Joy. 'We'll get your cholesterol checked too,' the doctor had added.

Her cholesterol was deemed to be high and another prescription was printed out. Bea made the decision to ask her lodger not to bake. From the expression on Joy's face, Bea guessed it was like asking Sherlock Holmes not to think. 'At least less frequently,' Bea added as a compromise. 'And not quite so copiously. You wouldn't want your treats to be the death of me, now would you?'

The problem with obsessions, thought Bea, when Joy nevertheless continued with her baking, is that they can't easily be shaken off. Joy simply became more secretive about her hobby. She'd close the kitchen door and attempt to waft the aromas into the garden. She'd sometimes bake in the night, believing perhaps that the smells wouldn't stretch to the top floor and rouse Bea from her sleep.

In the end, Bea was the one who had to be strong. She was eating Joy's food out of boredom, therefore needed to find more to occupy herself with. The days were becoming colder and shorter, and although the sprained ankle had returned to its normal size, it was still weak and never completely pain free. Another awkward twist could see her reversing up the stairs on her derrière again. More mental activity was called for, and after discussing possibilities with Bruno, he came and installed chess, patience and Scrabble on the communal PC for her. Bea then enjoyed many hours competing against the computer at the far end of the breakfast room – or kitchen/diner as they all insisted on calling it.

Having learned from Bruno how to find the BBC online, Bea would listen to her favourite programmes whilst playing these games. It was quite a lifesaver – dear Bruno – and an entire afternoon could pass in a flash. Miraculously, being in the same room as the frantic baking rather put Bea off the end results – as was often the way when one cooked a meal.

Bea's lodgers would come and go, and, regularly, when there were two together down at the kitchen end, they'd talk about the third party in an unflattering way. They were remarkably uninhibited, almost as though they thought Bea incapable of tuning into their conversation and the afternoon play at the same time. Perhaps they thought her hearing had been damaged as well as her ankle.

But Bea caught it all. Terry and Hugh discussing Joy's expanding rear, the way she'd mispronounced something or her unadventurous menus. Hugh and Joy on Terry's lack of hygiene and dress sense. Terry and Joy doing camp impressions of Hugh. On the whole, it was light-hearted – and, indeed, Bea had done the same herself, with Bruno. However, when the criticisms she heard were more venomous, and unpleasantries such as 'bastard', 'hag' or 'slob' were bandied around, Bea regretted being in earshot.

One Saturday afternoon, Bea herself became the subject under discussion. Joy had moved everything, including pot plants, to the dining table in order to clean surfaces, then had nipped to the shops for more scourers. When Bea was on the verge of checkmating, Hugh and Terry came in from the garden for refreshments. Not realising Bea was on the computer – hidden by foliage and without the BBC – they began to discuss her declining health.

'All those pills she pops,' said Hugh, 'seem to be making her doolally.'

Terry snorted unpleasantly. 'She called me Hugh the other day. Now who in their right mind could make that mistake? Wanna beer?'

'No, thanks.'

'And she takes fucking for ever in the bathroom these days.'

'Thank God I've got my ensuite,' Hugh said.

'Lucky bastard. Maybe me and Joy should lobby for ensuites. Mind you, I don't reckon old Bea'll be with us that much longer.'

'Mm, most definitely on a downward spiral now. Fancy one of Joy's flapjacks?'

'Yeah, ta. I often wonder what'll happen when the old girl pops off, don't you?'

'You mean, with the house?' asked Hugh

'Imagine if she left it to us instead of Simon,' said Terry, speaking through a mouthful of food, as was his custom.

'Golly, I've never thought of that.'

'Stranger things have happened. Maybe we should start buttering her up, then. Take a bit more interest in that bloody ankle. I mean, how long can a sprain take to heal?'

'Even if you are a hundred and ten?' said Hugh and both men laughed, slammed a few cupboard doors, clattered things into the sink for Joy to deal with, and returned to the garden, leaving Bea in an icy state of shock – her hand, she noticed, shaking the mouse.

After a while, she reached for her bag and took out her little phone. 'Hello, Bruno,' she spelled out carefully, shakily. 'Haven't seen you for days. How are you, dear?'

THIRTY-FIVE

Will could tell Bruno was running out of money. His mate Steve was no longer rolling up to work on the house. In fact, he'd left Bruno's ground-floor room half sanded, and the under-stairs cloakroom was still a big open space; the wooden wall having been pulled down weeks ago. Bruno was now working at his old pub again four nights and three lunchtimes a week, and when Will presented him with his second rent cheque, he kissed it and went straight to the bank.

'I'm trying to increase the mortgage,' Bruno told Will and Harrie one evening. 'But it's not going to be easy on a barman's wages. They only gave me one in the first place because I put a quarter down, and estimated a high rent income. Anyway, they say I'm at my limit.'

Harrie put a hand on his. 'At least you know I'm not a gold-digger now.'

Bruno smiled and squeezed her back. 'No. Listen, either of you two got a suggestion?'

'Hmm,' said Will, having a think. It really was time Bruno kicked Simon out. Another tenant would pay a fortune for that basement. But with Simon making himself tea just feet away, it wasn't the time to bring it up. 'If you need to increase my rent,' Will told Bruno, 'that's fine. I'm sure Harrie wouldn't mind paying a bit more either.' Will suspected Harrie wasn't paying any rent, and was just trying to make a point. When Bruno snorted and Harrie blushed, he guessed he was right. Maybe not a gold-digger but a bit of a leech.

'I'm still trying to get housing benefit sorted out,' announced Simon in the distance. 'There's something of a backlog, apparently.'

Will and Harrie stared at Bruno disbelievingly. Surely you needed a tenancy agreement to claim housing benefit? When Simon disappeared downstairs, Bruno said, 'What could I do? He's got nowhere to go because he can't come up with all that deposit-and-month's-rent-in-advance business. Basically, if I boot him out, he's stuffed.'

'I suppose he's no trouble,' said Harrie. 'But really...'

Will was surprised she didn't know Simon was an official tenant. Perhaps Bruno was a bit secretive. Personally, he tended to tell Melanie everything and hoped she wouldn't keep things from him. Naomi used to tell him everything, but rarely anything he wanted to hear.

Of course, another idea would be for Harrie and Bruno to share a room, then there'd be a whole floor of the house to let. Bruno could get a wall put up between Harrie's rooms and find two lodgers. Should he suggest that, Will wondered, just in a casual way? It was a bit of a sore point with Harrie, their separate rooms. Best not, Will decided, while it all went very quiet for a bit. Finally, he said, 'Shame you haven't got any spare rooms to let.'

Harrie shot him a look, which said *Careful* or maybe *Good on you*. Will couldn't tell because he was also taking in the strange look Bruno was giving him. Maybe it was time to go. He took his phone out and said, 'Ah, got a text,' even though he hadn't. 'Melanie.' He pretended to scroll. 'Wondering where I've got to.' He stood up. 'See you guys later.'

Melanie hadn't been expecting him, but one of the great things about her was that she was so easy-going. Naomi had definitely had a planner personality, always knowing what she or they would be doing next Sunday afternoon, or two weeks Thursday. Their August holiday in Portugal had been booked and paid for in January, which for Will had taken all the fun out of it.

'Hey, nice surprise!' Melanie gave him a kiss with both hands in the air. Play-dough, she explained, wiggling yellow fingers. 'Sam's asleep, so I'm cooking some up as a surprise.'

'Great. We used to make it with Mum.' Will felt funny every time he spoke or thought about his mother now. Unsettled, nervous even. Was she really coming home, alone, or would Ken – Will couldn't call him his dad – be with her? And would she come home at all? She'd already delayed her flight once, which meant missing the start of her course. Both he and his sister were too scared to call the number she'd given them, in case Ken picked up. 'God, I haven't played with dough in years,' he told Melanie.

'I should hope not.'

'Do you mind if I...?'

'It needs to cool down first.' She washed and dried her hands and smiled at him. 'We could always do something a bit more energetic while we wait.'

'What, like an egg-and-spoon race?'

She laughed and bobbed her eyes to the ceiling. 'How about a sack race?'

How he loved a woman who took the initiative.

'Oh, I know the answer to that,' she said. Will had been talking about Bruno's guardedness with Harrie.

'You do?'

'Bruno told me, confidentially, you understand...'

'Of course. Go on.'

'Well...' Melanie was all curled up in his arms in her virginal bedroom: white walls, white bedding, white curtains. 'Oh, maybe I shouldn't.'

'Look, I promise I won't say anything.'

'Well, we were just chatting in the garden. Bruno and I have known each other years, as you know. Always got on *really* well.'

'Hey, how well? I know you like younger men.'

Melanie tutted. 'Anyway, Bruno said that

when he first started seeing Harrie, this bloke he knows, Malc, who knows Harrie and was quite keen on her at one time...'

'Yes?' said Will in the silence.

'In fact, she'd sort of led him on...'

Melanie went quiet again and Will growled. 'Stop stopping like that, will you?'

'Thing is, she is your sister and I don't know how discreet you are yet.'

'Oh, for crying out–'

'OK, OK. Malc told Bruno that if he wanted to hang on to Harrie he should play hard to get. That as soon as a guy comes over too keen, she loses interest. Bruno said it goes against his nature, but he's mad about her and doesn't want to blow it. Thinks Malc's advice is working so far.'

'Ha! Good for Bruno. Mind you, he could be raking in money for those rooms she's got.'

'Must be true love, then,' Melanie sighed, turning and looking at him.

He and Melanie hadn't mentioned anything about love yet. Did this mean she wanted to? 'Like us?' Will ventured.

'Are you saying you love me?'

'Er... I don't know. I suppose I am.' He thought about her at least half his waking day, so maybe he did love her. 'How about you?'

'Probably. You're easy to be with and very pretty.'

Will was taken aback. 'And I think you're ruggedly handsome.'

Melanie tickled him in the ribs, which made him yell out, which woke Sam on the other side of the wall. 'Bugger,' Melanie said, and went off to see to him.

Will lay back, looking around the pale room and wondering if it was OK to be called pretty. No doubt the fair hair and blue eyes had something to do with it, not to mention the girlie wrists. Melanie was a nine out of ten when it came to looks. Not traditionally pretty but very attractive, in an athletic way. Thick dark hair. Tall, long legs and slightly bony shoulders. Very slim. Bordering on skinny, in fact. Lovely face, although she had her dad's nose. Perhaps an eight out of ten, but more than good enough for him.

He imagined what his mum would make of Melanie, but thinking about his mother made his stomach churn, so he turned his thoughts to Terry and Joy and whether they'd found a place to live yet. Would Melanie know her father's plans? She and Terry didn't seem all that close, so maybe not.

Should he call in on them? See how Patrick was bearing up too? Will had been busy at the shop with all the students arriving back, then seeing loads of Melanie in his spare time. Yes, he ought to pay a few more people some attention, he decided, and was about to get up when a two-year-old clambered on to his stomach with a large book.

'He's insisting you read it,' said Melanie. 'Sorry.'

Will went to the bathroom, then ushered Sam back to his little bed in his little room, and spent the next twenty minutes reading *The Quangle Wangle's Hat* over and over again. Melanie came in and said, 'There are lots of other books, you know,' but Will and Sam said they liked that one. It was fun, and Will wanted to follow it up with a play-dough session downstairs, only Melanie said a definite 'No' to that.

It wasn't far from Melanie's to his mum's house. Melanie rented a thirties semi in a quiet area full of learner drivers. Five minutes on his bike and Will was in the urban street he grew up in, approaching the front door of the small terraced house that was worth half as much again as Melanie's relative palace.

Will rang the bell and was let in by a glum-faced Patrick and led through to what felt like a packed kitchen. Lots of cooking seemed to be going on and Will sensed an atmosphere. Patrick went back to stir-frying what looked like tofu, while Terry prodded a meaty stew.

Joy, in tight jeans, black top, huge loop

earrings and a choker, offered Will a drink, which he accepted. He then followed her out into the narrow herb-filled garden, nicely lit up by a fullish moon, where they sat on the old bench that hadn't moved in decades.

'How's things then?' he asked.

'Oh, fine, fine,' said Joy. 'Well, not really. Terry and I are frantically looking for a place because we can tell we're getting in Patrick's way, and using his pans for meat when we shouldn't, and he doesn't like my bath cleaner, and anyway, we will be off, just as soon as we've found the right place. How's your G and T?'

'Er, powerful.'

'Just as it should be,' she giggled. 'Put hairs on your chest.'

'About time,' he said, and drank on.

'We saw a lovely little cottage to rent right beside the river. Those ones you get to by the towpath. Only Terry thought if it was night-time and he'd been on a gig and had a few, well...'

'Mm, could be iffy. Listen, do you know when Mum's coming back?'

'End of the month, we think. Patrick says her visa's expired, only she doesn't seem bothered. I'd be having kittens myself. Poor old Patrick, he doesn't look well, does he? I can't help thinking a dollop of Terry's stew would buck him up.'

Will nodded. Patrick always looked in need of a dollop of stew. 'Have you seen any other places?' he asked.

'There was a semi, quite near Melanie. But whilst we were going round, we heard the woman next door through the wall. She coughed, just the once, but she could have been in the room with us. Imagine Terry practising his drumming!'

Or Joy laughing, thought Will.

Patrick appeared, dabbing at his face with a tea towel and asking if he could speak to Will alone. He seemed pretty shaken and could have been crying, but it was too dark to tell. When Joy left, Patrick said, 'As you know, I'm normally a chilled sort of guy but my nerves are in shreds, Will. I've even taken to throwing things.'

'Oh dear. Have you tried your herbs?' Will waved an arm around the garden.

'Everything. I'm sorry but those two have to go. Before your mother comes home. If they're still here, I guarantee she'll be back on a plane within a week, then there'll never be a chance for us.' He sniffed and wiped his nose on the tea towel. 'They've filled the house with chemicals, there's dead animal everywhere, they don't recycle a single thing. Joy sings these dreadful songs, Terry watches car programmes, it's hell.'

'They are trying to find somewhere.'

'But nothing's right for them. Too small,

too near the river, walls too thin, kitchen cramped, not close enough to the shops. Honestly...'

'They were a bit spoiled in Bibury Road, that's the problem.'

'I have to listen to the lovemaking, as well.'

'No more!' said Will. 'Please, Patrick. He might be my father-in-law one day.'

'Forgot, sorry.' He sniffed again and Will wished he'd stop. 'How are you and Melanie getting on?'

'It's good, yeah.'

'She wouldn't have a spare room that—'

'No. Tell you what, I'll ask around and check out the agencies and stuff. There must be somewhere that suits them.'

'Want to stay for dinner, Will?' called Joy.

'Already eaten!' he lied.

'Wise move,' said Patrick, almost breaking into a smile. 'There's enough salt in that stew to float the *Queen Mary*.'

THIRTY-SIX

For several days Bea continued to smart from the words she'd heard. It was impossible not to feel like a befuddled old fool with a tendency to malinger. Not that long ago she'd been clear in head, strong in body

– what had happened? With a self-imposed gag on herself, she went about the house in relative silence. It was the only way to avoid calling Joy 'Terry' or doing something equally amusing for her tenants to use as ammunition. Yes, it had begun to feel a little like war.

She'd so liked to have discussed things with Bruno, but didn't want to bother him. He was busy with his life – and, after all, Hugh was his father. Instead, Bea talked to Dr French about it; not in any detail, but enough to convey her increasingly melancholic state.

'It's quite common for convalescents to feel low,' he said in his kind voice. 'Why don't we try you on a short course of antidepressants, Bea? They'll have you right as rain in no time.'

Although told they'd take a while to have an effect, a serenity came over Bea within minutes of swallowing the first pill. Her old self returned, only with a slightly foggier mind – which was really rather pleasant. She even forgave Hugh and Terry for their biting comments, realising it was the sort of thing people do all the time, herself included. A hundred and ten! It was actually quite funny.

A week or so on, Bea confided in Joy about the antidepressants, and how there were so many different tablets to take that she was getting in a muddle. Joy suggested Bea make a note in her diary of what she took and when, which seemed a sensible suggestion, but which didn't work too well in practice. Often, her diary wasn't to hand when she needed it and she'd tell herself she'd jot things down later. Other times, she'd write the initials of the tablet down, then couldn't remember if she'd actually taken the medication before making the diary entry. Oh, to be thirty again, she'd think, laughing off her confusion. Or even sixty! Eventually, Joy set her up with a medication organiser, which Bea was grateful for because it left her more time to re-read the Patricia Highsmiths she'd so loved in the fifties.

When the course of antidepressants was about to end, Bea phoned the surgery for a repeat prescription, only to be told she'd have to come in. She made an appointment with Dr French, who gently spelled out the perils of dependency on such drugs and said why didn't they see how she fared without them.

Bea didn't fare well. The blissful nights of deep prolonged sleep vanished, and she began each day far too early, increasingly with jangled nerves and a head full of pessimistic thoughts – the weather was bound to be foul, her ankle wouldn't last the morning, the postman would bring only bills. She'd temporarily perk herself up with strong tea and plan a little light work – raking the leaves, perhaps – before Joy, then Hugh, then Terry appeared and somehow dampened her spirits again with their own negativity. One complaining about the lack of milk/bread/cornflakes, another – usually Terry – not wanting to go to work and swearing like a trooper about it.

Bea would take herself back to her attic room and lie on the bed, listening for the front door to slam, then slam again, before breathing a sigh of relief. Joy and Terry had gone to their part-time work, Hugh to his basement.

But now what? she'd think to herself. The ankle was strong enough to get her to the Summertown shops, but what on earth for? Then again, if she stayed home, what would she do? She could no longer play games on the computer. When on the antidepressants, her intellect was somehow dampened. Off the antidepressants, she felt too apathetic to compete with the all-knowing software. More often than not, Bea would simply pick up her Patricia Highsmith and tumble into the world of the author's sinister protagonist. Learning how warped a mind could be wasn't perhaps the best tonic for a low-spirited old lady who'd begun to mistrust her tenants, but Bea had become something of a Highsmith addict.

This was how Bruno found her, late one Thursday morning. He'd first called in on his father, then come up to see how she was. Bea heard the sound of knocking and her name being called out, and quickly sat herself up and straightened her skirt.

'Did I wake you?' Bruno asked, kissing her cheek.

'No, no. In fact, yes. But I shouldn't drop off so much during the day because then I'm wakeful half the night. I've become quite an insomniac in my old age!' She heard the falseness of her laugh and saw the concern in Bruno's face.

'What's the matter, Bea?' he asked, and before she knew it, she was pouring it all out; even the remarks his father and Terry had made. This was so unlike her, she felt, but then Bea hadn't been herself in a long while.

'Come on,' Bruno said, when she'd finished. 'Let's go out for lunch.' He took her hand and helped her from the bed. 'Where do you fancy?'

'Oh, no, really,' protested Bea. 'Look at me. I'm not fit to be seen anywhere.'

'You look great. How about that place in George Street you like? I'll ring for a taxi. What, half an hour?'

Bruno didn't wait for an answer and forty minutes later Bea was being ushered to a corner table for two. Out in the big wide world again – marvellous – and in a restaurant full of interesting busy people.

'Goodness,' she said, sitting down and accepting the large menu she was being offered. 'This is so unexpected, Bruno. But surely you've things you should be doing?'

'No bar work till this evening, and it's not one of my drop-in centre days.'

'And how are you enjoying that?'

'It's great. I really like the people.'

'Even though they're depressed?'

'Sure. You don't stop being an interesting and worthwhile human being just because you're miserable.'

'Oh, I don't know,' sighed Bea. 'If one feels uninteresting and worthless, it's hard not to convey that image to others.' She chuckled. 'Particularly those one lives with.' Once upon a time her lodgers had respected her, now they were simply enduring her, as they waited to – they hoped – inherit her house. The fact that Bea had opted to fulfil their expectation no longer sat easily with her, but she wasn't sure what to do about it. But that was an issue she didn't want to discuss with Bruno.

'They're all really fond of you,' he was saying. 'Dad especially.'

'But not fond enough to come to the attic and have an occasional natter.' How she hated the bitterness in her voice. 'Listen to me, Bruno. I'm sounding like a victim. I've always despised that in people.'

'You're allowed to feel sorry for yourself,' he said, smiling at her. 'We all do at times.'

'Not me.'

Bruno looked at her quizzically. 'No?'

'Not out loud, at any rate.'

They both laughed, then ordered from the hovering waiter. 'And a bottle of wine, why don't we?' asked Bruno. 'Red or white?'

'Oh, I...' Had Dr French said she could drink with her heart and blood-pressure tablets? 'Why not?' she answered. It would, after all, be a splendid way to go. 'Red?'

Either the wine went to her head or Bea thought her time was drawing near, but, whatever it was, she felt impelled to tell Bruno about the life insurance policy she'd taken out some time back.

'I'm really the beneficiary?' he asked. 'Wow, that's amazing.'

'It won't be a huge amount,' Bea said, not wanting to build his hopes up, even though the sum assured was currently substantial, thanks to accrued profits.

'It's really kind of you, Bea. I'm sure I don't deserve it.'

'That's for me to judge,' she said. She wanted to reach over and stroke his smooth cheek. Such a lovely face, with his mother's oriental features blended with Hugh's more English-rose look. One day, a very lucky woman would get his attention and retain it. Bea pictured someone educated and fairly feisty, but with a feminine soft centre. How she herself might once have been described, in the days before a heartless son and the vagaries of an ageing body began to sap her.

And was it the wine that made her bid Bruno farewell outside the restaurant and head straight for the offices of Rogers, Rogers and Hope? How much better her ankle felt for the exercise – or again, perhaps the wine. She even took the stairs to the third floor, where the receptionist told her, in the politest of terms, that Mr Rogers senior was with a client, but if she cared to take a seat, she'd see what she could do. When Bea finally made it into his office, after a sobering cup of coffee, it didn't take much for Charles Rogers to, well, not quite talk her out of her new plan, but to at least go away and have a jolly good think about it.

Back at home, after an hour's sleep, Bea made her way downstairs, the aroma of Joy's baking growing stronger with each step. Her self-worth having been renewed, Bea decided to be charitable and forgiving about Joy's compulsion. As Bruno had once pointed out, it was most likely a substitute for something – a man, a baby – so the poor soul ought to be pitied. Often, Joy's produce ended up at the local nursery school or old people's home, so it wasn't an altogether pointless activity.

'Like an angel cake, Bea?' she was immediately asked on entering the breakfast room.

'Actually, I've just had a hefty and rather expensive lunch with Bruno.'

'No doubt you had to pay, then,' said Joy with a tut. 'Hugh does worry about that boy, and I don't blame him. A bright, nice-looking chap like that should get himself a decent office job, instead of frittering his days away on the emotionally challenged, as Hugh put it. And that pub work can't pay much.'

'More than a part-time doctor's receptionist,' said Bea, unable to hold back. 'He earns enough to pay his rent, I believe, which is more than can be said for anyone in this house.'

'Oh,' said Joy, her face reddening.

'And surely it's better to spend one's spare time helping others, rather than killing them with calories?'

'Well!'

'And no, thank you,' said Bea, 'I don't want a wretched angel cake.'

Inevitably, things were frosty for the remainder of the day. Barely a word was said over dinner, as Bea continued, she could tell, to scowl, and Joy was either reeling or sulking. The men seemed to be picking up on the atmosphere, or perhaps Joy had told them what had happened.

How had things come to this? Bea wondered. Her lodgers were grown people with a lot to be thankful for, but as she looked around the table, Bea saw only truculent children. She'd been a sort of parent to them, and now – as was so often the way with offspring – they'd come to hate her.

Hate might have been too strong a word, but children tended to be unappreciative of parents' efforts. In addition, the whole ageing business could be such a tiresome and unattractive process to witness, when one was in good health with life goals still to be achieved. Not that her lodgers appeared to have a single goal between them, merely a lot of spare time on their hands.

'So, how's the old ankle now?' asked Terry, breaking the silence.

'As though you care!' she replied.

Later, she wondered if it was the 'old' that had made her snap.

THIRTY-SEVEN

Harrie was practising her Beatrice on Bruno. "'O God, that I were a man,'" she said wistfully. No, wistful wasn't right. "'Oohh Gooodd, that I were a maaan,'" she wailed.

'You know that has an exclamation mark?' said Bruno, holding up *Much Ado About Nothing* and pointing to the spot.

'Ah.'

'Again?'

"'O *God*, that I were a man!'" she exclaimed.

'Great. Carry on.'

'OK.' Harrie got back into her pose. "'O God, that I were a man! I would ... I would..." shit.'

Bruno sighed. He gave his digital alarm a glance then went back to the page. "'I would eat his heart in the market-place.'"

'Oh yeah. God, that's such a vivid and satisfying line. Don't you just love Shakespeare?'

Bruno yawned behind a hand. 'Used to.'

'Oh, come on. I've been rehearsing for only–'

'Almost an hour. And it's such a short speech, Harrie.'

257

'I know. I'll have to cobble two of Beatrice's speeches together, if I'm going to fill one and a half minutes.'

'*Two* speeches? Listen, let's have a break. Might do you good.'

'You think I'm crap, I can tell.' It was stress and excitement and having to perform in front of Bruno that was making her rubbish.

'No, I think you're good. Or could be. You just have trouble with more than five words.' He laughed, got up and aimed for the door. 'Can't you do something from Pinter instead? Lots of useful pauses, while you remember the next line.'

'I have to do Shakespeare, they say. Then something modern, but I've already decided on a bit of Poliakoff.'

'Jesus. So much to learn before Thursday. Will you manage it?'

'Dunno. Patrick said I should take ginkgo biloba. It's good for memory, apparently, because it channels blood to the brain.' Harrie thought maybe she'd go and buy some at the health food shop. It was Saturday and it was half-past three. She had to do something drastic if she was going to get through the audition.

In the kitchen, Bruno put the kettle on. 'I went to see *Much Ado* with Bea.'

'Yeah, it was in her diary. She said you both loved it.' It was what had decided Harrie on that piece, in fact. Plus the character being called Beatrice. Once again, she felt Bea's diary was guiding her. 'Listen, nothing for me, I'm going to get some ginkgo.'

Harrie ran upstairs for her purse. How lucky she was, she thought again, walking into her fantastic adjoining rooms. She'd spent two work-free days painting the walls and ceiling a yellowish white, and with Bruno's help had got rid of Joy's ancient carpet. The floorboards needed sanding, but yesterday, when she'd bought some cheap colourful rugs and scattered them about, the place suddenly felt cosy – and very much hers.

Perhaps Bruno had been right all along on the space issue. Harrie wasn't the tidiest of people, Bruno was neat. Where she liked to listen to funk and R and B and, yes, Madonna, Bruno played blues and jazz. It would never have worked, totally sharing a room. Currently, they were spending three, sometimes four, nights a week together, in either his or her bed. It was all spontaneous, and no one's feelings got hurt if one wanted an early night, or a very late night. Not much, anyway.

Harrie went to the chest in the front bay window and rummaged through the pile of clothes on top for her purse. While she did so, her eye caught a taxi pulling up. Out got the driver, then out got Hugh. The driver went to the back of the car, opened the boot and took out two suitcases. Hugh paid him, the driver did a sort of salute when Hugh waved a hand at the change being offered, then the driver got back in and pulled away. Harrie felt as though she were watching a film, because surely this couldn't be happening. She wondered if it was another thing Bruno hadn't told her about, then she heard voices.

She hoisted one of the sash windows to listen in. Hugh was apologising. Bruno was telling him it was OK. Hugh offered to go to a hotel. Bruno said not to be so silly. Hugh asked if Bruno was sure he had room. Bruno said of course he had. Harrie turned her back to the window and took a look around her domain. Oh no, please. Surely Bruno would make Simon move out of the basement? And put him where, though?

She placed the purse back on the chest, then picked it up again. She was dying to know what had happened with Hugh but there was the blood-to-the-brain thing to sort out. Also, it might be more considerate to let Hugh fill his son in first. Harrie picked up her purse. But what if she went out for ginkgo and came back to no room? She put down the purse. She'd have to move in with Bruno. That would mean listening to John Lee Hooker and never leaving knickers on the floor. Bruno would resent the paraphernalia that kept her hair straight, and the fact that she took all her mugs to the kitchen once a week.

Harrie looked at the purse and thought of the forthcoming audition, then scanned her lovely rooms again.

No. Her brain would have to wait.

'Hugh!' she said. 'Nice surprise.' She went over and kissed his cheek, pretending she hadn't seen the suitcases by the table. She sat beside him on the sofa. 'How's life?'

Bruno was putting the kettle on again. 'Dad's er...'

'Left Anthony,' said Hugh.

'Oh, no. Are you OK?'

'I am now,' he told her with a faint smile. 'The man's a tyrant of the first order. I just wish I could have abducted those poor moggies too.'

Harrie rubbed his arm. 'That bad, eh?'

Hugh winced and rolled up his sleeve. He showed her a large purple and brown bruise, then rolled the sleeve further and showed her another.

'Oh, how awful,' she said, even though Hugh looked the type to bruise easily. 'What on earth made him...?'

'Just me,' he said. 'Just me being there. He couldn't bear the intrusion into his fastidious, routine-driven daily life. He also saw one of my bank statements.'

261

'Oh, poor you. But maybe you should have told him about the lump sum.' She leaned over and gave Hugh a hug, trying not to hurt his arm. 'He is your partner, after all, and it's not good to have secrets.' That was for Bruno's benefit, of course.

'*Was* my partner.'

'I'm so sorry it didn't work out,' Harrie said. 'So, where are you staying?'

Hugh pointed at his cases. 'I'm not.'

'Ah.'

'I thought we could squeeze Dad in here,' said Bruno. 'If you crashed in my room, Harrie–'

'No.'

'I'm sorry?'

Oh God. If she moved downstairs they'd be bound to go the same way as Hugh and Anthony, but she could hardly say that. On the other hand, she hadn't, as yet, paid Bruno any rent. She had no right to an entire floor of the house and she knew it. 'I meant *no* problem,' she told them, smiling nicely.

'Any chance of my old basement back?' asked Hugh.

Bruno shook his head. 'Simon's quite settled, I'm afraid. Even bought himself a second-hand three-piece suite with his back-dated benefits.'

'One shudders to think,' said Hugh, literally shuddering.

'O God, that I were a man!' said Harrie, as she moved her things down to Bruno's floor. 'Then maybe I'd inherit a house and boss my girlfriend around.'

Bruno laughed behind her. 'What *is* all this stuff?'

Harrie looked back at the basket of goodies he was carrying. 'It keeps my hair straight, my skin flawless, my nails polished, my legs smooth, my elbows–'

'OK, OK.'

Their relationship was going downhill already, she could tell. What was he going to say to all her shoes?

'Girls, eh?' he chuckled. 'Carly was even worse than you. Couldn't get out of bed before putting her slap on.'

Harrie turned, causing Bruno to come to a sudden halt. '"Is he not approved in the height of a villain,"' she said, '"that hath slandered, scorned, dishonoured, my kins-woman? O that I were a man! What! bear her in hand until they come to take hands, and then with public accusation, uncovered slander, unmitigated rancour– O God, that I were a man! I would eat his heart in the market-place."'

'Hey, perfect,' said Bruno. 'And consider-ing you don't know Carly, spoken with passion.'

'I'm not sure I need the ginkgo now.'

'Nah.' Bruno was reading something in

the basket. 'Do you really use a cellulite scrub?'

'Oh, that's Mum's,' she said, thinking quickly.

Later, when Bruno had gone off to a band practice, Harrie found another of Beatrice's speeches to add to the first. This time, without a handsome distraction, she memorised it quickly. She then timed herself, and the whole audition piece took one minute, forty-three seconds. Not bad. She'd only have to speed up a little.

The drama school was near Bath and had a great reputation. It would cost a bit but, should she get on the course, there'd be bursaries to apply for, plus she'd carry on with her extras work at weekends and in the holidays. At least she didn't have to worry about rent, unless Bruno suddenly turned funny about it. And if he turned really funny about everything and they split up, she could always live at home. Unless, of course, her real dad had installed himself there.

Last thing she'd heard – as usual, from Patrick – Ken was planning a two-week trip back home late autumn, and was desperate to see his kids. Harrie and Will thought they might be out of town that fortnight. All those years of neglect and he was suddenly desperate to see them?

'"He is now as valiant as Hercules,"'

264

Harrie said, "'that only tells a lie and swears it. I cannot be a man with wishing, therefore I will die a woman with grieving.'" She couldn't make out if Shakespeare felt sorry for men or for women. Both probably.

Had Bea died 'a woman with grieving'? Grieving over her son? Harrie lay down on Bruno's bed – her bed now. She nuzzled a pillow and breathed in her man's lovely aroma, all the while thinking how things might have been different if a ceiling had fallen on Simon years ago.

THIRTY-EIGHT

'Absolutely certain,' Bea told Charles Rogers. 'Now, may I wait whilst you draw it up?' The last thing she wanted was to have a fatal seizure before signing her new will.

'Um ... this "reasonable compensation" you mention, Mrs White.'

'Yes?'

'It's rather vague. And, should you pass away soon, the beneficiary would be terribly young to be making such a decision.'

'I trust Bruno implicitly. He'll know the right thing to do. Now, if you wouldn't mind, I have a dental appointment at three.'

'Yes, of course. If you'd care to take a seat

in reception, Sally will bring you a tea or coffee.'

On her way home, after a clean bill of health from the dentist – thank heaven some bits of her were working – Bea got off the bus near Little Clarendon Street and bought each of her lodgers a present.

For Hugh, she chose a modern and colourful tie. He liked to wear linen suits in the summer, and on special occasions would add a tie or cravat. For Terry, she chose a plain bedspread in the Indian shop. It had an exotic smell and was in a deep green that wouldn't show the dirt. As far as she knew, Terry had never owned one and they did so give a bed – or in his case futon – a much neater look. Joy was harder to buy for, but Bea finally plumped for a large, perfectly formed torte from the French patisserie.

When they congregated for dinner, Bea handed out the gifts, saying, 'Here you are, everybody. I'm sorry I've been such a grump recently.'

'Ooh, I say,' gasped Joy, 'doesn't this look yummy? Golly, if only I could bake this way.'

Bea could see Hugh and Terry wishing she could too. 'I thought the tie might go nicely with your collection,' she told Hugh.

'It's fab,' he said, holding it at his neck. And I've got *just* the jacket to wear it with. How clever you are, Bea.'

'Thank you. Here, Terry. Sorry it's rather mundane, but I felt the colour to be you.'

'Yeah, very macho. Cheers, Bea. I'm sure the birds'll like it too.' Bea wondered if he planned to spread it on the lawn, before she realised what he meant. Birds, chicks ... who on earth thought up these terms?

Bea knew she'd bought the presents out of guilt, but no amount of gushing over them, or the fawning that followed – 'Bea, you gotta come to one of my gigs again,' or, 'Would you like me to give your room a jolly good spring clean, Bea?' – could make her think she'd been wrong in her decision. Dear Bruno, who could be relied upon in a crisis and whose care for her was never conditional, would inherit 50 Bibury Road, and no doubt make an excellent job of managing it and its occupants. Perhaps a better job than she had.

When Bruno rolled up later, and they spent a good hour duetting on the piano and giggling over wrong notes, Bea felt even surer of her decision.

THIRTY-NINE

Having Hugh around changed the feel of the place. Before it was a young house, but with an old guy hidden away in the basement, now it felt as though someone's dad had moved in. Will was glad it wasn't his own father, but felt a bit sorry for Bruno, despite the fact that Hugh had obviously returned at least some of the compensation, for work had got going again. The old bath had been ripped out, a new one put in and the bathroom floor tiled. At last everyone felt safe while they cooked or washed up. A cloakroom was being installed and the remaining bare floorboards throughout the house were being sanded and varnished. Luckily, the attic conversion was relatively recent, so no one would be upsetting Will's little haven.

Because the rest of the house was in shambles – and maybe because Hugh spent a lot of time in the kitchen/diner – Harrie and Bruno often came and hung out in Will's room, or else sat quietly on the balcony enjoying the autumn sun. It was a view that Will had only just come to appreciate, thanks mainly to Harrie and Bruno's comments – how you could see the tops of so many beautiful trees (they named them), the spires of several colleges (they named those too) and, in the very distance, Boars Hill. Will wished he were a bit more refined and inclined to notice such things. All he'd seen were loads of rooftops.

He'd make an effort to become more of an aesthete, he decided. Although dealing with inner tubes all day and watching Melanie's TV at night wouldn't leave much time for refinement. He had to find a new career path, he kept thinking, and soon.

Following all the derision, Will had given up on the accountancy idea. It was just that he'd always been good with numbers, he tried explaining to people. Every now and then he thought he'd go to a career counsellor and take one of those tests, but in a way it was Hugh who finally clarified things. While work was carried out on the first floor, Will was letting him use the attic to teach in. Students were being passed Hugh's way again by the tutorial colleges, and one or two familiar faces had drifted back. Will didn't mind, so long as there was no hanky-panky.

When he got home one evening, Will caught the tail end of a tutorial on Delacroix. Hugh and his student were on the balcony and Will lay on his bed for a while, unnoticed and just listening. Hugh was pretty good, and afterwards Will told him so.

'I do my best,' Hugh said, still at the little table, where Will joined him. 'It helps that I love my subject.'

'You're very lucky.'

'Yes. And how about you, Will? Do you love yours?'

'Bikes? Er, yeah, I do actually. You'll probably find that hilarious.'

'No.'

'I'm not like passionate or anything. Just get quite a buzz from turning people on to cycling, making a cranky old bike run smoothly, that sort of thing. Trouble is, I've really got to get myself a proper career sorted out.'

'Not necessarily, Will. I nagged Bruno relentlessly after he dropped out, and now look where he is. Who knows what's round the next corner. I thought a leisurely life in the country with Anthony was my path, and here I am, tutoring in a shared house again. And quite happy, although I am missing the others.'

'Terry and Joy?'

'Ridiculous, isn't it?'

'And are you missing Anthony?'

'Yes. Also ridiculous, I know. I don't suppose there'll be any going back to what we had before.'

'Hmm,' said Will. Personally, he wouldn't

give someone who'd beaten him up another chance. Unless it was Melanie, of course.

Hugh leaned uncomfortably close. 'What I'm saying is, follow your heart. I had a mild dread of moving in with Anthony, but it was my head not my heart that drove me there.'

'Oh?'

'I always feared someone else would snap him up. He and his glorious house were quite a catch.' Hugh sat back and stared for a while at the distant spires, or maybe just the rooftops. 'None of this would have happened if I hadn't...' He continued to stare, then turned and looked into the room behind them, eyes suddenly wide, like pale blue saucers with a white rim.

'What?' asked Will.

'Mm?' Hugh said with a start, his head spinning back to Will. 'Sorry?'

'You said none of this would have happened if you hadn't...'

'Did I?' Hugh quickly stood and gathered his things. 'Must get on. Papers to mark. I wonder what Joy's cooking up for...' He stopped and chuckled. 'What am I saying?'

Will laughed too. 'Don't worry, I've thought the same loads of times. Listen, thanks for the advice.'

''Twas nothing,' he said, floating off.

Will remained on the balcony, wondering if he should just carry on at the shop, after all. The big question was whether he'd be secure enough to have a qualified pharmacist girlfriend who earned twice what he did. But then, years with an overachieving sister would surely have prepared him for that.

Will sniggered to himself. Harrie had only gone and done it again, beaten the competition to get into drama school. She seemed surprised by this, but no one else was. Harrie succeeded at everything she went for, with the exception – until now, at least – of relationships. Maybe she'd end up with it all, Will thought. Nice husband, big posh house and the acting career she longed for. He tried not to let that image depress him and, instead, gave her a call on her mobile to see if she wanted to go out and celebrate. One, it was Friday night, and two, it felt like the big thing to do.

'We've just finished shooting,' she said. 'I was an eighteenth-century courtesan. *Suuuch* fun. How are you, sweetie?'

Sweetie? 'Good, yeah. I just wondered if you wanted to go for a meal this evening, with Bruno. Celebrate getting into drama school.'

'What a super idea. Would Melanie come along? She's *suuuch* a darling.'

'Harrie, why are you talking like this?'

'What do you mean, silly? Listen, I'll be home in an hour or so. Speak then. Ciao!'

Will hung up, guessing she must have

272

been in earshot of Anthony Minghella or someone. Was Harrie going to become unbearable? He pictured her in a few years' time, getting her first Oscar … maybe thanking her brother for motivating her. 'We really couldn't have *two* losers in the family,' he heard her tell the world.

It was a nice evening. Melanie got a baby-sitter and they went to the best Thai restaurant in town. Will kept everyone amused with bike shop anecdotes, pleased that he was good at something, and Harrie's luvviness wore off after the first bottle of wine. Even Hugh's petulance when they got back – if they'd invited him, they'd have had to invite Simon – didn't dampen the general mood.

When Will and Melanie went upstairs for a quickie before calling her a taxi, he asked, a bit drunkenly, if she cared that he worked in a bike shop, while she was going to be practically a doctor.

'Christ, no,' she said, yanking his shirt off. 'Every time I pull a wishbone, I ask for a house husband.'

'Do you rea–' he said, but she'd clamped her mouth on his and conversation ended.

After she'd gone, Will lay thinking about being a house husband. He imagined them having a baby together. After the maternity leave, he, Sam and babe would wave Melanie off in the morning, then spend the day having fun with play-dough and colouring books. They'd read *The Quangle Wangle's Hat* and *Where the Wild Things Are*. If he needed to hear adult voices, he'd put on Radio 4. The baby would be a girl, and Sam would be helpful and protective towards his little sister. In the summer they'd go to the park; in the winter they'd do potato prints and make collages with lentils and kidney beans. Maybe he could do the odd Saturday at Neil's Wheels, just to keep his hand in. It all looked fantastic in his head. So fantastic that he picked up his phone and wrote 'I'll be your house husband' in a text to Melanie. Obviously, he didn't send it.

FORTY

Harrie still couldn't believe her luck. If two people hadn't dropped out of the diploma course the day before she phoned the school, she'd never have heard that they were holding another set of auditions for those places. It was short notice and previously rejected applicants were asked not to re-audition, which meant there wasn't all that much competition on the day. She was going to be an actor!

Meanwhile, there was funding to apply for. Help towards fees, help towards living costs. She'd already been to the bank and organised a career development loan, amazed they'd agreed to it, but apparently she passed the credit check and that was all that mattered. They'd expect her to start repaying as soon as the one-year course was over, but by then she'd be in a *Miss Marple* or something, so no prob.

She sat at the big table-cum-desk in the front bay window of Bruno's room – their room – filling in forms and trying to imagine everyday life at drama school. Would they all be younger than her? The other auditionees had been mostly late teens. You didn't actually need any qualifications to get on the course, so should she keep quiet about the Oxford degree with the other students? Just imagine, she could have gone straight to drama school at eighteen! But then she wouldn't know all about Spinoza and the rest, and surely the more life experiences you brought to acting, the better.

Harrie looked up from the forms and watched leaves and branches gently fluttering and swaying in the autumn breeze. She thought back to her 'O God, that I were a man!' piece. How good had *that* been! Well, not perfect, in fact, as that guy had pointed out. She tried to remember his name.

Something theatrical, with an x in it. Like Alexander, Felix, Maxwell. Anyway, he'd said there'd been a touch of the histrionics to her pieces – *Ouch* – but that they'd soon knock that out of her. Well, she was going there to learn, after all.

Harrie was chewing on her pen and wondering if she ought to buy some new clothes, when, out the corner of her eye she saw a body approach the house. It was a woman's body – in fact, Joy's body – dragging a big wheelie case across the gravel towards the front door. Harrie sat frozen for a while. Should she go and let her in, or would Joy still have a key? The bell was rung, then the knocker rapped twice, quite loudly and urgently, and Harrie reluctantly got up. Where on earth was Bruno going to put this one?

'Bold as brass and at eleven in the morning!' Her eyes were smudged from crying and Harrie wondered about recommending waterproof mascara. 'In our bed,' continued Joy, 'well, your mum's bed ... with this ... tart. All knotty black hair and bright red underwear.'

'Oh, how awful,' said Harrie.

'The underwear or the situation?'

'Well, both.'

'I honestly thought he'd put all that behind him.' Joy sniffed and reached up her sleeve for some tissue. She blew her nose, had another gulp of white wine and nodded towards the kitchen area. 'You've kept it nice,' she said.

'Thank you.' Harrie couldn't take credit, though. 'Simon's quite a cleaner. He says it's something to do.'

Joy tucked the tissue away again. 'I know what he means. So, who cooks the evening meal these days?'

'No one. We all do our own thing. Bruno and I usually eat together, but not always. Hugh, Simon and Will just seem to graze.'

'Oh, what a shame.'

'No, it's fine.'

Joy hoicked a large tartan bag on to her lap and unzipped it. 'I picked up a beautiful bit of beef yesterday.' She pulled a package out and put it on the table. 'Needs to be cooked today. Do you mind if I ... only we don't want it going to waste.'

'Er, no,' said Harrie. 'I suppose not.' She pointed at the oven. 'Help yourself.'

When Bruno got back from the drop-in centre, Harrie intercepted him in the hall. 'Joy's here. She's got a suitcase.'

'Christ, no,' he said, visibly slumping.

'She left the surgery early with a headache and found Terry in bed with a woman.'

Bruno looked tired, Harrie thought. A whole day with depressed people would make her tired too. She loved him for doing it, though. He said, 'Does she want to stay here?'

'She didn't say, but her sisters haven't got room and she's making a roast.'

'It smells really good.'

'I know.'

Bruno scratched at his head. 'There's that plasterboard left over from the kitchen ceiling. We could nail it across the arch upstairs and make two rooms out of dad's. The door's still there, from the landing. Maybe I'll get Steve over.'

'Your dad won't be happy.'

'Is he here?'

'No. He went to meet Anthony. For a post-mortem, he said.'

'Good.' Bruno got his mobile out and tapped at it. 'If we get the wall up while he's out, he won't have time to object.'

'True. Listen, Joy wants to know if we'd prefer apple crumble or lemon meringue for dessert.'

'Crumble?'

'That's what I said.'

Simon leaned back and patted his middle. 'May I say, Joy, I haven't feasted so well since I last dined at Claridges.'

'Ooh,' said Joy, giggling and flapping her eyes at him. She seemed to be over Terry already. 'Yes, you may.'

278

'And may *I* say,' chipped in Hugh, 'that I've rather missed your good old-fashioned cooking, Joy.'

'Me too,' said Will, although Harrie thought that might have just slipped out. Before dinner, he'd moaned like mad about Joy's return.

Joy, of course, was relieved and grateful that Bruno was going to accommodate her, for the time being at least. She'd had a little sob again when he made the offer, and this time Harrie had taken her to one side and slipped waterproof mascara in her hand. 'Really works,' she told Joy. 'I used it for my audition, when I had to cry over not being a man.' Harrie wondered every day if that had been a good idea.

After dinner the camp bed was carried up to the first floor for Joy, Simon having recently got himself a double mattress, which he slept on directly on the floor until he could afford a base.

'If Terry phones, I'm not here,' Joy said, when they left her to fill the chest in the window with her things.

Terry didn't phone, so Harrie decided to drive over to the house and see how he and Patrick were doing. She found Terry out and Patrick scrubbing the kitchen counters with Ecover.

'No more meat,' he said. 'I've made Terry promise.'

'How is he?'

'A bit down, so I gave him lavender spray.' He was working hard at an old bloodstain. 'Joy going is such bad news. She was the driving force on the finding-a-home front. Terry will never get it together, not with Pisces in the ascendant.'

'That's bad?'

'Believe me.'

'Maybe his new woman will take him in.'

'She's barely a woman,' said Patrick. 'Still lives at home, he said. No, he'll have to go to a hotel.'

'Right. So, er, don't you want to congratulate me?'

'What? Oh God, drama school! That's so brilliant, Harrie. Well done.' He came over and gave her a hug. 'Sorry, I meant to text back, but my mind's been on your mum coming home and ... well.'

'That's OK. But, hey, remember your hot flash?'

'Of course. Oh, by the way, I had another one.'

'Of me?'

'Mm, you're at a table ... a kind of big farmhousey-type thing, with high-backed chairs around it. I think there's an Aga. You're definitely in charge of food.'

'OK...' This was sounding good. Perhaps she and Bruno are entertaining members of an Ayckbourn cast.

'There's a dog, no two.'

'Oh, wow, I love dogs.'

'Spaniels, I think.'

'And what's happening?'

Patrick took her hand and squeezed it. 'You're feeding four children.'

'You what? Are you sure it's *four?*'

'Yep. Two are having a squabble, the other two are crying. It looks like a typical large-family teatime.'

Harrie gulped. 'Is Bruno there?'

'Um, no.'

'Don't tell me, the dogs are barking.'

'Now you come to mention it.'

'God, Patrick. Tell me it's all tosh. *Four* children? I'd die of exhaustion.'

'I can only tell you what I see, Harrie.'

'And there's no sign of an au pair?'

Patrick shook his head apologetically 'But maybe it's her day off.'

'Or she's just popped out.'

'Who's just popped out?' asked Terry, blasting his way into the house with a bashed door, then another. 'Joy?'

'No, she's gone for good,' said Patrick, 'And to be honest, it's time you were too.'

'But...' said Terry. He looked helplessly at Harrie. 'Where the fuck will I go? And how and where do I start looking? Then how do I choose, and will I end up somewhere that makes me bloody miserable?'

Patrick groaned. 'See what I mean,

Harrie? Pisces rising.' He returned to his scouring, and with his back to Terry said, 'You've got exactly six days.'

Harrie hoped her mum would like this new forceful Patrick and instantly drop Ken. Oh God, her father was going to be paying a visit. She'd almost forgotten in the excitement of the past week.

'I don't suppose there's room in Bibury Road?' asked Terry.

'No!'

Terry stepped back. 'Keep your hair on, sweetheart. I was only asking.'

'I'm sorry. It's just that we're ... suddenly full.'

'Oh, I see. Joy's there, is she?'

Harrie sighed. 'She said to tell you she wasn't.'

'Reckon I could come and have a word with her? She's a wonderful woman and I cocked up something rotten.'

'Oh, all right. But no suitcases!'

'OK. Not that I own one.'

'And another thing.'

'Yeah?'

'Don't call me sweetheart.'

'Sorry, darlin',' he said with a grin.

For some reason – drama school? – 'darling' seemed fine.

FORTY-ONE

On Monday, when Will arrived at work, Neil called him into the office – more of a cupboard with a window – and told him he was going to be taking a break from the Oxford shop to open another one in Banbury. Would Will be able to take charge in his absence, he wanted to know.

'You mean be manager?'

'Yep.'

'When will you be–'

'Day after tomorrow.'

'So soon?' Will was a bit thrown. Wasn't he looking for a proper job? And did he really want all the responsibility? But then he thought 'I manage a cycle shop' sounded pretty OK, and decided he'd cope.

'Yeah,' said Neil. 'Sorry about that. Been meaning to bring it up, then we suddenly exchanged on the property last week, so I gotta get cracking. I'll pay you more, of course.'

It dawned on Will that he was in a good position to negotiate a decent salary, there being no one else with anywhere near his experience. But first he'd see what Neil came up with. 'How much more?' he asked, and Neil said he'd do his sums and talk to him later.

For the rest of the morning, Will saw the shop in quite a different light. He thought about changes he'd make. Move the locks from where they currently hung because they were hard to reach when bikes were piled up for repair. Clean the window and create a nice display of helmets and lights and things, instead of that pyramid of oil cans. Stop Jake and Shaz taking so many fag breaks. He'd take down all the old dated posters, clean the place up a bit – paint it even. Make it somewhere female customers felt comfortable in. Will often saw in their faces how squalid they found it. Some of the blokes too.

When Neil cornered him again after lunch and came up with a not-bad-at-all salary offer, Will said he'd have to think about it for a while, because he had actually been considering becoming an accountant. Neil seemed, not unexpectedly, a bit surprised and dubious, but said could he have an answer before five-thirty.

At the end of the day, they'd settled on a figure higher than Neil's but not as high as Will's, and shook oily hands on it.

The first person he told was Hugh, who said, 'Congrats, dear boy. What did I tell you?'

Harrie said, 'Oh, how splendid!' in a sort of Maggie Smith voice. She'd just got back from a costume drama at Windsor, so Will let it go.

Simon seemed the most excited by his news. 'Does that mean you'll be hiring and firing?' he asked. They were in the kitchen/diner, or breakfast room, as Simon called it. 'Only I'm quite a bike enthusiast now, and a fast learner.'

Simon wasn't fast at anything, as far as Will could see. 'We'd have to advertise and Neil would want the final say, but, yeah, I'll definitely let you know if a vacancy comes up.' But maybe after it had been filled.

Simon was making himself the usual something-on-toast for dinner. 'It's just that they keep making me apply for jobs, and they're all so high-powered. I suppose I shouldn't have mentioned being a company director.'

'No.'

'Anyway, I'm very pleased for you, Will. Excellent news.'

'Thanks.' What a nice bloke, Will thought, when Simon picked up his plate and headed for his room. And how good it would be if he stayed that way. Every time Simon left the kitchen to go to his basement, he had to duck to get through the doorway. Any day now, he'd forget, knock himself out and come round a total bastard. People held their breath when he walked through that door, just as Will was doing now. 'Cheerio,' Simon said, ducking. 'And jolly well done again.'

Melanie was pleased too, when he called round. 'No chance of you being my house husband, then?' she said smiling.

Damn. But, no, he'd committed himself to the job now. And really, how many potato prints could you do before boredom set in? 'Not just yet,' he told her, keeping his options open. He might, after all, make a crap manager, lose Neil thousands and get fired. 'It's very appealing, though.' It was almost as though they were proposing to each other, and after only a few weeks. Not that the length of time mattered, he decided, thinking of Hugh and Anthony.

'I'd give you housekeeping money,' said Melanie. 'When I'm fully qualified, that is.'

God, she was being serious. Two job offers in one day. Not bad.

By the end of the week, Will had settled into his new role and already made one or two changes. Melanie went to her mother's for the weekend, so he spent most of Sunday alone in the shop, cleaning, painting and rearranging. It was knackering but satisfying, and a whole lot better than being at home, where a bit of a dodgy atmosphere had developed.

Bruno had confided in Will that the house was eating up way too much money, way too quickly. That, plus Simon being a permanent presence were getting him down. What was wrong with Hugh, though, Will had no idea. One minute he'd be morose, then he'd become agitated, then he'd be back to normal for a while. Will guessed it was something to do with Anthony. On the other hand, Bruno and Hugh weren't communicating much, so the problem might lie there. Or it could just be that the house now felt rammed, since Terry had got his futon out of storage and was sharing it with Joy in the front first-floor bedroom.

Will mulled over these things while he worked away on walls and floors and cupboards and counters. Then at half six he packed up, tidied up, got on his bike and went home.

He'd declined dinner and was lying in the attic and listening to Radio 3. He'd been doing that a lot recently; it was soothing and blocked out the rest of the increasingly busy house.

It sounded like Brahms but he'd have to wait for the end of the piece to find out – and assumed he'd be wrong because he always was. Some people have a way with the high arts, some have a way with a brake cable.

Whatever the piece was, it was nice, and made him think of running naked through cornfields with Melanie on a glorious summer's day. Fantastic. Although probably an offence – indecent exposure, trespass – and also a bit scratchy and painful. Then they'd have to wear shoes too, which might not be a good look...

'That was Johannes Brahms,' the man on the radio told him. 'Symphony number four, opus ninety-eight.'

Hey, he was becoming a classical music buff. He punched the air, looked up at the ceiling and said, 'Thank you, Bea.'

FORTY-TWO

To Bea's chagrin, not to mention fury, her ankle went again. The same ankle. She'd become complacent and far too adventurous and had set out on a walk along the Ridgeway, when an unseen dip caught and twisted her stout walking boot. Luckily, she and Meg hadn't gone more than half a mile and it was possible to limp, with the aid of Meg's shoulder, back to the car.

Again, the foot had to be kept raised, and again Bea's spirits plummeted. The difference this time was that her lodgers rallied round. It was almost as though a 'Be nice to Bea' campaign had been launched. Terry offered to exchange floors to make things easier for her. She gave it some thought, but only briefly. Being so close to the hub of the house would be most disturbing. She'd grown used to the peace in the attic, and so declined Terry's generous offer. He then said he'd look into stair lifts for her, in order, as he put it, 'to save that poor old rear of yours'. Bea opted not to react to the 'old' this time.

Joy bought a new recipe book and produced delicious things called smoothies and assorted tasty soups. 'We don't want you putting on that weight again,' she said. 'Best cut out the wheat too.' Joy not cook with wheat? It would be like Fred not dancing with Ginger. But Joy had been watching all sorts of healthy-eating programmes and so managed it, if only for the dishes she produced for Bea. The result was that, during her first fortnight of immobility, Bea lost a good half stone – a feat that Dr French declared, 'Most welcome, if a little overdue.' He hoped her blood pressure would take a similar dive, but it showed no signs of doing so.

Hugh's practical help consisted of coming up to the attic and reading to her. This she found useful, partly because cataracts had begun to form in both eyes, but also because the tablets she took at night to help her sleep were almost certainly remaining in her system the following day. Often, Hugh's lilting delivery kept her gripped, occasionally it sent her off. Either way, it was kind of him to read to her, when he must have all sorts of other things to do. Earn money, for example.

Each morning before going to the surgery, Joy would hurry upstairs with a mug of tea and Bea's mail, if it had arrived, and plump up the pillows and ask if there were things Bea needed, whilst she was out. Bea could rarely think clearly first thing, but then would remember something after Joy had left and end up trying to text her at work. Somehow, text messaging didn't come as easily as it once had. 'I'm sorry, Bea,' would come back from Joy. 'Don't understand. What's arovn raube?' Bea would reply, very carefully tapping out 'brown sauce' or whatever it was she'd got wrong. Such silly little phones.

In her more alert moments, Bea would grow mildly suspicious of her lodgers' care and attention, for it was almost excessive at times. Terry had organised the stair lift now, although Bea was to pay, of course. Joy regularly returned from work with some of Bea's favourite flowers. Hugh worked one entire afternoon on a sketch of the attic, which he subsequently framed and hung just where she indicated, on the wall by the foot of her bed.

But these moments of suspicion were fleeting, and Bea assumed her lodgers did genuinely care, for she could detect nothing in the manner of any of them to think otherwise. Whether someone had had a word – possibly Bruno, or perhaps Dr French, who occasionally dropped in – was of no importance really. Bea enjoyed the attention and tried not to entertain thoughts that their behaviour may be suspect.

For one thing, she had neither time nor energy. Each day was filled with a routine, albeit a fairly relaxed one. Rising, bathing, breakfasting on the healthy things Joy had left, being read to by Hugh, napping, lunching on the healthy things Joy produced when she returned from work, napping, watching a little late-afternoon TV, discussing any house maintenance issues with Terry, dining on more healthy things, listening to the radio and retiring.

Bea's life had slowed substantially, and how she'd ever managed to fit in the gardening and the trips to the shops and the walks around University Parks, she'd never know. Walks in the country, even! When she looked back to that former life it was rather like a video fast-forwarding.

Bruno was still a regular visitor, but more and more frequently he'd be there and they'd be having a super chat and then she'd suddenly wake to find a note from him. 'I expect I wore you out!' or 'Had someone to meet but didn't want to wake you to say goodbye.' Sometimes, Bea would try to recall what they'd been discussing, but it had gone.

What a bother she found her sleepiness, but, as Dr French said, 'The more you rest the quicker you'll heal.' Bea had reservations about her GP's advice, though, feeling he was simply covering himself for the drowsiness caused by her cocktail of prescription drugs.

The weeks turned into months and although Bea's ankle healed, she didn't recover her former dynamism; not that she particularly wanted it back. She'd grown to appreciate the comfort of her calm existence, as well as the continued pampering she received from her lodgers – or family, as she now felt them to be. When her birthday came round, they organised a small party, consisting of a couple of her friends – Meg and Lionel – and the neighbours, plus Bruno, Melanie and themselves. Joy made what she called 'a low-cal cake', and Bruno played his guitar. It was all terribly touching and uplifting and for the first time in months, Bea stayed up beyond ten.

She began to ask herself if she could have found better people to share her home with during her twilight years. She might well have ended up all alone like poor Meg, whose only daughter and grandchild lived in Canada, and who'd now been struck off the language schools' list as too elderly to be a host mother. A ridiculous decision to Bea's mind. Meg had the stamina of a twenty-year-old.

Yes, she was extremely fortunate. Fortunate to have people who'd find her reading specs for her half a dozen times a day. Easy for her lodgers to find, of course, when they were simply dangling against her chest on their chain! Bea often felt if she gave anything at all back to Hugh, Terry and Joy for their kindness, it was amusement value.

One morning, when Joy was straightening Bea's bedding for her, stirring the tea and passing the medicine organiser, Bea had yet more faint and foggy thoughts about her will. She remembered having left the house to her lodgers and Bruno, and she vaguely remembered deciding against that. What she couldn't recall at all, was whether she'd acted upon that decision and in what way. Did she make out another will? She thought perhaps she had, but couldn't be certain. She'd wanted to leave the house to Bruno, but hadn't the solicitor talked her out of it?

Oh dear, she hoped he had, for Bea now wondered if the responsibility would weigh too heavily on such a young chap. She considered phoning Charles Rogers to enquire, but would he think her a befuddled old thing, slowly losing her mind? What was that thing Simon had brought up ... power of something? She remembered not trusting her son over house issues... Would Charles get in touch with Simon to inform him his mother was now unhinged?

'What's that legal thing,' she asked Joy, 'where one gets so old and crazy that one's rights are taken away? Power something.'

'Power of attorney?'

'Oh, of course.' Now why hadn't she been able to remember so familiar a term? Bea sipped at her strong tea and felt the caffeine fighting the sleeping pills. 'Joy,' she said, 'do you think you might fetch me a will today?'

'You, mean a blank one? Like they have in the post office?'

'Yes.'

'But haven't you got one already? You know, with a solicitor or something?'

'Well, possibly. However, I'm a little fuzzy on the matter. So to be on the safe side, I'd like to write another. I'm sorry if I'm imposing on you, dear, only ... well, let's just say it'll be to your advantage, as well as Hugh's and Terry's.'

'Oh, crikey,' said Joy. Bea watched her face flood with colour. 'Are you sure?'

'Completely. You've all been so terribly

good to me, the least I can do is give you peace of mind on the home and property front. I'd hate to think of you being turned out of here.'

'I don't know what to say.'

'That's not like you,' said Bea with a smile, feeling far more alert than at eight fifteen most mornings. Mind you, Joy's lipstick choice for the day was enough to wake the dead.

The Last Will and Testament duly arrived after lunch, with one of what Joy called Bea's 'special detox' teas. Bea never drank the things, but her weeping fig did and seemed to be flourishing.

'Thank you so much,' said Bea. Joy hovered, as though waiting to help her fill the will out. 'Thank you,' Bea repeated, tucking the form away in her desk. 'Now, one other request. Since Terry hasn't organised a second stair lift, would you mind being in front of me whilst I go down this first flight of stairs? Only one gets so terribly dizzy these days. Silly, isn't it?'

'But you haven't drunk your tea yet.'

'Later, dear. My fig prefers it cold.'

Joy shook her head and looked prematurely bereft. 'Oh, Bea,' she said. 'Those blinkin' pills.'

FORTY-THREE

Harrie had projected her voice so much over the past few days, it must have reached her mum in Melbourne by now. While Patrick concocted something to soothe her throat, she talked croakily about Bibury Road.

'It was so cool a few weeks ago, with just me, Bruno and Will there.'

'And Simon,' said Patrick.

'Yeah, but he was no trouble. Still isn't. Unlike Hugh, who's gone *so* moody and no one knows why. Then Bruno's all stressed about things. We haven't made love for ... well, never mind.'

'I could make him up a–'

'Uh-uh. I'm pretty knackered anyway, what with the driving and the classes and getting to know the others. It's great fun, but then when I get home the atmosphere hits me and I'm just like *uurghh* and go to bed.'

'And how are my favourite people?'

'Terry and Joy? Fine, I think. They're just a bit annoying.'

'You don't say?'

'And they've slipped back into their old

roles. Joy's baking and polishing like crazy, Terry slobs out a lot. What's good is that Joy goes to all his gigs now, to keep an eye on him. That means they're often out in the evenings, but sometimes, perversely, you want them around, since everyone else is wound up.'

'Not Will, surely?'

'God, no. He's on such a high.' Harrie rolled her eyes. 'Loves his new managerial–' she drew quote marks in the air – 'position. Seems to love being with Melanie and Sam. And when he's home, he's got the nicest spot in the house. No, he's happy. Mind you, he's dreading seeing Ken too.'

'You're not calling him "Dad", then?'

'You kidding?'

'Here,' said Patrick. He handed Harrie a warm mug. 'Fenugreek, goldenseal, slippery elm, garlic and honey. It's not too hot, so try and gargle a bit first, then just sip slowly.'

'Cheers.'

'I'll bottle the rest, so you can take some with you.'

'This is really nice of you.' Harrie blew on the drink for a while then gargled some. It was so utterly foul that it would definitely mean another night with no sex. Did that bother her? Yes, but she'd carry on being extra nice to Bruno, just so he'd know it was OK and that she wasn't about to run off with a hunky drama teacher. He didn't need to know there weren't any.

Bruno had a lot going on. He wasn't telling her much about it, but she guessed it was to do with mortgage payments and how much Terry, Joy and Hugh should give him back, even though they weren't permanently living in Bibury Road. Or so they said. Things had got complicated and a bit out of hand, and Bruno kept saying how much he enjoyed going to the drop-in centre and doing his odd hours at the pub. How much he missed playing. The band was on the back burner for a while, not surprisingly.

What Harrie had found upsetting were the three white hairs she saw on him in bed on Sunday morning. They were sprouting from his crown and stood out so vividly against the black. Stress, she thought. She'd cuddled him from behind and told him lots of old houses have dry rot.

He'd stroked her hand and said miserably, 'There's woodworm too, on the ground floor. And Steve's found some lead pipes. They'll have to be replaced...'

'That's the very best thing,' Patrick was telling her.

'Sorry?' She'd been miles away.

'Not having to listen to Joy singing "I Know Him so Well".'

Harrie laughed and carried on sipping and gargling, then when she got near the end was convinced her throat was fully recovered. As a test, she broke into the Lady Macbeth she'd been practising, just in case an opportunity came up. "'Nought's *had*, all's *spent*,'" she enunciated, placing her mug on the counter and clutching her hands to her chest, "'Where our desire is *got* without *content*. 'Tis *safer* to be that which we *destroy*, Than by destruction *dwell* in *doubtful joy*.'"

Oh yes, the throat was so much better. She'd take the remedy to classes with her and have the odd glug or sneaky gargle in the loos. 'Brilliant!' she said. 'Thank you, Patrick. Hey, are you all right? Patrick, you're not crying, are you?'

'That was so ... moving.'

'You don't think it was a bit over the top?'

'A little,' he sniffed. '"'Tis safer to be that which we destroy." How true.'

Harrie was suddenly worried. Lady Macbeth committed suicide. Patrick wouldn't think of... Surely he was more secure than that? The trouble was her mother was coming home soon and no one knew what was going to happen then, least of all Patrick. Harrie went over and gave him a hug. 'Everything's so up in the air, isn't it?'

'It'll be all right, though,' he said when she let go. 'Jupiter's retrograde, but moves forward again next week.'

'I take it that's good. So, listen, Patrick, on a scale of one to ten, how over the top was it?'

'Nine?'

'Right. Thanks.' As if Patrick knew anything about acting.

Back at Bibury Road, Joy had made toad-in-the-hole with gravy and mashed potatoes. Harrie thought it was the perfect meal for the household – stodgy and boring and a bit ugly, just like the diners themselves that evening. She helped Joy put everything on the table, then filled the big water jug.

'There!' said Joy, breaking the silence and wiping imaginary sweat from her brow. 'Now all we need is Simon.' She crossed the room and called, 'Simon! Dinner!' into the basement, then took her seat on the end nearest the kitchen. 'Does anyone know if he's in? Now, let me slice this up, then you can help yourselves to a bit.'

No one said a word while Joy hacked at the batter and sausages with a spatula. Harrie wanted to catch Bruno's eye, but he was staring at Joy's dish, just like everyone else. Will looked pretty happy, in a little dream-world that had nothing to do with the house, the dinner or the people around him.

Joy finished slicing and sat back. 'There. Eight portions, even though there are only six of us.' At the sound of footsteps hurrying up the stairs, she added, 'No ... seven. Jolly good. That man would live on toast, if–'

She stopped because a loud thump had startled them all. It was followed by a *thump*, *thump*, *thump*, *thump*, *thump*, then silence.

Joy and Harrie got up at the same time, rushed to the basement door and peered down. Joy gasped at the crumpled Simon, motionless at the bottom of the stairs. 'Heavens above! Ring for an ambulance, someone.'

Will, Hugh and Terry came to have a look, while Bruno stayed at the table and got his phone out. 'This is all I need,' Harrie heard him say.

'No, honestly, he's fine,' Harrie told the woman. 'He's just sleeping now, so we don't think we need the ambulance. But thanks, anyway. And sorry to be a nuisance.'

Harrie hung up, forgiving the woman for her rudeness, on account of her having a stressful job, but not forgiving the ambulance driver, who still hadn't arrived after forty minutes. Although, thinking about it, they'd have more worthy cases than a bloke who'd walked into a doorframe

'Cancelled?' asked Hugh.

'Yes.'

They were all in the basement, sitting on Simon's leatherette three-piece suite, watching him sleep and hoping he wasn't going to show signs of concussion. Harrie had been on the Internet and was told that 'the patient must be monitored for 24 hours after the loss of consciousness. Once an hour, he or she should be asked to repeat something, such as name and address.'

Joy had brought dessert down and they were all digging into bread-and-butter pudding. As she ate, Harrie tried not to look at Simon's Y-fronts in his laundry pile at the foot of his mattress. She wondered how many years he'd had them and if he'd worn them through any serious relationships. He'd never mentioned anyone, but mostly you talked about the weather with Simon.

'Do you think it really needs six of us watching him?' asked Will. 'Surely one's enough?'

'But what if that person falls asleep?' asked Joy.

'Two then.'

'They might both fall asleep.'

'But,' said Will, giving his watch a quick glance, 'that could apply to any number. Six people might fall into a heavy night-long sleep.'

Harrie thought being a manager might be making her brother more clever and assertive. But not as clever as her. 'There's a probability factor,' she told him. 'Chance of two falling asleep, against chance of six falling asleep.'

'Oh, for Christ's sake,' snapped Hugh. He put his uneaten pudding on the floor, got off the slippery sofa and walked to the French doors, hands in the pockets of his pale blue cotton trousers. 'It's obvious why we're all watching him. It's because we're keen to know who he'll be when he comes round properly. New Simon or Old Simon.'

'Simple Simon or Sodding Simon,' chortled Terry.

'And what do we do,' continued Hugh, slightly shakily and now pacing up and down the room, 'if he is Sodding Simon? If he demands a big chunk of capital, then when he's given it, decides to contest Bea's will regardless? Mm? Mm? Mm?'

'Are you all right, Hugh?' asked Harrie. She got up and went and gently rubbed his back. First Patrick, now Hugh. It was her night for comforting sensitive and troubled men. 'You seem a teeny bit wound up. Is there something–'

'Oh, please, cut out the acting, Harrie. Don't you ever stop?'

'Hey!' said Bruno, coming to life at last and leaping to his feet. 'What's got into you, Dad? You've been a pain in the arse recently. Is it Anthony, or what?'

'There's a little more custard in the jug,' said Joy, 'if anyone wants it. A bit tepid, mind you. Terry?'

'Yeah, ta.'

Harrie said, 'Bruno, do you think we should ask Simon his address now?' She wanted him to sit down and calm down.

'No, it's *not* Anthony,' said Hugh. He dug his hands deeper into his trousers and puffed out his narrow chest. 'As a matter of fact, it's something altogether ... something ... well...' He paced away from them, then swung himself round. 'It's ... just that ... I, er ... oh God, you wouldn't believe how wretchedly torn I've been.'

'About what?' asked Harrie. Talk about *her* being an actress.

'About...'

'For fuck's sake,' said Terry. 'Spit it out, man.'

Hugh held his head in one hand, his elbow resting on the other hand. 'I'm so sorry, Bruno, but ... but...'

'*What?*' everyone but Joy shouted. She was wiping a custard ring from the wooden floor with her napkin.

'Honestly, Terry,' she puffed.

Hugh walked back to the sofa and flopped down in a defeated manner. 'It's just,' he said, his eyes lifting themselves and going round the group slowly, 'that I've found the will.'

Joy stopped wiping and joined in the '*What?*' this time.

'Oh my God!' cried Harrie. 'Where?'

Hugh did a strange titter. 'Of all places, in Bea's compost bin. Thought I'd spread a little round my marginals, and when I lifted the lid, there it was.'

Harrie and Will exchanged glances. Don't say anything, they were telling each other.

'I expect she thought she was posting it, or something, ha ha. Poor old love.'

'And have you read the thing?' asked Terry.

'No. She'd sealed it. I mean, actually sealed it, with candlewax.'

'Wow,' said Harrie. She didn't want to look at Bruno, but then when she did, his face wasn't as shocked and miserable as she'd expected. He looked unusually happy and said, 'This might change everything, then. And, hey, could be great news for you lot.'

'But not for you, dear boy,' said his father.

'Oh, I don't know.' Bruno went over to Simon, kneeled down and shook his shoulder to wake him. 'Simon,' he said. 'Simon. Wake up. What's your address, Simon? Simon, can you tell us where you live?'

To Harrie's relief, Simon's eyes opened a little. 'Bag End,' he told Bruno in a husky voice.

'Really?'

'Near Hobbiton,' he added, and went back to sleep.

While the Last Will and Testament of Mrs Beatrice White was being passed around and inspected unopened, Harrie offered to make coffee. 'Come and help?' she asked her brother.

Up in the kitchen, she dragged him to the den end and whispered, 'No way was it in that compost bin.'

'No. What's he up to?'

'Maybe Bea gave it to him, then he lost it but was too embarrassed to tell the others, then he genuinely found it again, somewhere stupid, like in his briefcase or somewhere. It's the only explanation. I mean, he wouldn't want to hide a will that might have left him a third of this house.'

'No,' laughed Will. Then he stopped and said, 'Oh Christ.'

'What?'

'It's just ... something he said when he was packing. How, in the past, Anthony hadn't seen any reason for Hugh to move out, but now he had no option but to take him in.'

'Hmm, interesting.'

'Yes. And then, when we were in my room once, he sort of came over weird and started thinking out loud about something he wished he hadn't done.'

'What?'

'Well, he didn't tell me.'

'Hide the will, maybe? Listen, we should make some coffee.'

'Yeah. But we keep quiet about this for now, right?'

'Right.'

Down in the basement Terry clutched the will, while they all discussed what to do about it. One thing they all agreed on was that they shouldn't open it themselves.

'I'll call the solicitor tomorrow,' said Bruno. 'Find out what the procedure is in such cases. I expect we'll all have to go along for another reading.'

'You're sounding dead chilled,' said Terry, 'for a bloke who might have just lost his property.'

Bruno shrugged. Harrie could see relief all over his beautiful face and had to admit to herself she was disappointed in him. What was so hard about owning a property? Judging from Patrick's hot flash, she'd have a big place too, one day. Harrie shivered again at the thought of all those kids and carried on feeling a bit let down by Bruno. If he couldn't cope with a house, how would he manage with four children?

'Now,' said Joy, 'let me get this straight in my head. If this is a more recent will – which I think it must be because it's exactly like the one I fetched Bea – then, the house would be put into my, Terry and Hugh's names, depending, of course, on what Bea wrote. Trouble is, there'd still be your mortgage, wouldn't there, Bruno?'

Not to mention the inheritance tax, Harrie wanted to say. God, this was going to be complicated.

Bruno nodded. 'But the three of you could put the lump sums I gave you towards paying off the mortgage.'

'Yeah, right,' said Terry. 'We might have started off with thirty K each, but, well, I don't know about you lot, only I–'

'Ha!' cried Simon, slowly sitting himself up and turning his pale face and dark-rimmed eyes to everyone. 'I knew it!'

Joy screamed and Harrie almost did. It was like Boris Karloff rising from the laboratory table. Those that weren't screaming were backing hard against the leatherette.

'Swindlers! Total bastards! But this time you're not going to get away with it. Sodding Simon will see to that!'

Joy heaved herself up using Terry's knee and dashed to the stairs. 'Oh dear, I don't think those sausages agreed with me.'

'Er, me neither,' said Terry, following her.

Will suddenly remembered Melanie was expecting him. Then Hugh looked at his watch and announced he'd forgotten to phone Anthony, and soon Harrie and Bruno were alone with the ashen and completely terrifying Simon.

'Bag End,' he said with a red-lipped grin and a nasty bruise on his forehead. 'Pretty damned hilarious, what?'

Once they'd established that he really did know where he lived, and once they'd got some food and a couple of paracetamols inside him up in the kitchen, the horrible truth came out. Simon had been conscious and listening all the time.

'Bloody stroke of luck, bashing into the door. Suddenly remembered things, like Joy discussing her thirty thousand at the surgery. Stupid cow. The whole waiting room was listening in. Then there was that party ... here.' Simon's eyes wandered up to the ceiling. 'Could sue you, of course, but I'm sure we're going to come to a reasonable settlement. Aren't we, Bruno? Mind you, the place might not be yours any longer.' He laughed cruelly, then went to the fridge and took out a beer. 'Did Mummy change her mind about her darling boy, eh?'

'To be honest,' said Bruno, 'I don't care. It's been a nightmare, juggling money, juggling needy people...'

Harrie gave his knee a sympathetic squeeze and hoped he wasn't referring to her.

'You know what I'd like to do?' he continued. 'Travel. Get as far away from here as possible.'

Simon drank some beer and burped. 'Yep. I can relate to that.'

Harrie removed her hand. 'You should do it, Bruno. I mean, there'll be nothing to keep you here.'

'Only you, of course.' He slipped an arm around her waist and kissed her. 'But you could come too.'

Harrie suddenly found herself exasperated with her boyfriend. It was always the same. She took a step forward, he took one back. She stepped back, he moved towards her. 'No, I couldn't,' she told him firmly. 'And you know that.'

Simon came and sat down. 'Now, now, you two. You're far too young to be tied. I've seen many a whiz kid felled by a possessive wife. I put my career first from the word go.'

'And look where it's got you,' said Harrie. She wasn't sure she'd meant to say it out loud.

But Simon merely guffawed. 'Oh, I'll be back on track soon. Especially now I've got a few more spondoolies coming my way.'

Harrie felt she'd heard enough talk of money and wills. She wanted to go and cuddle Bruno in their room. Make up with him and feel reassured. But if she suggested it, he'd be bound to be cool.

'Well,' she said instead, getting up from the table, 'I think I might go and check on Patrick.'

'Hey,' said Bruno, leaping up. 'Don't leave, Harrie.' The arm came round her again. 'Of course I wouldn't go travelling without you. Come on, let's go to our room and talk about it.' He made a face that implied they might make wild wonderful love after their weeks of nothingness.

'Patrick was very low earlier,' she explained, now actually wanting to go and check on her stepfather. 'Think I might stay there tonight.'

'But...'

She gave him a quick kiss. 'See you tomorrow.'

Walking down the hall, she heard Simon say, 'Women! Best just to pay for it, that's always been my motto. If you're ever in Hong Kong, I can recommend–'

'I wouldn't do that to Harrie,' Bruno told him and Harrie stopped, wanting to turn back. Why couldn't he say sweet things like that to her? Why so guarded all the time? Tears stung her eyes as she grabbed her bag and jacket from their room. If she'd gone back to him, he'd have turned frosty on her.

'Aarggh!' she cried, when she'd set off down Bibury Road on her bike. 'Aarrgghhhh!' They'd done frustration and rage in class the other day, and Max had praised her for being so convincing. Of course, all she'd had to do was think of Bruno.

FORTY-FOUR

For a while, Bea mulled over what to write in her will, although mulling wasn't coming easily these days – confusion and forgetfulness and lost trains of thought came far more easily. Although she didn't feel at death's door, Bea was aware of the urgency to get something done and dusted before all thoughts of a new will left her head altogether. 'If only Donald were here to help,' she often said out loud. Sadly, and rather strangely, her bereavement was almost more acute now than it had been in early widowhood.

One morning, after her first cup of tea, Bea decided today would be 'will day'. After waiting for her morning fuzziness to pass, she settled down at the bureau, unfolded the document and found her best fountain pen – once Donald's. She'd leave the house to Joy, Terry and Hugh. Bruno would have the insurance payout. Perhaps he'd like to use it to travel, she thought – something he still talked about. He could have all her possessions too, for what they were worth. Although he might appreciate the piano. Simon, she decided, would have nothing. Was it necessary to write that? 'To my son, Simon, I bequeath nothing,' she added leadenly.

When Hugh came up to read Highsmith's *Ripley Under Water*, Bea requested that he go instead to the retired Clive and Valerie next door, and ask if they would kindly be her witnesses. This they agreed to, and within an hour of her first sitting at the bureau, the will was signed and sealed. Sealed, in fact, with several drops of wax from the rosemary-scented candle that Joy claimed would help keep Bea alert during the day. Bea often felt Joy watched far too many self-improvement programmes than was good for a person.

Hugh had been straining to see the contents of the will, whilst Bea and her neighbours signed, and once Clive and Valerie had left, she put him out of his misery. 'You'll inherit a third of the house, Hugh. As will Joy and Terry.'

'Really,' he replied, almost dully. One might have expected a small whoop of glee. 'Right. Well, thank you, Bea. That's very generous.'

But not generous enough for a smile or a grateful peck on her cheek? It was possible Hugh was in shock, of course, and that once the information had sunk in, he'd pick her up and spin her round, plant a kiss on her and run out for flowers.

'I've had a bit of a change of heart about

the previous will,' she told him, 'about leaving it all to Bruno.'

'I'm sorry, do you mean the house? That you left the entire house to Bruno?'

Oh dear. Ought she to be telling him this? 'I … er, yes. I believe I may have made out a previous will along those lines. I recall, I think, a compensation provision for you, Joy and Terry.'

Hugh looked stunned. His eyes then darted around the room and landed on the document in her lap. 'I see,' was all he uttered.

'Now be a dear, would you,' said Bea, 'and make sure this is safely deposited with my solicitor, Charles Rogers in George Street.' When she handed over the envelope, Bea thought she detected a little twinkle in Hugh's eyes. Perhaps he was thrilled after all. Hugh had never been one for displays of emotion.

'Don't worry, Bea,' he said, at last bending and kissing her cheek. 'I'll take very good care of it.'

FORTY-FIVE

Profits for the shop were already on the up, thanks to Will's business skills, his sense of decent décor, and the thousand flyers he'd made the lads distribute and Neil pay for. Students were definitely a good source of income, and so they were the ones being targeted in their little shared houses and their big shared houses and their halls of residence. A lot of them arrived with cars, but a car was of no use for zipping around town, not unless you were happy feeding your student loan into pay-and-display machines. Buses too were expensive.

No, the only sensible means of transport was a bike. Bikes were handy, bikes were cheap, bikes were green – that was the message Will tried to get across. And not to worry should something go wrong, the flyer reassured them, because Neil's Wheels provided a fast and friendly service. How he wanted that to read 'Will's Wheels', but still.

Will would arrive half an hour before opening each morning. He'd sweep the floor and usually wash it too. He'd wipe and sometimes polish the wooden counter and make sure everything on it was straight and neat. Before Jake and Shaz rolled up, he'd light one of the joss sticks Patrick had given him, because he, Patrick, thought the shop had a bit of a young-man odour.

Today he chose patchouli because the last time he'd used that loads of people had said, 'Mm, patchouli,' in a positive way. The old hippies mainly, but some young ones too. The whole incense thing also fitted in with the row of businesses Neil's Wheels was part of: healing centre, deli, holistic vet and veggie café. Some thought Brian the butcher should move somewhere more suitable but, as an enjoyer of Brian's hot Cornish pasties, Will found himself on the fence.

He wheeled the eight second-hand bikes that were for sale out the front and chained them all together, then turned the Closed sign to Open and waited for his staff to arrive half an hour late. Every day he ticked them off, but Will's new opening time of eight-thirty – designed to catch people on their way to work or lectures – was confounding Jake and Shaz's body clocks. Still, he could cope with the first thirty minutes alone. In fact, it was quite a nice time, especially on a sunny morning like today.

Will nipped out the back to make a coffee, listening for the bell that tinkled when the door opened. He hummed to himself and felt good about things – the shop, Melanie and Sam ... not Bibury Road, but then he hadn't been there for days. Deliberately avoiding it, in fact. He'd heard from Harrie that the new will left the house to the three lodgers, and that it was all legally and financially complicated now. The whole situation over there was one huge messy cock-up, and nothing to do with him. For that reason he'd stayed at Melanie's and not enquired any more. A person could easily get caught up in the ill feeling and general tension, and not have time to make a success of his bike shop or his relationship. Best to leave them to it, he thought once again, though he might give Harrie a call later.

Will took his coffee through and slipped Mozart – 'that classical bollocks', according to the staff – in the CD player. He sat on the stool at the counter and waited for the first customer to tinkle the bell. Male or female? he wondered, since there was nothing else to do. A repair or a sale? Regular customer, or a new one propelled here by the flyer? Fat … thin … tall … short … beautiful? When the bell finally tinkled, the last person Will reckoned on seeing was Simon. The sight of him pushing his bike over the long rubber mat was a shock, but, when Simon looked up, he seemed even more surprised than Will.

'Christ Almighty,' he said, 'it's you. So this is your famous bike shop. Listen, what would you give me for this?' He leaned the bike against the counter and pulled his bicycle clips off. 'Oh, and these,' he added, dangling them.

Will got off his stool and inspected the fairly old mountain bike – battered, but a Giant, so he knew he'd sell it on quickly. He shook his head at Simon in an oh-I-don't-know way and said, 'Giving up cycling, then?'

Simon snorted. With his piercing gaze and still-bruised forehead, he might have frightened Will, were it not for the fact that he was desperately trying to sell his pushbike. 'Yes,' Simon said. 'Taking up flying instead.'

'Oh?'

'Job offer. Madrid.'

Will wondered if the blow to the head had been pretty serious. 'Is that so?'

'Did a bit of networking and an old pal put me on to his brother, who needs a marketing manager. Interviewed me over the old blower and I start next week. Flight's booked, first three months' accommodation paid for too. Just think, I'll be back in the land of the living and away from bloody wills and Joy's intensely annoying laugh.'

'Great,' Will said, now sort of believing him. 'So what's happening about the house and stuff?'

'The others have popped a nice amount in my bank account, I've signed something to say I won't contest the will, everyone's happy, and I can't wait to do eighteen holes again.' Simon played air golf with his hands, still clutching the cycle clips. 'Anyway, what do you think? Eighty quid?'

Now it was Will's turn to snort. 'Thirty tops.'

'Aw, come on. Their money won't clear till tomorrow and I'm off first thing. Absolutely have to get a suit. Being met at the airport, you see. I suppose I could touch the others for a bit more...'

'Forty, then. And two for the clips.'

'Sixty for the lot?'

Will could feel Simon breathing down his neck, literally. Suddenly, he wanted the guy out of the shop, so agreed to the sixty. He gave him cash, then went and opened the door for him. 'See you before you go, maybe.'

'Possibly. Listen, you don't know where I could buy a secondhand suit, do you?'

Will directed him to the Oxfam shop, then, once back inside, couldn't make out if it had been a good or a bad start to the day. Simon was getting out of everyone's lives, but Will had paid over the odds for the bike. He picked up the phone and called Harrie.

'Oh, you are alive,' she said. 'Ignore my texts, won't you. Talk about unsupportive.'

Will thought he wouldn't rise to the bait. 'I've just had Simon, in selling his bike. Said he's going to Madrid.'

'Yeah, well, I would have told you that days ago, if you'd been remotely concerned.'

'And that all the money business has been sorted out. How's Bruno feeling about it?'

'Overjoyed, I think. Owning a house was *way* too big a burden for his little shoulders.'

'You're pissed off with him, then?'

Harrie groaned. 'Oh, I don't know. Anyway, I've got to get to class now. See you one day.'

Will laughed. 'Yeah, maybe.'

After hanging up, he started to wheel Simon's bike out the front, but something wasn't right. He looked down and saw the front wheel was badly buckled. He swore. Why hadn't he checked the thing out properly? He pulled on the brakes and found the back one didn't work, then noticed the smashed reflector. He guessed he'd been so intimidated by Simon that he just hadn't noticed these things. He also realised he'd have given him the sixty quid, even if he had noticed. Large unpredictable men with big bruises had that effect on him.

He hauled the wreck of a bike out to the workshop, then called Melanie to say he'd be staying the night at Bibury Road. He suddenly felt the need to touch base, he told her, plus, he was running out of clothes.

'Oohhh,' she kind of wailed. 'Do you have to? We'll miss you.'

Will smiled. Could life get any better?

Later, he discovered Bruno, Hugh, Terry and Joy extremely on edge. Apparently, Simon kept saying he was going to stay the night at a hotel near the airport – all booked and paid for by the house-mates – only he wasn't leaving. Instead, he was going round scrounging things. Sunglasses, toothpaste and bigger things. 'I can hardly turn up with a tatty old rucksack, now can I?'

In the kitchen, Joy handed over her wheelie case and a set of tiny keys. 'It's not as though I'm always holidaying,' she said slightly miserably.

'Most grateful,' said Simon, ramming things into it. 'OK, anyone wear size tens? Need some decent shoes to go with the suit.'

Will was a ten, and he had those black lace-up jobs he'd bought for a wedding. They'd rubbed badly and he'd never wear them again, but he'd paid too much for Simon's bike, so said nothing.

'Terry?' asked Simon.

'Take a twelve, mate.'

'Hugh?' Simon looked down at Hugh's feet. 'No, far too small.'

'A *nine*, I'll have you know.'

Simon came over to Will. 'Yours look about the right size.'

'Good bike you flogged me, Simon.'

Simon threw his head back and laughed. 'First rule of business, Will. Always check the merchandise.'

'Actually, I'm a twelve too. Sorry.'

'Oh, sod it, I'll get some when I land. The money will have cleared by then.' He slipped his suit jacket on over the striped shirt, and Will was impressed by Simon's charity shop outfit, ruined only by the holey trainers. 'Now,' he said, *'tempus fugit* and all that. Who's going to give me a lift to the station?'

'Well, Harrie's the only one with a car,' said Bruno. 'And she's out in it.'

Simon smirked. 'Looks like it'll have to be a taxi, then.' He held out a hand.

'For fuck's sake!' snapped Terry. 'How much more are you going to fleece us for? Jesus, you never bloody stop. Now take your crap out of Joy's case, put it in your rucksack and get the helmet from the shed.' He unhooked the key and chucked it Simon's way. 'I'll take you.'

'Terry!' cried Joy. 'No! It's getting dark!'

'Oh, stop your fussing, woman. I got you to work that time.'

Simon threw a panicked look at the kitchen clock and cursed. 'Get the thing fired up, then.' Will guessed no one had filled him in on Terry and his bike.

Joy said, 'But, Terry, don't you remember that red light you went through...' her voice trailing off because Terry wasn't listening.

'Now,' he was saying, excited and rubbing

his hands together as he pushed past Will. 'Where's me leather jacket?'

Terry went to the coat rack in the hall and Simon came in from the garden, fastening his crash helmet.

'Oh blimey,' said Joy, 'let me give that a clean.' She opened a drawer and took out a yellow duster. Simon rolled his eyes and bent down, and Joy wiped away bits of cobweb. 'There. Now, when he tells you to lean *with* the bike on sharp bends, do as you're told or he'll shout horrible abuse and shock passers-by.'

'I have ridden a bike myself,' said Simon. 'Now, where the devil is he? If I miss the seven-fifty, I'll have to wait yonks for the next. Terry!'

But Terry had obviously taken another route to the garden, for an engine could be heard cracking to a start.

'Oh, cripes,' said Joy, holding her stomach.

Hugh put a hand on her shoulder. 'Think positively, Joy. You and I would have half the house each.'

Will joined Hugh and Joy out on the pavement. After Simon hoisted himself on to the bike, rucksack on back, he turned and waved to them. Will found himself waving back, but in a piss-off-and-good-riddance way. Hugh waved too, but Joy was still cuddling her stomach and mumbling something that could have been a prayer.

Terry revved up and switched on his lights, then they were off, at first meandering down the thankfully empty Bibury Road, then sticking to the central dotted line and keeping to a straight course. Will and the others walked up to the bend to watch them safely to the Banbury Road.

'Well,' said Joy, 'I don't suppose he's that bad a motorcyclist. I mean, he got to the garage and back last week for the MOT.'

A car then turned into Bibury Road and Will felt his stomach tighten. 'Oh shit, what's Terry doing?'

'Oh Lord,' said Hugh, covering his eyes.

The car pulled right over to the left to let him pass, but Terry continued to aim straight at it. Will closed his eyes too, then heard Joy scream and the vehicles crash at more or less the same time. 'Christ,' he said, opening his eyes to see Terry on the car's bonnet and Simon sprawled at the foot of a lamppost.

'I love you, Terry,' sobbed Joy, clutching at Will's arm.

He shook her off and ran as fast as he could. On reaching the increasingly familiar car, he first checked Harrie. She was conscious, thank God, but just staring at Terry's still face through her windscreen. Will stretched through the open window and turned off her engine.

'"Oh God, that I were a man,"' she whispered in the sudden silence, before turning to Will and locking her big pale eyes on his. '"I would eat his heart in the marketplace."'

'Harrie?' Will said, then leaned around the windscreen. 'Terry? You all right?'

There was a groan, then, 'Leg. Pain. Can't move the fucker.'

Simon began groaning in a similar way, squirming around on the pavement and mumbling to himself. Will thought he heard 'lawsuit'.

'Did I kill anyone?' asked Harrie.

'Unfortunately not,' said a breathless Hugh, casting a glance at Simon. 'Oh Lord, what am I saying? Listen, I've called 999. An ambulance is on its way, or so they say. I asked for the fire brigade too.'

'Why?' asked Will, realising straight away that Hugh might just want some firemen rolling up.

'In case the car explodes, of course. Like they always do in the movie–'

'Oh shit!' Harrie said, and in the blink of an eye, she and Terry were on their feet – one foot, in Terry's case – and halfway down the road.

FORTY-SIX

After three days in shock, Harrie felt it was time to get back on the horse, so to speak. She offered to drive Simon to Heathrow. Bruno was coming with her, in case Simon did a runner, although that might have been hard on crutches. Harrie and Bruno had to promise the others they'd stay and see him go through to the departure lounge.

It was a wet and dismal drive, not helped by the lack of conversation in the car. In the passenger seat, Bruno was engrossed in a Lonely Planet guide. Which one, Harrie didn't know. He'd recently bought a whole stack of the things, trying to decide on a travel plan.

Every now and then she looked over at his hung head. That lovely shiny hair, that perfect profile were soon going to leave her life and get on a 747. Well, once all the money was sorted out. He'd be bound to meet loads of beautiful interesting women, and maybe hook up with a fellow kindred-spirit traveller. A woman with a fantastic blues voice ... who did voluntary work with addicts on a sink estate ... and wouldn't want to own a house if you gave her one.

'You OK, Simon?' Harrie asked, as they took the Heathrow turn-off. Since Oxford, his face had scowled at her in the rear-view mirror. More to do with the sprained and bandaged foot, than with her, she hoped.

'It's hardly a stretch limo, but I suspect I'll live.'

'Nearly there.'

'Are we?' said Bruno, looking up and straining to see the sky. 'Ah, yes.' Planes were dotted around; one was coming in to land. He grinned, knowing he'd be up there soon, no doubt.

As she crawled along in the stream of cars aiming for their terminals, Harrie felt a flicker of excitement at the idea of getting on a plane and being somewhere else. No, more than a flicker. On such a drab day, it seemed like the only thing to do, in order to stay sane. This miserable, wet, dreary, boring country. God, no wonder Bruno wanted to travel. 'Yes, OK, I'll come!' she wanted to cry. He'd invited her loads of times over the past couple of days, perhaps just feeling sorry for her after the accident. Hard to tell. Not that sorry for her, though, since he was going anyway – which was a bit unilateral of him, to say the least.

'How long do you think you'll be away?' she asked him now.

His eyes left the circling planes and he put a hand on her leg. 'Six months, a year.

Come with me?'

'She's got her bloody course to do!' shouted Simon from the rear. 'How many times does she have to tell you?'

Harrie said, 'I've got my course to do,' and Bruno laughed. Then Harrie laughed too, but secretly wished she could be more of a pushover.

They saw Simon safely through to the departure lounge, gave the housemates a quick call, then had a livelier drive back to Oxford.

Bruno didn't look at his travel books once and they talked about anything but his big adventure – stuff in the news, the house-mates, some of the things she'd been made to do at drama school, the extras work coming up at the weekend.

Before they knew it, they were home and walking into the kitchen/diner, where Joy, Terry and Hugh were huddled around the computer screen. Harrie joined them.

'Still taxiing,' said Terry, in charge of the mouse, his plastered leg to one side of the desk. He was on the Heathrow 'Live Flight Tracking' page.

'You mean Simon?' asked Harrie. She thought he'd be halfway to Madrid by now, boring his neighbour with his lost inherit-ance tale.

'I just want the bloomin' thing to take off,'

said Joy. 'Then I can get on with my toad-in-the-hole.'

Harrie sighed. Not toad-in-the-hole again.

Hugh said, 'Should have gone forty minutes ago.'

'Forty-three,' said Terry. 'Right, let's refresh the page and – hey! Eu-bloody-reka!'

'Airborne?' asked Hugh and Joy.

'Airborne!' confirmed Terry.

After a general cheer, they all seemed to deflate, but in a happy way.

'Anyone for a celebratory drink?' asked Joy, already pulling wine from the fridge.

'Nothing fucking else to do,' grumbled Terry. He hauled himself off the chair and gathered his crutches, then limped towards the sofa on them, clonking bits of furniture on the way. One trouser leg had been cut off at the thigh and, at the other end, some very ugly toes stuck out of the plaster. *I used to have a handle on life, but it fell off* said his T-shirt.

Bruno settled himself at the table with his guide book. 'Not for me,' he told Joy.

Harrie guessed he'd be engrossed and ignoring her again for ages. 'Me neither,' she said, suddenly needing to escape. 'I've got to go out.'

Bruno dropped the book and jumped up, then came over to her. 'Where?'

Harrie tutted and said, 'Just out,' like a stroppy teen. What was her problem? He wanted to travel. He wanted her to go with him. She was choosing not to. Not that choice really came into it, since she didn't have the money and had taken on a loan for the course, and anyway, *wanted* to be an actor. Actually, he'd offered to pay for her to go with him, but that didn't seem right, even though the money had fallen into his lap. Oh God, it was all too hard.

'See you later, then,' Bruno said, more nicely than she deserved. He kissed her on the lips, which made her want to weep and hug him and thump him, all at the same time. Talk about infuriating! Still, it was all stuff to draw upon when improvising.

Harrie walked in on Patrick cuddling a woman on the sofa, their heads sort of buried in each other. One of them was sobbing, but she couldn't tell which. 'Oops,' she said, backing out of the room. 'Sorry.'

As she slowly pulled the door to behind her, the woman called out 'Harrie!'

Harrie stopped dead. 'Mum?' she said. She pushed the door open and there was her mother, dabbing her eyes with the corner of a cushion. 'I thought you were coming back on Sunday?'

Her mother got up and came to give her a hug. 'Change of plan,' she said. 'Listen, Harrie, never, never, *ever* have anything to do with men. Not unless they're just like

Patrick.' She kissed Harrie's cheek damply, then drew back, still holding her. 'You look fantastic.'

'You too, Mum. So blonde!' Her mother was as petite and athletic-looking as ever, but now had such an amazing glow. 'How come you're tanned when it was winter over there?'

'The bastard had a sunbed.'

'Ah.' Harrie wasn't sure she wanted her father referred to that way, just when she'd begun to forgive him. But obviously, she was supposed to hate him again now. God, her mum was annoying. But perhaps everyone was today. 'What did he...?' Harrie began, then realised she didn't want to know. 'Oh, never mind. Let's phone Will and tell him you're home.'

'There's lots of veg and couscous,' said Patrick, 'if you want to stay for dinner?'

Harrie had to sit down. She fell into the beanbag she'd never got rounding to chucking out and was overcome with something. Relief, happiness. A sense of being home. Of being back in the fold. Her, Mum, Patrick. It was familiar and cosy and oh so easy. No eggshells to walk on, not a toad-in-the-hole to struggle through. She dialled Will's number and heard the crack in her voice when she told him the news.

He brought Melanie and Sam with him

but, even so, there was enough food. For someone on a low budget, Patrick always cooked vast amounts. Harrie told her mum all about the course, the minor car crash and the odd goings-on regarding Bea's will.

'So you think Hugh hid the thing?' asked Patrick. 'That was a scenario we didn't come up with.'

Harrie nodded, and her mother said, 'I can see I've missed all the fun!' in a jolly sort of way, even though she was drooping over her plate. She'd worn herself out playing with Sam – plus flying from Australia, of course.

'Er, before you fall asleep, Mum,' said Will, 'there's something I want to tell you ... *we* want to tell you.'

'There's going to be a baby?' she asked through a yawn.

Will laughed and Melanie said, *'No.* But I've asked Will if he wants to move in with me, and he does.'

'Wow,' said Harrie, elbowing her mother awake. 'Mum, Will's moving in with Melanie.'

'Is that such a good idea, Will?' drawled her mother. 'I mean, remembering Naomi?'

Melanie flinched and Will said, 'Do you think you need to sleep, Mum? Jet lag seems to have made you tactless.'

'Oh God,' she said. 'Sorry. And, *really*, who

am I to tell anyone how to conduct their relationships?' She laughed but her eyes welled up. 'Listen, I'm very happy for you, honestly. And you're nothing like Naomi, Melanie. Christ, she was–'

'Bed, Mum.'

'Yeah, OK.'

Patrick returned from tucking her up, just as Will, Melanie and Sam were leaving.

'Nice to have Mum back?' Will asked Patrick.

Patrick beamed. 'What do you think?'

'And, thank God, Ken isn't coming,' said Harrie.

'He still wants to see you two, apparently. I think he'd like you to go over there. Said he'll pay.'

A paid-for trip to Australia? Didn't sound bad. Maybe in the summer break... Who said Bruno should have a monopoly on travel?

'Huh,' said Harrie. 'He'll be lucky.'

FORTY-SEVEN

Bea was discussing her health with Donald, who was perched on the stool with an arm on the piano lid, wearing his listening face: chin forward, a trace of a frown.

'Angina,' she told him. 'They've got me taking aspirin every day now, on top of everything else! Oh, Donald, do you remember how I shunned medication? How you'd have to cajole me into taking aspirin for my headaches? Now look...' Bea pointed at her medication organiser. 'It's like the Pick'n'Mix in Woolworths!'

'Well, so long as you *don't* pick and mix,' said Donald, laughing.

'To be honest, I have been tempted. Down the lot with a measure or two of whisky.'

Donald wagged a finger. 'Now you're being silly, Bea. And besides, you're stronger than that.'

'Am I?' Bea asked. 'Am I really?' Donald began to fade, while Bea wondered how he'd reached that conclusion. Simply living a long time didn't make one emotionally strong – rather the opposite, she'd found. The first attack on the stairs had seen her crying like a baby, long after both the pain and Dr French had left. Bea felt it was only Bruno's insurance policy keeping her from picking and mixing, for she believed it might well become null and void following suicide. However, she wasn't sure, and could hardly phone the company to ask, or get Hugh to read each clause to her because she'd never manage that tiny print... And, besides, where was the policy? In her bureau? She hoped she hadn't let it lapse somehow. Not kept up payments. Oh dear, now she feared there wasn't a policy at all for the child.

'Look at how you've coped,' Donald was saying, back again. 'Kept the old house going, provided a wonderful home for three lost souls. Been a splendid grandmother figure for Bruno. I admire you enormously, Bea. And so do many others.'

Bea smiled and said, 'Thank you, darling.' No one could boost her confidence the way Donald did, although Bruno often managed it. 'And listen, Donald, before you go... I'm so sorry about your vegetable patch ... the fruit bushes, the greenhouse... It's just that–'

'Knock knock!' came a third voice. 'Anyone home?' It was Hugh, here to read to her. Donald faded, then Hugh took his place on the stool. 'Let's see what the dastardly Bruno's up to, shall we?'

'I beg your pardon?' said Bea, sitting

straighter and wrapping her bed jacket tighter. It wasn't an adjective she'd ever have attached to Bruno.

'He's just strangled Miriam at the pleasure park?'

'I'm sorry?'

'Strangers on a Train?'

'Ah, silly me.'

Hugh opened the Highsmith and lifted the corner of the page he'd turned down. How Bea hated that, but she couldn't chastise someone who took time out to read to her and occasionally run errands. Which reminded her...

'Tell me, Hugh. The will I made out the other day...'

'Yes.'

'I did sign it, didn't I?'

'Yes, you signed it *and* it was witnessed.'

'And I gave it to you to take to–'

'Don't worry, Bea, it's in a safe place. A very safe place. Now back to Bruno.'

'What about him?' she asked, trying to recall what they'd been saying about the boy. Was Hugh still despairing over his lack of a career plan? Should she tell Hugh about the insurance policy and put his mind at rest? If there was a policy...

Hugh double-crossed his legs and peered at her over his reading glasses. 'As I said, he's just killed Miriam.'

'Of course.'

'And why has he done that?'

'Because ... he wants the other chappie...'

'Guy.'

'That's it. Bruno wants Guy to kill his father, in exchange.'

'Yes! Well done, Bea!'

If Hugh had been closer, she might have delivered a firm slap and told him not to patronise. Instead, she leaned her head against the pillows and said, 'Fire away.'

FORTY-EIGHT

On Saturday, Harrie found herself being picked out of the crowd, along with three other blonde women. They stood in a row and were inspected by a large middle-aged woman with a clipboard.

'You,' she said, pointing at Harrie, 'the very blonde one. Want to come with me?'

The woman was walking way too fast for Harrie, still wearing, as she was, a cling-film evening dress for the scene they'd be shooting later. The woman disappeared into an outbuilding and Harrie reached it, just as she was leaving. 'You'll have to change quickly,' Harrie was told, before the woman zoomed off again.

Inside, a short baby-blue T-shirt and

almost shorter skirt were waiting for her. 'Here,' said a young girl, 'let me help you. Someone went sick at the last minute, apparently.'

'Really?' Harrie's heart soared. Was she about to get a walk-on part? Or, better still, a speaking part? 'Do you know who?' she asked, as the girl yanked the tight skirt over Harrie's hips.

'Uh-uh. OK, breathe in while I zip you up.'

Harrie did as she was told.

'No time to redo the make-up. Let's go.'

Harrie was led to the house, then through it, then to the vast kitchen where, at one end, a group of actors milled around mouthing their lines. If she too was given lines, she'd need to do some voice exercises – something she'd been learning, luckily. She spotted two well-known actors in the group and tried not to look overawed while she approached.

'No,' said the girl leading her. 'Not that way, this.'

Harrie followed her to the far end of the vast kitchen, where someone else took over and asked her to sit. 'On that chair. No, that one.'

'I'm sorry,' said Harrie, sitting, 'but could someone tell–'

'OK, bring in rentacrèche!' a man shouted.

Someone was combing Harrie's hair.

'Only, I haven't actually been told what I'm supposed–'

'Fuck, where have they got to?' said the shouting man, storming off. Who was he? What was happening? She looked resentfully at the real actors in the distance. She'd bet they knew what was going on.

Suddenly, her hair was being pulled into bunches. 'You're kidding?' she protested.

The young girl doing it wound a band tightly round one bunch. 'That's what they said.'

Harrie heard the children before she saw them enter.

'Emily on that side of the au pair,' said the shouter, maybe an assistant director. 'Archie opposite, Sophie next to him.'

What au pair? wondered Harrie, before realising he meant her. The children sat at the table.

'Where do you want the high chair?' someone asked.

'Other side of the au pair. Right, can we wheel in the baby?'

Two dogs appeared on leads. One barked, which set the other one off. They looked like spaniels.

'Food on the table now, and let's get a bib on the baby.'

The baby cried when the bib was tied round his neck. Nearby, stood what must have been his anxious mother, chewing a nail. When the food arrived, two of the toddlers started squabbling over the one cake with a cherry on. That made toddler number three cry and the baby scream louder. A bowl of mush and a plastic spoon were placed in front of Harrie.

'Great!' shouted the maybe-director. 'Now start feeding the baby and let's get rolling.' He shot down to the other end of the big farmhouse kitchen, where the actors took their places and filming began.

'Cut!' Harrie heard after a minute or so. 'Can someone ask the au pair what's so friggin' funny?'

FORTY-NINE

'Donald?' said Bea. Hugh had gone and Joy had left her some lunch she couldn't face. A faint Donald had once again perched himself on the piano stool.

'Yes, dear?'

'Do you remember Rome?'

'Of course.'

'I berated you for flirting, do you recall?'

Donald looked sheepish and recrossed his legs. 'Vividly.'

'Have you any idea how it ruined my

holiday, and many many other holidays and outings, Donald?'

'I have now, Bea. And I'm so dreadfully sorry for all those years I hurt your feelings in that way.'

'Not to mention humiliated me.'

'And that. I had the most wonderful wife in the world, and I'm truly sorry. Do forgive me, Bea.'

Bea closed her eyes and hummed a familiar little tune – what was it? – and when she lifted one lid, just a little, and looked towards the piano stool, Donald had gone. 'Yes, dear,' she whispered, smiling contentedly. 'I forgive you.'

FIFTY

Bruno had gone to stay at his mother's, to let the housemates sort themselves out, and Harrie had moved back home. Will thought that would have ended the relationship, but it wasn't so. If anything, they were getting on better, according to Harrie.

After boxing up the last of his things, Will tried not to get emotional about leaving his attic. Only good things had happened to him in the time he'd spent there – Melanie, then promotion. Would his luck take a dive, with Bea not watching over him? He looked at the ceiling and asked her, but it seemed Harrie was the only one she'd communicate with. Well, no turning back now. With Melanie and her car not due for a while, Will trotted down the stairs and knocked on Joy's door.

'Come in!' she called out. 'Only mind my hostess trolley!'

Will pushed the door and bashed the trolley, and wondered when Joy ever did any hostessing in her own room. 'Sorry,' he said rubbing at the gaudy gold metal. 'No damage, I don't think.'

'Sentimental value, that's all. Wedding present. How's your packing going?'

'All done. How's your spreading out going?' Joy now had the entire first floor again, the plasterboard having come off the arch.

'To tell the truth, Will, I'm missing my carpet.'

He'd thought she was going to say Terry. 'But these floorboards are beautiful.'

'I know, only it's not the same. Still, mustn't grumble. Now, shall I hang this picture where it was, or what? Where do you think?' She held a colourful cottage scene up and moved around the room with it.

'Er, behind the wardrobe?'

'Oh, you,' she said, flapping a hand at him. 'Listen, I've got you and Melanie a house-warming gift. Now, where did I put it?'

Will's insides filled with dread. Rightly so, it turned out, when Joy handed him a set of place mats featuring National Trust properties. 'Hey,' he said.

'Didn't get round to wrapping it. Apologise to Melanie, won't you?'

'I certainly will.'

'Oooohhh,' went Joy. She put her arms around him and squeezed. 'You will come and visit?'

'Of course.' Actually, he probably would. 'And you must come and see us.'

'Well, if I've got time. What with the two part-time jobs! You've no idea how much this house is going to cost us a month, once it's properly in our names.'

'You know,' Will said into her slightly coarse hair, 'you could charge a fortune for the attic. Much more than I've been paying.'

'Don't worry, we're going to. Already advertising.'

'Good.'

When Joy finally peeled herself off him, Will had lipstick and a smudge of foundation on his shirt. He quietly cursed her, then decided he'd leave it on and make Melanie jealous. Didn't want her getting too complacent, just because he was moving in.

'Anyway, this is just a quickie,' he told Joy. 'I'm going to say goodbye to the others too. Better this way, than having you all on the doorstep, waving me off. Dead embarrassing.'

'And I'd be bound to blab!'

'Me too,' he said, and she broke into her giggle. It was quite an endearing one, really.

'Fetch us a beer?' said Terry. He was stretched out on the futon in the ground-floor room that had yet to be sorted. There were black bags everywhere, just waiting to trip up Terry and his plaster cast.

'Anything else?' asked Will.

'A woman of the night, if you come across one. Only she'd have to be a bloody contortionist.'

How Melanie found herself with such a father perplexed Will. He'd yet to meet Melanie's mum, currently living in Leeds, but when he did, he might ask if there was a paternity secret she'd like to share. 'One or a couple?' he asked Terry.

'Women?'

When Will returned with two beers, Terry sat up and took one. He saluted him with the can, then pulled the ring out. 'You will take care of Melanie?' he said before knocking back the lager.

Will was taken aback. 'I'm not sure she needs taking care of.'

'Trouble is,' Terry said through a burp, 'they change. Soon as they've nabbed you.

Look at Joy. Bossy little cow she was, when we had our own love nest. Now we're sort of separated, living-wise, again, she can't do enough for me. Bloody great, it is. Anyway, I'm sure my Melanie won't bollock you for overboiling the cabbage.'

'I don't suppose we'll be boiling cabbage.'

'No. Anyway, I expect I'll be seeing a bit of you, now I'm teaching young Sam the drums. That kid's definitely got it.'

'Mm.' At two, Sam was barely co-ordinated enough to feed himself, but Terry had splashed out on a ridiculous set of mini drums for him. Melanie approved, though. Thought it was a good bonding thing.

'Well,' said Will, no longer wanting to look at Terry and his three-day stubble and the uncomfortable-looking cast that Joy had written 'I told you not to get plastered!' on. 'Better go and say bye to Hugh.'

'Right. Tell the bugger to stop ignoring me, would you? Tell him if I bang on the floor with a crutch, it's a fucking emergency.'

'Will do.' He gave Terry's sweaty hand a shake and meandered his way out through the bin bags.

Strangely, Hugh wasn't organised. 'That slob, Simon!' he declared on seeing Will. 'Mug rings etched into the floor, Sellotape on the walls, peeling my paint off. I'll have to start again, but will I manage, now I'll have to work full time?'

People do, Will wanted to say. 'Can't you just cover the rings with the sofa and slap some more white paint on the walls?'

'Oh, *really*,' Hugh said, but then didn't expand. He just stood in the middle of his vast basement room, surrounded by furniture and still packed cases. 'It's one's worst nightmare come true.'

Will thought living with Anthony might have been top of the list. 'Listen,' he said, 'Melanie's on her way, so just wanted to say goodbye, and good luck with the new job.'

Hugh was going to be teaching at a new and desperate crammer school. Not just art history, but various other subjects they hadn't yet filled the posts for. It would surely kill him, but it seemed the house-mates were determined not to lose their home again. Even Terry, once he was up and about, planned a motorbike repair business on top of his IT work. He'd be starting with his own bike, of course.

Hugh came over with open arms and Will willed himself not to reverse. He let Hugh hug him, and even patted his slim straight back. 'It won't be the same without you,' Hugh said.

Will eased himself away. 'Has there been any response to the ad?'

'Funnily enough, I had a call this morning from a chap. Just got a job in publishing, new to the city, twenty-six and a *très* husky voice.'

'You don't think someone a bit older might be good?'

'Dear boy, we hardly need another old wreck in the house. Now, where are my Yellow Pages? I need to hire a sander, if only to drown out the noise of Terry bashing the floor with his crutch.'

Will laughed. 'Listen, I've got to go. But one thing before I do. Um, that will you happened upon.'

'Yes?'

'Well, it couldn't have been in Bea's compost bin because Harrie emptied that.'

Hugh stopped his search and shook his head at Will. He was quiet for a while, then said, 'The other bin, silly. The old one, beside the greenhouse.' A hand went to his chest. 'Golly, one would think you were accusing me of something.'

'No, no,' said Will with a wave. 'See you soon, yeah?'

'You've been in a clinch with Joy, then?' laughed Melanie, pointing at his shirt. She unlocked the boot and lifted the lid, then pushed the back seats forward for extra room. 'Hope you haven't got a lot of stuff,' she said before going in the house to see her father.

Will didn't have much, but even so, he

could tell from the limited space that they wouldn't be calling at the lock-up for Angelina Jolie. He had his clothes and his stereo, but was leaving the microwave for the next tenant – who might well have been the young guy now hovering on the pavement with a scrap of paper in his hand. 'Can I help you?' Will called out.

'Er, maybe. I'm looking for "Delightful accommodation in easy-going shared house for right person". I thought the man I spoke to said fifty, but this doesn't seem...'

'Yeah, right house,' said Will. He looked the bloke up and down. He was tall and skinny and dressed in a cool way, with a cool haircut and a badge that said 'Stop Climate Chaos'. He was handsome enough for Hugh to go for, Terry would relish being non-PC with him, and Joy would enjoy fattening him up with her plum duff. Trouble was, what if things didn't work out with Melanie, and Will needed a room?

'Wow,' said the guy, looking up at the house. 'Incredible.'

'Yeah. Only, listen, I'm afraid it's taken.' Will shrugged and made for his boxes in the hall. 'Sorry, mate.'

Having loaded the car, he closed the boot then nipped round the house to the back garden, in order to check out this other compost bin. It wasn't there. He looked down both sides of the greenhouse and even behind it. 'As I guessed,' he said to himself.

As Will approached the house on his way back, Hugh appeared on the basement steps. 'Anthony took it to the dump,' he said. He was flushed and looked slightly cross. 'Rusty old thing.'

The publishers hope that this book has given you enjoyable reading. Large Print Books are especially designed to be as easy to see and hold as possible. If you wish a complete list of our books please ask at your local library or write directly to:

Magna Large Print Books
Magna House, Long Preston,
Skipton, North Yorkshire.
BD23 4ND

This Large Print Book, for people
who cannot read normal print,
is published under the auspices of

THE ULVERSCROFT FOUNDATION

... we hope you have enjoyed this book.
Please think for a moment about those
who have worse eyesight than you ...
and are unable to even read or enjoy
Large Print without great difficulty.

You can help them by sending a
donation, large or small, to:

**The Ulverscroft Foundation,
1, The Green, Bradgate Road,
Anstey, Leicestershire, LE7 7FU,
England.**
or request a copy of our brochure for
more details.

The Foundation will use all donations
to assist those people who are visually
impaired and need special attention
with medical research, diagnosis
and treatment.

Thank you very much for your help.

ituh 7am